WEB OF LIES

Truth or Die Series, Book Two

Alex Clayborn

Web Of Lies - Truth Or Die Series, Book Two

Copyright © 2021 by Alex Clayborn

eBook ISBN 978-1-7350695-3-1
Paperback ISBN 978-1-7350695-4-8
Hardcover ISBN 978-1-7350695-5-5

Printed in USA

Cover Photograph: Malcolm Wright

Cover Design: Rusty Apper

1

Lindsay and Robert stood staring at each other. Lindsay because she couldn't wait to hear what his first words were going to be and Robert because he didn't know what to say at that moment. A moment he prayed most of Lindsay's life wouldn't happen.

Lindsay Phillips was rarely at a loss for words and the thoughts in her head were swirling faster than she could form sentences or questions with them. She had, after all, just found out that the father she believed had died when she was five years old was still alive and standing in front of her. Not only was he still alive, but he had been orchestrating her entire life.

Robert Langston, the head of a secret, elite special ops empire, stood in front of the daughter who had believed him dead almost her entire life. Born and died as Greg Phillips. Lindsay's dead father, now reborn as Robert Langston.

Yes, he had orchestrated her life, but as Kendall Thomas. Lindsay Phillips is her birth name and the identity she uses in her "normal" personal life. Kendall Thomas is the secret agent he created her to be, under the guidance of Jack Cooper. Robert Langston asked himself how he would ever explain to her why he did what he did and would she ever forgive him? These are the two questions he had been asking himself since Lindsay was five. These are also the only two questions he has never been able to answer.

Since Lindsay had walked into the room, the only thing that either had said was Lindsay when she said, "Hello Daddy." After several more minutes of silence she had then said, "What's wrong? You don't know whether to call me Lindsay or Kendall? We are one and the same, remember?" Neither had said a word since.

Down the hall, waiting in the living room, were Sam Stone, Lindsay's boyfriend who had also just returned from the grave, and Derek Stevens, the mystery man known to most as "Cowboy." Also waiting was Joe, the ops driver and apparently a whole lot more Lindsay didn't know. The three of them were holding their breath, not knowing what to expect from the other room. They did not expect extended minutes of uncomfortable silence. Sam stood up and suggested they go outside to give Lindsay and Robert more privacy.

Once outside, Derek looked uneasy and didn't have anything to say. Joe was fidgety, which was completely out of character for him, and made Derek more uneasy. Joe mumbled almost to himself, "Man, he's one of my best friends. I can't imagine what he is thinking being face to face with her after all these years."

Derek let out a long breath and looked at Sam. "Do you think it's a good idea for us to leave them alone?"

The hurt on Sam's face was apparent. "I don't know how she is going to react. Hell, I don't know if she will ever forgive me. I can't imagine what she is feeling with me being alive and then facing her dead father. Jack aiming his gun at her, willing to kill her, getting shot himself. It's too much for anyone. Do you think we should be out here with Jack in there?"

Joe had an easy answer to that, "Yeah, Jack isn't moving too much. You guys brought him in since he couldn't walk on his own. The doctor that's with him is Robert's personal doctor and, naturally, he's armed. Jack's not going anywhere."

The guys stood there looking around, lost in their own thoughts and not knowing what else to say. It was very quiet on Langston Drive that sunny afternoon so the sound from a gunshot was intensified.

Joe was closest to the door and grabbed the door knob but it was locked. "Damn it! It auto -matically locks when closed." He began pounding on it as hard as he could. Sam ran to one side of the house while Derek ran to the other side. Both were headed toward the back of the house where the gun shot came from. Where Lindsay and Robert were seeing each other for the first time in many, many years.

2

Just as Robert started to take a step toward Lindsay, the bullet hit him in the arm, jolting him. He went to the ground and looked at her, not expecting her to have shot him.

Lindsay was looking dead at him as she hit the floor, thinking he fired at her. At the same time she saw the bullet had just hit his arm, she realized the bullet had come through the window.

She scrambled back toward the door to the hallway while grabbing her own gun from her back. She was glad Derek had picked it up at Jack's office before they left. Once at the door, she crossed the hallway and scurried through a door that opened to a family room across from the office where Robert was starting to move toward her. He had his gun drawn.

The room was all windows and sliding doors that led to a deck. Beyond the deck was the well-maintained lawn and the woods. The woods Lindsay had been in a few times herself. Lindsay moved into the large open room and took cover behind the sofa that faced away from the windows. Just then she saw Derek and Sam coming across the deck toward one of the sliding doors. She ran to open it.

As Derek and Sam ran through the door she yelled, "Shot came from the backyard! I don't see anyone." They were lucky they weren't shot.

"Are you both okay?" Sam's voice was a little shaky.

Lindsay and Robert both said "yes" at the same time. With that one word, they knew Lindsay was pissed.

Still looking at the woods in the back, Lindsay didn't hesitate to add, "If anyone is going to shoot him, it should be me."

Sam and Derek glanced at each other and only Derek said, "We thought maybe it was. Are you two alright to stay here while we go check it out?"

"I'm going, too. Move!" Lindsay was already moving toward the door leading to the deck that they had just came through, gun raised and ready.

"Lindsay, stay here. With all that you have been through today, that would be best. Can you check and see how bad Rob..., he's hurt?" Derek was already moving out through the door.

"No, I'm going!" Lindsay was almost on Derek's heels already.

As the three of them sprinted through the backyard, they joined Joe who was already at the edge of the woods. That guy didn't miss anything.

3

"Lindsay, are you sure you don't want me to come with you this time?" Sam wasn't sure he liked this, but at least this time Lindsay and Robert would be meeting at his office in Philadelphia. It was safer than Jack's house in the suburbs with all the windows.

"Are you afraid for me or him?" Lindsay couldn't take Sam's doting. She wanted to remind him that she had survived just fine between his death and resurrection. She was a little edgy with all that had happened the previous week, but she would never admit that to Sam or anyone else.

"I know you must be feeling better. Your sarcasm is back."

"Did it leave? I didn't notice." Lindsay wasn't sure how she felt about anything at this point in her life. She didn't mean to snap at him and felt badly for doing it.

Sam couldn't think of anything to say. He couldn't blame her for being confused and unsure of her feelings. He had never seen her hurt so he wasn't sure if she overused her sarcasm. He didn't want reports on her after his supposed death. He knew she would be in pain and grieving and he didn't want to experience it along with her. He was dealing with his own grief knowing she was suffering and knowing he couldn't do a thing in the world to soften it.

"I'm sorry, Sam. I don't mean to snap at you.

We're going to talk. But I can only deal with one thing at a time. I was going to ask you how Jack is doing but I'll save it for an open with…Robert." She messaged her forehead with her palm, squeezing her eyes shut in frustration. "I can't even call him Dad. I'm not really sure what to call him. His name isn't Robert any more than mine is Kendall."

"I was going to offer to drive you to Philadelphia but I figured you'd say no to that, too. I just want you to know, I want to be here for you. It's important to me that you know that. It's also important you know I love you. None of that has changed for me. I want a future with you, Lindsay." Sam stood still and held his breath. He hated not knowing where he stood with her and was wearing his heart on his sleeve. This was something new for him, but where Lindsay was concerned, it always had been easy. And after all he had put her through, he felt the need to be completely honest and transparent with her.

Lindsay's heart almost broke at the hurt she heard in his voice and the hurt she could clearly see on his face. It made her mad. It was painful to be with him and it was painful to be away from him. She wanted to touch his face and tell him everything would be okay. But she wasn't a liar. She truly didn't know.

Not knowing what else to say to Sam at that moment, she picked up her purse, gave him a sad smile and said, "See ya in a few days." As she headed toward the door, Sam asked from behind her, "Why a few days? Are you staying in Phili?"

Still facing the door and not turning around, she simply said, "I need some time." She didn't look back. His hurt was his own fault for the decisions he made. Her pain was because of him and the other people in her life. Every single one of them had made decisions for her, without discussing any of it with her. Every decision they had made on her behalf had altered her life. And she had no say in any of it. She wasn't sure which emotion was bigger, the hurt or the anger. And then they lied. Almost every aspect of her life had been a lie.

What Lindsay didn't know yet, was that it was all a lie.

4

"Hey, come on in." Joe leaned down and gave Lindsay a kiss on the check then a big hug. He was a great hugger for such a big guy.

"How are you, Joe?" Lindsay found comfort in Joe and she wasn't sure why. He had held a gun on her in the woods behind Jack's house that day he found her snooping around. He'd always been straight with her except when he gave her the information she had been researching on who the "boss" of the organization was. He had told her the boss's name, Robert Langston. But he hadn't told her that Robert Langston was her father. She had pieced all the information together and came to that conclusion because as crazy as it was, nothing else made sense. The fact that Jack was willing to shoot her to stop her from finding out the truth, sealed her suspicion. It wasn't easy and it was still a guess by the time she demanded Jack take her to him.

"I'm doing well. You're looking good but I can't imagine what is going on inside of you. I'm truly sorry for all that you have been through. You know I will always have your back." Joe reached out and touched Lindsay's shoulder tenderly. "He's waiting for you. End of the hall."

Lindsay knew where his office was. She had been here and had seen his office. It was where she had seen the pictures of herself. That had been the pivotal point for her guessing Robert was the boss. And her father.

Lindsay walked to the end of the hall. It was much the same feeling as she had the last time she walked down a hall to see him for the first time, just last week. She forced herself to maintain her composure and speed up her steps. She really had nothing to dread, right?

As she walked into his office, he took a step away from the window sill he had been leaning on.

"You might want to stay away from those." Lindsay nodded toward the window.

He couldn't help but smile at her sarcasm. He had been hearing about it for years and finally the opportunity to witness it firsthand arrived. Her sarcastic comment was well deserved he supposed. He motioned for her to sit in one of the chairs in front of the wall of shelves.

"I trust your drive here was good?" Really? He couldn't think of something more intelligent than that to say to her.

"Yes, as good as can be expected under the circumstances. How are you feeling?"

"I'm going to live. I'm sure it will take some time to heal since the bullet went through the muscle. I've taken worse."

Lindsay almost said something sarcastic like, "Well, Daddy, I wouldn't know." She let it go. "No idea who shot you?"

"No, as you know, no one was found and no clues. Disappeared into thin air." Robert didn't look her in the eyes and his gaze went beyond her to the door. Lindsay didn't miss the gesture that he was uncomfortable, and probably lying.

"Who knew you were going to be there that

day? It was Jack's house so they had to have followed you or knew you live next door, if you do live there, I mean?"

"The guys and I are still investigating and looking at who it may have been. We'll figure it out. They'll make another move." Just like that, Lindsay was dismissed from that conversation. She let it go for now since she had more pressing questions.

"How is Jack?" Lindsay asked this question first because she was judging what Robert's response and body movement would be. There was no reason for him to lie and Lindsay wanted to gauge a truthful statement from him. It was also a safe question.

"He will also live. He is going to be sore for quite some time. He'll need physical therapy. I'm sorry he pulled his gun on you. I guess we had never talked about you actually finding me. We knew you may find me but we didn't think you would figure out who I really am. When you met Jack that morning, he suspected you knew and told others, although he wasn't sure how you figured it out. Let me be blunt.... we underestimated you. I'm sorry. Would you like something to drink?" Robert Langston was not a rambler, but here he was, rambling on.

"Are you sorry you underestimated me or are you apologizing for not offering me a drink sooner?" She gave him her most amused smile. "You had to know I would know you the minute I saw you. At least, saw you up close. I did see you leaving the airport one night with a few others and get into Jack's Mercedes from the private airport. There was too little light to see you closely enough to put it together. And of course, I couldn't know you were the boss."

He got up and went to the wet bar. He poured two waters and handed her one before he sat back down. "I suspected it was you that followed us. I had been told about your 'research' and curiosity. I had a gut feeling. I will admit I considered telling you the truth then."

"What stopped you?" Lindsay crossed her arms and waited.

"As I said, we didn't think you would figure it out. If I'm being totally honest, I didn't know what I would say to you or how you would take it. I was scared for the first time in my life. At least this way, or how things were, I could keep you in my life from a distance and keep you protected."

Lindsay's blood pressure went through the roof. Robert didn't need to see the red creep up her neck to know. It was clear when she spoke. "Protected from what, or who? You?" She didn't bother to hide her frustration.

"Yes. No. The people that could come after you to get to me. If anyone finds out who you really are, it could put your life in danger."

Lindsay didn't miss a beat, her anger taking control, "And that would be different how? I'm pretty sure with what I do, being Kendall, the one you created, I'm in danger every day. Maybe you should have thought about that before you created her. Why do you get to be in my life but I don't get to be in yours?" She stared at him expectantly, demanding an answer with her eyes.

Robert noticed the stare but instead of answering right away, he took a few minutes to think that over. He also wanted to give her time to calm down. He leaned forward in his chair and clasped both hands between his legs, while resting his elbows on his knees. All he could do was look at the floor in front of him. That didn't work as hoped. It gave her time to think. She continued.

"I see. You needed me and my photographic memory. It didn't matter to you that I needed you? You had to know how my childhood would be with my mother and brother. You remember them? Your wife and son?" Her voice was rising with every word. Not that she cared about them and the effect it had on them. They had had a punching bag. Her. "I don't suppose they know this truth? My God, my whole life has been one lie after another after another. You could have prevented every single one of them! But you didn't. Inconsiderate bastard!"

She was now standing. She felt her ears pulsating from anger. He hadn't moved. She stormed out. He jumped to his feet and called after her but she kept going. By the time he caught up to her, she was opening the door to exit out of the office. She ran smack into Joe.

"Please don't leave yet. There are things you need to know." Joe put his hand on her arm.

She stopped and looked at his hand, then at him. "Are you detaining me?"

"No, but if you leave, I leave with you."

From behind her, Robert pleaded, "Lindsay, please don't go. Wait!"

She turned sharply and looked at him with so much anger, he flinched. "At least you know my name." With that, she walked out.

5

She didn't slow down until her vehicle was in sight. Joe kept pace with her. "Lindsay, you can let me go with you or I follow you, but I would prefer to go with you."

Lindsay stopped before he realized she was going to and he almost plowed into her. She didn't turn around to look at him. She stood there for a few moments, taking deep breaths. "This is how it's going to be? Fine. But you're driving."

He took the keys from her and waited for her to go around the Tahoe to the passenger side and get in. He didn't miss her wiping her eyes as she did. He had never known her to cry. Except when Sam died. But that was it. She wasn't a crier, or emotional at all for that matter. Neither of them said anything for the first ten minutes. Joe was letting her digest their conversation so far and waiting to see if she was going to ask him anything. He hoped not. But he had a few things to tell her.

Lindsay had been looking out the side window and without turning, quietly said, "You guys are watching me. Who?"

"Protecting you is more accurate than 'watching' you. Me and Derek. Kendall, it's for your own good."

"We are back to Kendall? Who is in danger, Kendall or Lindsay?" The sarcasm was dripping.

He looked over at her. He wanted to grin, but didn't dare. "I'm sorry. I've known you as Kendall longer. Well, I've never known you as Lindsay, actually. It will take conscious thought when I address you."

"Call me either. I think I still have a job as Kendall, don't I?"

"I'm not sure. It depends on how the rest of this plays out. There is still a lot the boss wants to tell you. There are things that you need to know now that you've come this far. Unfortunately, there is no going back. But you'll have to hear most of it from the boss."

"The boss, huh? You said you and Derek are watching me. What part does Sam play in this now?"

"That's up to you. You're the only one that can decide that. We don't feel safe with Sam watching out for you. He's too involved. I don't think I've ever known two people who love each other the way you two do. It's actually refreshing to know true love exists. Don't be too hard on him. I saw him and I swear, he was torn up. There wasn't one time I saw him that he didn't need reassurance that you were okay. Ken…Lindsay, that man loves you more than life itself. There isn't anything he wouldn't do for you. He would die for you."

Lindsay could only look at Joe. He felt the cold stare more than saw it. It took him a minute to realize what he had said.

"I'm sorry. Inappropriate. But he would. He values your life over his." Joe was never uncomfortable talking to anyone until now.

"He died to protect me from the truth. Really, Joe? Think about that. It's like this is a game of truth or die. My father dies. I get lied to. Sam dies. I get lied to. They die so I don't get the truth. My whole life has been one big lie. What next? Or should I not ask that? Will more people around me die to protect me from the truth? Is there more? I feel like I'm circling a drain and any minute, it's going to suck me in."

"There is more. Not more that I can say but more you need to know. You father... ummm, Robert, has enemies. Those enemies will now be yours, at least if they find out you're his daughter. Just please promise me you aren't going to tell anyone about any of this?"

"Who would you suggest I tell? No one knows I lead a double life except for those in the organization."

"They all do. Most of us do. But not many know the extent of your double life. Only me, Sam, Derek and Jack know the boss is your father."

"Do I need to worry about Jack?" Lindsay felt the ringing in her ears again. She was still slightly in shock that he pulled his gun on her and would probably wonder the rest of her life, if he would have shot her had Derek not shot him first.

"I don't know yet. Brutal honesty. We don't know yet." Joe didn't think Lindsay had to worry about Jack but until they could be absolutely sure, it was best to keep her guard up. There was so much left to tell her.

"Sometimes the one you would take a bullet for, is the one standing behind the trigger. Seems to be about everybody in my life, Joe."

Joe couldn't look at her. He wanted to understand, but he had to admit he didn't. "It's not like that. Really, it's not."

"Joe, I need you to be one hundred percent honest with me." She didn't say that if he hesitated, she would know he was lying. She wanted to see if he would. "Did Sam know Robert Langston is my father?"

Joe didn't hesitate, "Yes, but I don't know how long he's known." Joe was surprised it took her that long to ask. They had all agreed this would be the answer they would give unless she asked Robert or Sam herself.

Robert and Sam disagreed on the answer. Sam wanted to be honest with Lindsay. Robert told Sam to lie because she would never forgive him. Sam argued that was one of the most hypocritical things Robert could ever say. One of Robert's biggest worries was that Lindsay would never forgive him for his lies. There were more reasons he didn't want Lindsay knowing who he was, but those hadn't been disclosed yet.

Lindsay got lost in thought and didn't hear anything Joe said after, "Hello" when he answered his phone. She was mad that she had left before she could ask Robert that same question herself. She wasn't sure she would believe anything that came out of his mouth though.

6

"Hey, Kendall? I hate to do this right now, but we have a situation." Joe looked over at her expecting an acknowledgement but didn't get one. "Kendall?"

"Sorry. What? Why Kendall?"

"We have a situation. That was the FBI. They are requesting your presence at a scene in Philadelphia. I hate to ask right now but are you up for it?"

"Yup, fill me in." Lindsay could use the distraction. One thing that she wouldn't do was compromise her focus while working. She was all business and compartmentalized everything else. She loved her job with the organization.

"Are you sure? I don't want to put you back to work before you're ready and well, I....., but they did request you personally." Joe was speaking slowly to make sure that she was comprehending what he was saying.

"What's going on? Fill me in. And turn around and head over." Lindsay's whole demeanor changed right before Joe's eyes. She was a professional.

"Details are sketchy. They are sending the helicopter to meet us. It'll be faster. They need your photographic memory."

"That's not difficult then. Let's get it. It'll be good to be back at work."

Joe stayed on the phone making arrangements and trying to get as much information as possible about the situation they were walking into. He wasn't happy with the lack of information coming in. He continued working on it while Lindsay continued trying to figure things out in her personal life. She decided that was a lost cause for the moment and turned her focus on previous cases with the FBI to get back into work mode.

The helicopter met Joe and Lindsay at a helicopter pad on the roof of a business office building and took them to an FBI office on the outskirts of the city. As they drove to the scene, two agents caught Joe and Lindsay up on the situation. Within the last two hours, the FBI had followed a suspect to a house in a prestigious neighborhood. The house is owned by what now appears to be the Mexican cartel, under a bogus South American investor. The house is filled with fine artwork and most of it believed to have been stolen.

Lindsay thought back to one of her favorite trips to Mexico. Caro Aguilar. He thought he was suave inviting her to see his most prized artwork, in his bedroom. She was sure he would never forget her after that meeting. Of course, she had gone in undercover as Mr. Cabrera's wealthy wife. She had gotten the best of him. With a smile, Lindsay asked the FBI agents if this had anything to do with Caro Aguilar.

The agent continued, "We believe this is tied to Caro Aguilar. It's why you've been requested, Ms. Thomas. You are one of the few that has been in his house and parts of it that no others have and you have been in his offices. You have also been closer to him, physically, than any FBI agent."

"Surely you don't think the suspect is Caro himself?"

"No. We need you to go in and see him and check the artwork in the house. See if anything ties it to Caro."

"This could have been done electronically. Why am I really here? I want the name of the agent who specially requested me." Lindsay was excited to be back to work but there was definitely something off. The FBI had pulled Lindsay, as Kendall of course, in on cases before but Jack had usually orchestrated the contact.

Stepping out of the SUV at the scene, Lindsay pulled Joe aside and demanded to know who requested her. Joe reassured Lindsay that his contact was legit and she would be meeting the agent in charge, an old friend of his. Before Lindsay could say more, two men hurriedly strolled over. One handed Lindsay FBI gear to put on. The second one shook Joe's hand and told him it was good to see him. Then he quickly stuck his hand out to shake Lindsay's. "Miss Thomas, thank you for coming so quickly. I'm Special Agent in charge, Deacon Wyatt. It's a privilege to meet the legend."

If his reference to her being a legend hadn't struck her as odd, his stunning good lucks would have. He looked like Robert Langston, her father. There was no time to question or ponder either of these thoughts. There was work to do. Lindsay didn't bother to acknowledge what that was supposed to mean.

As Deacon was bringing Lindsay and Joe up to date on the situation, they walked into the house where their suspect was detained. It was a beautiful home and obvious that everything in it was top of the line from the floors to the furniture to the wall coverings. It was somehow familiar to Lindsay. She had taken all this in while walking from the doorway through the expansive entryway into the even more expansive living room.

Lindsay didn't waste any time in getting down to business. She walked over to the suspect and sat down, never taking her eyes off of him. She studied him for a moment then in Spanish she told him it was nice to see him again, although he looked nothing like the last time she had seen him. She knew the minute he realized who she was. She saw it in his eyes. First fear flickered, unnoticeable to the untrained, unfamiliar eye. Then he smiled and this confirmed she was right. Standing very slowly, she walked away from him but didn't take her eyes off of him. She asked Deacon to show her around the house. Smiling at Caro, she asked him if the master bedroom was worth a trip. She saw the familiarity flicker in his eyes this time, along with anger. But that too was short lived when he masked his expression and still said nothing.

Walking out of the room, Lindsay let Deacon know her cover was now blown and she would be no good to them in Mexico. Deacon simply said, "Your cover was blown when you injected Caro in the neck in Mexico, or at least you weren't going to be invited back."

"True but he had not known who I worked for, until now. Was that job for you guys? I usually don't know which side of the fence we're playing on."

"Wait. Are you saying this IS Caro himself? He doesn't look like any photos of him that we've seen. What makes you so sure it's him?" Deacon had stopped walking.

"Take the silicon off his face and you'll see a man that looks more like the photos and the Caro you were expecting. I'm sure that transformation cost more than anyone I know makes in a few years." It was a mixture of more than just silicon but Lindsay didn't need to explain that to them.

They ended in the master bedroom where Lindsay looked over the artwork. At first, she didn't see the art piece that he claimed was his prized possession he had shown her in his bedroom in Mexico. She did recall the size of it and walked over to one appearing to be the same size. Pointing at it and looking at Deacon she grinned. "Take this apart and you'll find what you are looking for." Then for a moment, Lindsay stood very still without saying anything. Deacon waited.

A slow smile crossed Lindsay's face and neither he nor Joe missed the flare in her eyes. You could see the excitement. "I saw the blueprint for this house the last time I was in his office. Follow me."

Deacon was intrigued. Lindsay led him and Joe to the kitchen. She began looking through the cupboards. Not finding what she was looking for, she began feeling under the counter ledge that hung an inch over the bottom cupboards. Still nothing. She looked at the gas stove and was still for a moment again. She closed her eyes this time. Picturing the blueprint, she realized there was no gas going to the stove. She walked over to it and turned it on. Nothing happened. She opened the oven door and began looking around inside.

"There it is!" Turning around proudly, she watched their faces as the entire wall where the pantry was slide away to reveal a staircase. "Shall I lead?" Lindsay lead them down the stairs into a large, long room spanning the entire width of the house. "You wouldn't have known this was here with the basement only being partially exposed to the back of the house. This part is all below ground and not able to be seen from the sides of the house. Pretty clever, huh?"

"Clever on their part, amazing on your part. You're right, we wouldn't have known." Deacon spoke without hiding his amazement as he looked around.

"Listen, I think my job is done here. Happy hunting. I'm sure you'll find enough for a conviction of Mr. Aguilar. I have to go." Lindsay headed back to the stairs with a nod to Joe to follow.

"You aren't sticking around to see what we find?" Deacon knew they could handle it but wanted Lindsay to stay.

"No, I have somewhere to be. It was great meeting you, Special Agent Wyatt. Good luck."

"Please, call me Deacon. Thank you, Miss Thomas. You far exceed any expectations. I owe you." Deacon shook her hand and gave Joe a slap on the back and a handshake. "Joe, let's do dinner soon." Joe nodded and followed Lindsay up the stairs and out to the Suburban.

"You aren't curious what they will find? Do you mind my asking why the hurry?" Joe wasn't one for questions so he surprised Lindsay with these two back-to-back. She suspected it was to keep the conversation on a professional level and avoid the personal.

"I have a meeting. I'm sure you will fill me in later. What's the deal with Deacon?" Lindsay wanted to ask how he was related to her but waited to see how much Joe would tell her. She didn't comment on how much he resembled her father. More lies would probably follow. Could none of them tell her the truth about anything?

Joe chuckled, "Deacon and I grew up together then joined the military together. Been best of friends forever."

"Then why is he with the FBI and not us?"

"He finished college while on active duty then was snatched up by the FBI, but finished out his tour first. It was a childhood dream of his. He's pretty straight and narrow. Not sure he would like some of what we do."

"And what exactly is that? Oh wait, I know, you would tell me but then you would have to kill me." Lindsay wasn't sure why she asked questions. She wondered for the thousandth time how much of what they told her was truth and how much was fiction. She sadly had a visual and she didn't like it.

Joe shook his head at her sarcasm. He wondered if it was safe to assume she still had her senses about her as long as she had that. "Another time. There is still information you need. You really do need to sit down with Robert and hear him out. You're going to have to find a way to stop getting pissed at him and walking out before he can fill you in. It's for your own good."

"Since when is anyone concerned about my good?" Lindsay held her hand up to stop any comment from Joe. She knew anything he would say was just fluff. God forbid anyone give her a straight, honest answer. She couldn't help add, "I'll say it again; the person you would take a bullet for, is sometimes the one standing behind the trigger."

Joe had nothing to say to that. The fact that she had said it twice already was a clear indication of what her mindset was.

7

Nothing more was said on the drive back to the Tahoe or the rest of the way to Lindsay's house. Joe put the SUV in park and reached for Lindsay's arm just as she reached for the door handle. "Lindsay, you have my number. Please know that I am available at any time for you."

"Who is your loyalty to, Joe? I know it's Robert first. Then Sam or me?"

"I didn't realize there is a pecking order. I can't imagine why I would ever have to pick one of you over the other. Is there something I don't know or something I need to know?"

"No, Joe, we're good. Thank you."

"I hope you can forgive him. I don't think he will be able to forgive himself if you can't."

Lindsay just gave Joe a nod, got out of the Tahoe and headed for the front door. Joe was following her to the door and when Lindsay stopped suddenly, Joe stopped just as quickly. He thought she had stopped because she realized he was coming in with her. She pointed to the door. It was ajar.

They pulled their guns and quietly went into Lindsay's house. Once inside, they listened intently. Nothing. Dead silence. But it was obvious someone was there or had been. Everything was strewn all over the place. Joe went to the back of the house toward the kitchen. Lindsay went downstairs.

Nothing was touched. The safe was still locked.

Coming back upstairs, Lindsay headed in Joe's direction. Joe was looking out the window into the backyard. He shook his head as if to say he hadn't seen anything yet. Lindsay pointed a finger at Joe then pointed it up indicating she wanted him to check upstairs, then indicated she was heading outside.

Lindsay made her way back to the front door and went around to the side of the house then to the back corner. The neighbor's house was fairly close with no room for trees and fences weren't allowed. She waited for Joe to come out and join her.

"Should we call Sam or Derek? Sam was headed home when I left earlier." They were now walking back to the front of the house outside.

"No, he was going to wait here for you to come back and give Derek some time off. I'll call Derek."

Lindsay didn't like this. She thought Sam was leaving, especially since she told him she would see him in a few days and she needed time.

Lindsay watched Joe pull his phone out. "Derek, where are you? Is Sam with you?" Then a moment of silence before Joe said more. "Okay, I see you now."

Joe nodded his head toward Derek's truck coming down the road. "Sam's with him."

As they pulled into the driveway, Derek hadn't stopped the truck before Sam jumped out and went straight to Lindsay. "What's wrong? You're back a lot sooner than I expected. That's not a good sign. How'd it go?"

Before Lindsay could answer, Joe cut in and told them someone had been in Lindsay's house and the front door was ajar when they walked up.

Derek looked mad and headed for the door. "We were only gone about thirty minutes. Had to go the store. Is anything missing? Sam, you didn't set the alarm?"

Sam just shook his head. "We weren't going to be gone long."

Lindsay told them she hadn't done a thorough check. The safe was still locked. "The last time someone was in my house that I didn't know, it was you, Derek. How did you get past the alarm? Oh, Sam gave you the code." She just shook her head and headed upstairs.

She was exhausted thinking about the argument with Robert, the boss, her father. She didn't know what to call him at this point. She still hadn't brushed the surface with all the questions she had.

Since her first meeting with Robert last week, questions got put on hold with the gunman on the lose and trying to figure that out. Plus, Lindsay had the boys home with her from then until last night. She needed time to process everything that had happened since her meeting with Jack, demanding answers from him, him getting shot, Sam coming back from the dead, formally meeting "Cowboy" and walking into the room to finally meet the boss. Her father. Robert Langston. Head of the very secret special ops empire. The very one she had been chosen for because of her photographic memory. Was it just that or that the boss was her supposedly "dead father"? She wasn't even sure who she was anymore.

8

After checking things out, Derek, Sam and Joe had cleaned up the mess in the living room. Lindsay reappeared looking refreshed.

Lindsay thanked them then asked them to leave. They weren't so eager.

"I think I should have one of my guys come in and do some fingerprinting if that is okay with you, Lindsay." She was sure that wasn't a question by the tone of Derek's voice.

"You know, I had thought about that, Derek, but I'm pretty sure that they won't find any and I would bet that it's the same person who shot at... the boss. What do I call him?"

No one was quick to answer so Sam walked over and gently took her by the arm, leading her to the couch. "Call him whatever you are comfortable with. We need to set up another meeting between the two of you." When Lindsay looked at him without saying anything, he explained, "Joe told us what happened."

"Not right now. Every few sentences with you all, I just end up with more questions. I would like for you all to leave. By the way, it won't be necessary for any of you to be watching me anymore. I can take care of myself and the boys."

She knew they wouldn't take that easily. "Protecting you, Lindsay. We aren't watching you. We are protecting you and more so now than ever."

Derek held her stare.

"From Who? Answer me that much!" Lindsay's frustration was palpable. No one answered, just as she suspected so she continued, "Listen, if this situation involved one of you instead of me, you wouldn't be watching each other. This is ridiculous. Jack was a bigger threat than whoever this is. As the boss said, they'll make a mistake and we'll get them." Lindsay glared at each of them and they each put their head down instead of meeting her eye to eye.

Sam was the first to speak again. "We'll talk it over with the boss and see what other options we have or come up with another plan."

"You do that. In the meantime, I need some regular girl time so I'm off to see Robin and Courtney." What she didn't say was how much girl time she would be taking.

Lindsay got up, walked to the front door and opened it. She stood waiting for them to leave. Joe hugged her and walked out. Joe was hugging her a lot lately and she wasn't' sure why. He had never done that until last week. Derek patted her shoulder and followed Joe out. Sam hadn't moved off the chair. "You, too."

"Really, pretty lady? I was hoping that we could talk. I know you've had a rough day, week, but I can't wait any longer to talk to you. Please?" He wanted to give her that grin that he knew made her melt, but didn't think now was appropriate. He stared at her intently, trying to gauge her thoughts.

"You have ten minutes. The girls are waiting." She walked away from the door, but left it open.

"Okay, that's a start." Now he gave her the grin. As she sat down in the chair opposite him, he knew she was trying to keep her distance. "I know this is sudden after all that's happened and I don't expect an answer right now, but I can't stop thinking about it. And with what just happened, it may be the best scenario as far as needing protection. I want to move in. I want to spend the rest of my life with you and I don't want to waste a minute more. At least consider it, please. I love you more than ever, if possible. I still want to get married but I know you have a lot to work through first and I'm okay with that. But I think this would be best for everyone."

"Do you always ramble when you are nervous or is it just because I only gave you ten minutes?" She had a smile of her own now. She had never known him to be nervous. Not even on their first date at the blues festival along the water. If he had been, he hadn't shown it.

He gave her that disarming grin again and walked over to her, kneeling in front of her, taking her hands in his and quietly said, "I love you."

She pulled him up as she stood. She was still holding his hands and looked down at them. "I need some time to digest everything and we still need to talk. You know the next question that is coming and I expect complete honesty. How long have you known the boss is my father?"

Sam didn't hesitate. She was right, he knew the question was coming and he had played it in his head a thousand times. "I found out right before I 'died.' It was one of the reasons I agreed to it. I wasn't originally so agreeable, then Derek and Robert told me. They told me so that I would understand what Jack was trying to protect and the extremes he would go to. Robert and Jack had been discussing the options of letting you go or letting you keep trying to find out. I don't think Robert really thought you would figure it out and Jack was tired of playing the wait and see game. He tried scaring you and distracting you, but nothing seemed to be working. Then when Jack messed with me, it got more serious because we knew then that he was making decisions on his own and getting nervous about you."

"So how long were you going to play dead?"

He didn't see that coming. "Until we decided what to do with 'Kendall' and figure out what to do with Jack."

"Why didn't the boss just let Jack go? I guess he knows too much and he is the boss's right-hand man. Have they been together in this since the organization was created?"

"These are the things Robert wants to explain to you. Robert had started the company and Jack joined a few years in. That's just what Derek told me so I don't know much. Can we talk about us?"

"No, I have to go." During the conversation, Lindsay had made her way across the room to put distance between them. She could see in Sam's face it was painful for him. The only thing that prevented her from giving in to him was his lie.

Sam smiled a sad smile and headed for the door. "I understand. Call you later tonight?"

Lindsay hadn't moved from her spot but watched him walk to the door and close it behind him. She slowly walked to the window and watched him until he was down the road and out of sight. Then she ran upstairs, grabbed her laptop, signed in and opened the tracker app.

She now could see where Derek's truck was

and where Sam's truck was. Derek and Joe were at the bar two miles from her house and it looked like Sam was joining them. Perfect, she thought as she closed her laptop and headed downstairs to the safe.

9

Lindsay was thinking clearly for the first time in weeks. She suddenly felt refreshed and like her old self. Whoever that was. She wasn't completely sure anymore. But she was definitely thinking clearly as she made her way down to the safe. Maybe it was because she had a plan.

As she entered the combination into the safe, she thought she heard something. She continued to open the safe as she listened more intently. The house was completely quiet so it wasn't difficult. She felt his presence before she saw the reflection in the mirror that she had put in the safe for this purpose. For as big a guy as he was, he moved silently. But that was part of his training. Tall One was standing behind her, moving slowly toward her.

She turned around quickly, acting surprised. Smiling she said, "Tall One! What are you doing here?" Before he could answer, she jumped across the room like she was going to jump into his arms. He was smarter than Lindsay gave him credit for. As she got close enough, he grabbed her right arm expecting to see a knife or syringe. Lindsay was smarter than him and had put the syringe in her left hand. She stuck him in the neck with her left while he was looking at her right hand.

His reaction was quick but not quick enough to stop Lindsay from hitting him hard with the injection. She got it in his neck at the prefect spot and it would only take a moment to take effect and put him down. As he dropped to the floor he asked, "What did you do that for?"

"Why are you here and sneaking around?" Before he could say anything, he was out. She hadn't expected him to go out that fast. Lindsay had to move quickly. She dragged him into her laundry room. Since the room was so big, she also used it for storage. It's where most of her job accessories were since no one came in here but her. She grabbed handcuffs for his hands and fishing line to tie him up. Once she was sure he wasn't going anywhere, she went back to the safe.

She took out two passports with different identities along with matching licenses, insurance cards and loyalty cards with the new names on them. She didn't use the loyalty cards but liked them to fill up the wallet of the day for authenticity. Each identity had three credit cards.

As she walked back in to the laundry room she pulled out her phone and snapped his picture. She only considered for a moment that he might be here for good. Then why was he sneaking in instead of ringing the doorbell? He didn't make for a very charming picture since he was tied up and out cold, but at this point in her life, she figured charming was overrated. Sam and Jack had been charming and look where that got her.

Lindsay didn't want to wait around for Tall One to wake up. Whatever he was up to, Sam could try to get it out of him when he found him. She had no doubt that once they all realized what was going on, her house would be their first stop.

As Lindsay headed for the door, she grabbed

her car keys and overnight bag, set the alarm and locked the door behind her. She didn't bother with the cameras in the house. She had disabled them. The guys were already aware since none of them suggested they look at them to see if anyone showed up from the break-in. She wouldn't be questioned or cause concern taking her car to Courtney's since she had already told Derek, Joe and Sam where she was headed. Let them track her. It would be the last destination they would be able to locate her.

10

Lindsay arrived at Courtney's a half hour later. Before going inside, she opened her laptop and checked the tracker information for Derek's and Sam's trucks. It appeared Derek was on his way to Courtney's, but Sam's truck was on his way to her house. She hadn't planned on them moving so quickly. When they said they were 'protecting' her, they meant it. Now she had to move faster.

Lindsay, Robin and Courtney had agreed to go riding when Lindsay got there. Lindsay grabbed her overnight bag out of the car and headed inside.

"Hey hey girlies! Let's go!" Lindsay wasn't wasting any time getting out of there.

"What's the hurry? I thought we would eat first." Robin never missed a meal and never gained any weight. She also worked out religiously.

"I'll tell you what, I'm anxious to hit the trail and get some fresh air so you guys eat then catch up with me." Lindsay never stopped moving toward the door that led to the back of the house and on to the stables.

Robin hollered after Lindsay, "Ok! But I get Broomstick!" Courtney didn't get a chance to say anything. She only had time to turn around and look at Lindsay with a blank look, while standing there with a hot pan in her mitted hand.

It would work out best for Lindsay since she had planned to ditch these two on their ride. Lindsay felt badly about it, but it couldn't be helped. Robin and Courtney had no idea that Lindsay led a double life. They had never heard of Kendall. And they never would. She shouldn't even be here right now and hoped she wasn't putting them in any danger.

Lindsay kept her eyes moving as she jogged through the expansive backyard toward the stables. Unfortunately, it was difficult to really see anyone in the woods surrounding Courtney's house. The backyard to the stables was four acres that Courtney spent every other weekend mowing.

As Lindsay entered the stables, she passed by Broomstick and considered taking him. But she had already decided on Gunner, who was 16.2 hands, making him the fastest horse. He was her favorite after Broomstick. He would be better for this ride and Lindsay knew he would easily find his way back home. Gunner was a lot wilder than Broomstick so Lindsay only rode him when she wanted a challenging ride. He would love this ride because Lindsay was alone and planned to keep it that way until she got where she was going. Gunner loved to run so he wasn't fun when there were two or more of the girls together. Hence, the name Gunner. Courtney's horses all had bloodline names but Lindsay and Robin had given them all nicknames.

Lindsay noticed Broomstick had his saddle on and was ready to ride. Gunner did not. Could Lindsay do bareback with Gunner? If she remembered correctly, he liked it better. Lindsay was about to find out. As she entered his stall, he snorted. Lindsay told him to relax as she put the reins over his head. Lindsay reached down into the overnight bag she hadn't dropped until inside Gunner's stall.

She now pulled the backpack out of it and threw the empty overnight bag in the corner of the stall. Gunner walked calmly to the door of the stable with Lindsay. She pulled him over to the side of the stable right inside of the door. She needed a place to mount him and even though she was 5'9", with his height she couldn't just swing herself up onto his back without help. She jumped up on the wooden railing to the last stall by the door and mounted Gunner easily. He hadn't moved.

Lindsay did have to wonder why he was being so easy. Maybe it was because she hadn't put the saddle on him. She led him through the door of the stable and steered him toward the far left of Courtney's property, away from the trail that they usually rode. They hadn't gotten far when Gunner took off into a full speed run. Lindsay was good with that. She needed to get out of here as quickly as she could. They wouldn't be far behind her.

11

———————

Gunner ran like the wind across the open field. Lindsay felt free and able to do anything. For a few minutes, she forgot about all the lies and manipulation from people who she should have been able to trust. She forgot about the old friend, one time flame, tied up in her laundry room.

Gunner slowed as he neared the edge of the woods. Lindsay knew she would have to go in them to lose anyone who might attempt to follow her and to get where she was going. She couldn't stay out in the open for too long. As much as she hated the woods, they seemed to be what gave her the most protection. She ended up in them much more than she would have preferred. She was definitely a city girl.

Gunner grunted as Lindsay led him in to the woods. There wasn't a trail here so they would have to take it cautiously. Lindsay led Gunner through the trees, thankful for them, yet cussing them at the same time. She turned him toward the stream. She had carefully mapped this out and wanted to walk him upstream for a few minutes. The water was rarely deeper than eight inches. Gunner was a strong horse and the best one for this trek.

Once they reached the point where Lindsay wanted to get out of the steam, she stopped and looked back. For as small as the stream was, it was still loud. It wasn't deep but it did move fast. She didn't stay there long but she did take the time to pull her gun out of the side of the backpack and tuck it into her waistband.

Lindsay turned back around after she was satisfied she hadn't seen anyone. They made their way through the woods for about a mile. Just short of the road that Lindsay knew was up ahead, she stopped Gunner again. She listened quietly and looked back behind her. She didn't see or hear anything. She pulled out her cell phone and dialed a number. "How far away are you?" She had turned the location off on the phone but knew that wasn't a complete safeguard.

"I'm coming around the corner. Be there in about two minutes. Are you there?"

"Yes." As she clicked off, she dismounted Gunner. She gave him a pat and a kiss, thanked him for being a great horse, turned him back toward home and slapped his backside hard. The slap didn't have the affect she had hoped. He snorted and looked at her. She told him to go home. She turned and headed off toward the road on foot. She jogged about fifty feet when she turned and looked at him. He was still looking at her but started moving toward home.

She jogged the rest of the way to the road and jumped in the car waiting for her. "Thanks for being here."

He put the car in drive and sped off before saying anything. "No problem."

"Did you get the cars lined up? The first one in Frederick, Maryland. The second one in Massanutten, Virginia, the third one in Roanoke, Virginia?"

"Yes, they're all set. Now are you going to tell

me where you want the last one?"

"The fourth one in Charlotte, North Carolina. That one will have the two suitcases with clothes in it. You have the shopping list to order the clothes on line then have them put in that car. I will be in Charlotte in three days. Do you have any questions?"

"Still not going to tell me where exactly you're going? You trust me enough to do all of this for you. C'mon. Who am I going to tell?"

"Drama Llama, I only trust people so much and that includes you. You already know too much. Any more could be a danger to both of us."

"At least tell me how long you're going to be gone." Drama Llama, whose real name was Dave, was concerned. He knew Lindsay could take care of herself, and he knew that her life was turned upside down lately. He didn't know exactly what was going on, but he was worried Lindsay was in trouble and he didn't like her going off on her own.

"I appreciate your concern. The less you know, the better off you are. I'm fine, really. I'll be gone at least a few months. The boys are with their dad, then going to visit their cousins out west at their ranch. They love it there. Did you pick up the cell phones I asked you to get?"

"Yes, here are the six for you. I have the other six for them. Here are the numbers for each one."

"Great. Did you number the six for them so they'll know which one to turn on when I send them a request?"

"Yes. You scare me with how well planned out this is. Has this, whatever this is, been going on for a while?"

"Good. Just follow instructions and quit asking so many questions and worrying. Just be sure that your steps aren't traceable. Are you making sure that we aren't being followed?"

"Yes. There's a car behind us that has been keeping up with us for a few miles. He's staying close behind and maybe being too cautious. I'm watching."

"Yeah, I noticed. Turn into the next fast food restaurant. See if he follows. I need a sweet tea anyway."

Drama Llama pulled into the next drive-thru. The car continued on and that was the last they saw of him, or any other prospective tail. They had a three-hour drive to the drop off point and only because Lindsay insisted on looping around a few times. Lindsay needed sleep. It was a long day. "I'm napping, please stay awake."

12

"Lindsay. Lindsay. Wake up. We're almost there."

Lindsay jumped at the voice. "I was out! All good? I haven't slept like that in weeks. Too bad it was so short."

"Yeah, all good. I thought you were going to start snoring any second."

Lindsay slapped his arm and informed him she never did any such thing, ever. "I heard you snore loud enough to wake the dead."

"Yeah and who would have told you that?" He looked sideways at her, not believing her.

"Your girlfriend. She was a wealth of info."

"I might believe that if you had ever met her."

"I may have to meet her since she's been around for a while now. Must be good if she's kept you this long. Here are my cell numbers back. You can keep this. I have them memorized." Lindsay realized the mistake as soon as it was out of her mouth. She needed caffeine.

"Damn, did you read them in your sleep to remember them?" He had no idea Lindsay had a photographic memory.

"Yeah, just keep them safe and only use in case of emergency. Let me be clear. The only emergencies are if anyone contacts you, you believe I've been compromised or if the boys are in any danger. Thank you for watching out for them for me.

Keep your distance. No one knows of our connection and I would like to keep it that way. Talk to no one ever. I doubt Sam figured out we are anything more than customer/bartender and I've certainly never shared with him who you are or what you do. By the way, if anyone comes around asking about Kendall Phillips, I need to know."

"Who is she?"

"Will you never learn to stop asking questions? No one you need to know but I mean it. I need to know if anyone does."

"You got it. Are you sure there isn't any more I can do? I'm worried about you, Lindsay."

"There is no time to worry about me and things you can't control. Have to go. I appreciate all that you've done. Here's payment." Lindsay handed him an envelope, gathered her bag, stuffed the phones in it and got out. She disappeared from Drama Llama's sight once she went through the door of the restaurant. He hoped it wouldn't be the last time he ever saw her.

Lindsay walked straight through the restaurant and out the backdoor. The car Drama Llama parked there was waiting for her. She didn't hesitate but jumped in and drove off through the back entrance of the parking lot. It was a two-mile drive back to the highway and another mile to the first rest stop. Lindsay was glad it was later than they had originally planned. The job for the FBI earlier that day had set her behind, but it worked out since it was now dark.

Lindsay drove to the first rest stop and pulled the car in between two semi-trucks. She waited five minutes. With nothing happening, she got out and opened the trunk. She found the equipment she had asked for. It looked like everything was there. She pulled out the electronic device tracker and went over the car twice to make sure there were no trackers on it. Finally satisfied, she got back in and drove away.

She only went past five exits before getting off the highway to her first destination. Lindsay had picked this hotel because there was more than one way out of the parking lot and she was able to get adjoining rooms. She always had an escape route. If only all of life had one.

Sadly, this adventure was planned out as an escape from her current reality and she just needed time to figure her life out and all the new revelations. She hated that she had to go through such extremes to get away for a little while. She would also be doing some research to get more answers now that she knew the players in this game of life. She couldn't do it at home with so much 'supervised protection'.

Her mind drifted to Sam. The love of her life. Lindsay didn't doubt that she loved him. She wasn't sure how to feel about what she couldn't help but think of as betrayal. She wouldn't think about him right now. She needed time to process it all. She wanted to find out more about him and would have time later. For now, she needed more sleep. Tucked safely in this hotel, she gave herself time to do just that.

She had been sleeping solidly until the banging started. Her eyes flew open, she immediately jumped out of the bed and grabbed her gun, all in one swift motion. She walked confidently to the door knowing it was locked along with the safety latch firmly in place.

Lindsay peered out the peep hole to see a woman dressed in a housekeeping uniform. She took a deep breath and asked, "Who is it?" just as the door started to open. The safety latch caught. The woman was quick to apologize. "It's housekeeping. I'm sorry. No one answered when I called out."

Still staying behind the door where the woman couldn't see her, Lindsay informed her she wasn't needed. She had told the hotel last night no interruptions. The housekeeper apologized again and left.

Going back to sit down on the bed, Lindsay realized she had slept the best she had in weeks. It was 11:00 am. She never slept that late, no matter what time she went to sleep. She got up and made coffee. She had checked the trackers on Derek's and Sam's trucks last night before she had gone to bed. They were both at her house. She had texted Courtney not long after she had been picked up by Drama Llama and told her that she was sorry but she had to leave and if anyone came asking for her to say that she was out riding. Lindsay told Courtney not to worry and not to tell anyone that Gunner showed up without her.

Lindsay knew Courtney would have questions but that she would also cover for her and trust whatever she was doing, she could handle herself. Lindsay had wanted to tell her friend about finding out that her father was alive as well as Sam, but she would have too many questions and Lindsay wouldn't have any answers. She wasn't willing to tell Courtney about her double life and put her in any danger.

Lindsay sent Courtney a text asking her if

anyone had shown up asking for her. Instead of Courtney texting back, she called her. Lindsay almost didn't answer but thought better of it. "Hey, what's up?"

"Ughhhh what is going on? I had two extremely handsome guys here last night and then another this morning looking for you. Are you in trouble?"

"No, of course not. Did you happen to get their names?

"Derek Stevens was the nicest looking. Joe something or other was the guy with him. Then this morning a guy who said he was from the FBI showed up. His ID, which you know I insisted on seeing closely even though he tried flashing it, said his name was Oliver Nicks. He asked the most questions. The two from last night didn't ask much. The guy this morning asked a ton of questions. You know I didn't tell him anything but it was weird. Lindsay, what is going on? If you are in some kind of trouble, let me help you. I can hire an attorney if you need one."

"Courtney, I'm fine. It's just a misunderstanding. I'll catch up with the two from last night. Just friends worried about me, unnecessarily. I'm not sure who the guy was that he said he was from the FBI and I doubt he really is. Just play dumb if any come back. Any descriptive, identifiable features of Agent Nicks?"

"Not really. How did they know to check here?"

" The two from last night were friends with Sam so he had probably mentioned your house or horses."

"Sam? Now you really need to tell me what

is going on! Did you find out more about how he died? Does it have anything to do with that?"

"No and no. I may be out of service area so, if you call, leave a voicemail. I have to go. Just stick to playing dumb. We'll chat soon and don't worry." Lindsay hung up before Courtney could ask any more questions. She hated not telling Courtney the truth, but at least she wasn't lying. The less said though, the better.

Lindsay let her thoughts wonder for a moment. How would she ever explain to anyone sane that she had just found out that her dead father was alive and controlling her life as Secret Agent Kendall Thomas. And that Sam was also alive and only played dead to get close to the guy from the secret organization. The same one that her very alive father created. Where they worked for the bad guys and the good guys. Where you never really knew who else worked for the organization. Where you couldn't trust anyone, especially those closest to you. Lindsay rolled her eyes at the ridiculousness of it. If it was so ridiculous, why was she so angry and frustrated? Why was she about to disappear from everyone? She needed time to think. She had to determine how she really felt about her life up to this point. She also needed to make decisions for her future. She would be in control of that much of her life.

Lindsay stopped the musing and decided to hit the road. She dumped her cell phone in the hotel garbage and didn't look back.

13

Lindsay's next planned stop was Frederick, Maryland where she would switch to car number two. She decided to leave that car and go on to Massanutten and get the car that Drama Llama left for her there. It was only a few hours drive and she needed to clear her head. The great night of sleep certainly helped.

Lindsay had carefully planned where each car was located. She had them parked in shopping areas where she could check them out by day; then, at night right before closing, she could walk into a store and out the back door. She would slip behind the shopping center and come out at the other end where the next car was. Her backpack looked like a big purse and, for now, that was all she had with her. The tracking device scanner fit neatly in the backpack and she scanned each car before taking it.

After getting the car in Massanutten, she drove to the hotel where she had dinner, worked out in their gym, checked Derek and Sam's trackers and took a long bath, which she never did. Then she finally went to bed. Had it been winter, she may have strapped on some skis and taken a few trips down the slopes. She hadn't skied since the last time she was here, years ago. She would need to come back.

Lindsay got up early, had her coffee and hit the road again. She was anxious to get to Charlotte and spend some time there. She had never been and she wanted to check out the courthouses. Something she usually enjoyed. Every courthouse she had been in on her last several trips, Derek, known only as "Cowboy" then, had shown up. Since no one knew where she was, maybe she would be able to spend time there and enjoy it.

Right before starting her drive, Lindsay had checked the trackers on Derek's and Sam's trucks. They were all over the place between her house, their houses and the boss's in Philadelphia. She knew Sam had found Tall One in her laundry room. She would love to know how that went. As she drove, she could only imagine that conversation. She was also sure by now that the boss and Jack were involved in conversations with Tall One. She had been turning her phone off when not in use and had seen the missed calls when she turned it back on. All thirty-two of them. She also saw the voicemail notifications, but hadn't bothered to listen to them. Maybe she should have before she dumped the phone.

Lindsay had thought about her time with Tall One. He was a good guy. His issue though of jealousy was just plain weird. He, undoubtedly, had absolutely no reason to worry about anyone cheating on him. He had everything going for him. Lindsay didn't know if him showing up now was due to Jack or something else. Whatever it was, she was sure it wasn't good. Tall One had no reason to knock on the door, let alone sneak into her house. They had parted ways on decent terms. The fact that he broke in and was sneaking around didn't sit well with Lindsay. She would have to do research on Tall One and try to figure him out more. Maybe she should have waited until he had woken up and questioned him. She couldn't wait around though. She wasn't sure how long before Sam would have shown back up, even though she told him she needed time.

For a moment, Lindsay felt badly about skipping out and not telling anyone where she was. That feeling didn't last. Why should she care? She was a grown adult. She could make decisions on her own. Although, the boss and Sam may disagree since they had been making decisions for her, even if she didn't know or realize it. Now they were just smothering her. Since she had found out that her father was alive and Sam was working with him, everything had changed.

Lindsay had a lot of figuring out to do and that was the reason she was taking this hiatus. During her drive to Charlotte, she thought about what it would have been like to have grown up with her father. Something she had tried not to think about all these years since it was a moot point. Now, it wasn't so moot, and she was angry and hurt.

By the time Lindsay reached Charlotte she was mentally exhausted. She had told Drama Llama she would be here in three days and she was a day early since she skipped Frederick. She headed straight to the hotel and was able to get a room immediately. She ate dinner, hit the gym and went straight to bed. She didn't bother to check Sam's and Derek's trackers.

The next morning, Lindsay decided to stay by the pool most of the day and read a good book. She napped in the afternoon, which she rarely did and just enjoyed the day, acting like she didn't have a care in the world. She refused to let her mind wander to reality.

The second day in Charlotte, Lindsay was up early and ready to explore the city. She preferred the city. She started with the courthouses, taking her time, walking around them and taking it all in. Then she walked along Romare Bearden Park. She loved the Charlotte landscape.

Lindsay chose a quant Italian restaurant in the food district. Sitting outside along the brick street, she truly felt at home. This beat the woods any day of the week. She found herself relaxed for the first time in a long time. Sadly, that relaxation was short lived. She felt her nerve endings start to tingle sparking a keen sense of being watched.

Lindsay slowly moved her head up and looked around, as if searching for her waiter. She took in everything around her quickly. The only thing that was odd was the lady across the street, staring at her. She had fabulous green eyes, much like Lindsay's. Her hair was pulled back and under a wide brimmed hat so Lindsay couldn't see what color it was. She was dressed in what was easily recognizable as expensive, designer clothing. Lindsay casually smiled at her. The lady kept glaring. Lindsay figured she was mistaking her for someone else. Apparently, someone the lady was furious with. Lindsay finished her lunch, the whole time keeping her head down but watching the lady across the street through her upper eyelashes. Every once in a while, the lady would do something on her phone. Lindsay finished her lunch, paid the bill and stood up. As she did, she looked the lady straight in the eyes and started moving toward her. The lady got up, turned around and started walking away, quickly.

Curiosity got the best of Lindsay, so she followed her. The lady walked briskly up the street and turned into a store. Lindsay continued to follow her. The lady took the escalator to the second level, then breezed through the door to a parking garage. Lindsay followed her but just as Lindsay got to the door, the lady jumped into the passenger side of a sports car and screeched off.

As Lindsay walked back to her car, she scanned her memory for the lady with the fabulous green eyes. She would have remembered seeing her before today. Maybe the lady had realized that Lindsay was not who she thought and that is why she left without contact.

Lindsay wasn't going to let anyone ruin her tour of Charlotte and continued exploring the city. It was beautiful and the weather was perfect for being outside. Lindsay loved the outdoors, in the city, not the woods.

14

Lindsay ate dinner in the hotel restaurant, then relaxed by the outdoor pool for a while before heading up to her room. She walked into the elevator and turned around to face the doors. Just as the doors shut, she caught a glimpse of the lady with the fabulous green eyes staring at her from outside the huge lobby windows. She tried to open the elevator doors but wasn't quick enough. It couldn't be a fluke that she had seen her twice in one day, and both times the lady was glaring at her. If she knew Lindsay, why wouldn't she approach her and get out whatever was bothering her. Surely, she wasn't hired by her father to follow her. She wouldn't be so obvious nor would she openly glare at Lindsay and draw attention to herself.

Lindsay got off the elevator on the second floor and took the stairs back to the lobby. The lady was nowhere to be found. Lindsay approached the desk clerk and described the lady she was looking for. The clerk said he hadn't seen anyone with remarkable green eyes other than Lindsay.

Now, taking the stairs back to the third floor, Lindsay peered out the glass in the door leading to the corridor she needed to go down to get to her room. Not seeing anyone, she ran to her room, unlocked the door quickly and went in, shutting and locking the door. Lindsay was not typically paranoid, but something wasn't sitting well with her.

She pulled out her laptop and opened the tracker app. Derek and Sam where both in Philadelphia at the boss's house.

She decided even though it was late, she would leave Charlotte during the night. She wanted to get a few hours of sleep then she would leave. She didn't want to leave right now with Green Eyes around. Fortunately, Lindsay could do what she called "sleep on demand." As soon as she closed her eyes for more than two minutes, she was asleep. She could do this standing if needed. She was also a few days early leaving Charlotte and hoped Drama Llama had the car with the clothes ready.

Lindsay sent Drama Llama a quick text from one of the burner phones asking if the car was in place. He responded immediately with, "Yes".

At 3:00 am, her alarm went off. Lindsay jumped in the shower, put her hair up under a baseball hat, packed her few things into the backpack and carefully made her way to her car.

There wasn't a soul around. She was confident she wasn't followed as she drove to the shopping center where car number three was with her new clothes. She pulled up next to it and parked. She debated on whether to check it for trackers, even with the dim light from the shopping center parking lot. Feeling like a target out in the open of the empty parking lot, she decided against it. She did take time to open the trunk and check for luggage, which was there. Some of Drama Llama's best qualities are his speed and efficiency.

She drove out of the parking lot and headed for the highway. No one followed. She decided she was being paranoid and that no one knew where she was. Green Eyes still gave her an uneasy feeling that she couldn't shake.

Lake Dare was a few hours' drive west of Charlotte. Lindsay had considered going to a beach somewhere, but she had the lake house she had bought years ago, under the fake identity of Kendall James. She had considered not using that identity since it was close to Kendall Thomas, her secret ops identity. But it couldn't be helped now.

For the first several years after Lindsay bought the lake house, she had an older lady, Elizabeth Johnson, live there and establish an identity in the small town. Lindsay had intended on visiting her, but never took the time. Elizabeth had done a great job establishing herself in the small town as an artist and a widow. Elizabeth was a lady who had lost everything and needed a fresh start. Lindsay had met her at a street market where Elizabeth was selling paintings to make money. Fascinated with her work, Lindsay befriended her over the course of a few weeks, frequently visiting the market. When Elizabeth confessed her problems, Lindsay knew she was the perfect person to live in the lake house and establish a town presence. The town was very small, everyone knew everyone; but Lindsay didn't want anyone knowing her.

Lindsay had Drama Llama make a new identity for Elizabeth. Elizabeth would now and forever be known as Ava James. Once the new identity was established and Ava was comfortable with it, Lindsay moved her to the lake house to live, paint and establish her presence as a local. Ava had done a great job of playing a widow with only a niece as her last living relative. Ava had told everyone that her niece, Kendall James, was busy with her job as a writer traveling the world. Once a year or so,

Lindsay bought Ava a ticket to any place she wanted to go and had Ava tell everyone she was going to visit her niece.

Ava was no longer at the lake house. A few years ago, she had met and married a gentleman on one of her trips to Europe. She was now living overseas, and still using the name Ava. She and her husband had returned to the lake house for short visits at least once a year. The trips were to check on the house since Lindsay never made it back.

The lake house was one of many places Lindsay had bought in the event she needed a hide out. Like now. The lake house was meant for an extended stay and she had thought she may bring the boys here over the years. It just had never worked out the way she had hoped. The other places she owned were in busy tourist areas where people came and went all the time and no one noticed new faces or extended absences.

On the drive, Lindsay went over all the things "Aunt Ava" had told her friends at Lake Dare. Thankfully, there were not a lot of details. Ava was very good about keeping details simple and to a minimum.

Lindsay had been keeping an eye out for anyone following her. She was sure no one was, but she knew all too well, you could never be one hundred percent confident in that. And this is why she had switched cars in towns along the way and was using different identities. Once she reached the lake house, she would be Kendall James, niece of Ava James. At least she could remember Kendall easily enough since that name had been used half of her life, when she wasn't Lindsay.

Shortly after Lindsay left Charlotte it had

started to rain. Now it was pouring and still dark since she had left at a ridiculous hour. Lindsay wasn't one for having bad luck, but when she did, it was at the most inconvenient of times.

She knew immediately the moment the tire went flat. She didn't hear the thumping noise over the downpouring of rain, but felt the car pulling badly. She had no choice but to pull over. She was only twenty minutes from Lake Dare. Lindsay wasn't impressed with having to change a tire at 4:30 in the morning, in a downpour, but at least she knew how to do it. Jack had made sure of that when she first got her license. She wouldn't think of Jack right now. His betrayal was still raw, too, along with the others.

She pulled over onto the shoulder of the road and contemplated on waiting out the rain. After only a minute, she decided against taking any longer than necessary to get to the lake house. She put her hazard lights on and got out. Lindsay opened the trunk, took out the two suitcases put there by Drama Llama and put those in the backseat. She was soaked already but got the spare tire and necessities to fix the flat. Just as she knelt beside the flat tire, a car pulled up behind hers on the shoulder of the road. She didn't wait to see who it was or if they could help her. She wanted out of the pouring down rain as quickly as she could.

She glanced over toward the back of her car, but couldn't make out if the person approaching was male or female. She decided it was a male by what little she could see of his size through the rain. She continued working on the tire. He approached and stood beside her for a few seconds and watched her. Lindsay looked up at him through the pouring rain but couldn't make out his face for the rain hitting hers so hard. She hollered up to him that she was fine and thanked him for stopping. He didn't move.

Lindsay continued to work and, without looking up again, hollered to him to leave as there was no sense in them both getting soaked. She was struggling to get the last lug nut off the tire. The man standing near her, knelt and took the wrench from her hand. Lindsay moved over and let him get it off. As soon as he did, she tried to move back in to finish the tire change. The man didn't move but continued to fix the flat. Once he was done, he grabbed the tools and the flat tire and put them in her trunk. He didn't look at her as he closed the trunk, but instead turned and jogged back to his car. From the brief encounter while kneeling at the tire, Lindsay could see that under his raincoat hood, he had sharp, angular features. For a moment, while he was changing the tire, she had watched rain drip steadily off his nose and chin.

They had never made eye contact nor had he said one word to her. He definitely never gave her time to thank him. Lindsay always heard people around here were some of the friendliest one could meet. This had been two people in less than twenty-four hours she had contact with who never said a word to her. It was just as well. She wasn't here to make friends. She wanted peace and quiet to think about her life. A life she hadn't intended. Tangled with lies, betrayal and deceit.

15

Lindsay made it to Lake Dare half an hour later. The rain had slowed her down, but she didn't care. She was glad to be out of Charlotte and away from the green-eyed lady. There was a familiarity about her that Lindsay still couldn't shake.

Lindsay passed through the small town, taking it in. Nothing had changed since her last visit here when she bought the house. Making her way through town and stopping at one of the few traffic lights, she noticed the sign directing people to the campground, which was not here years ago. She made a right toward the lake and wondered why the campground was in the opposite direction. She loved that the lake was five miles out of town, but not completely remote. As she made the last left onto the road leading around the lake, she noticed the new convenience store. It wasn't a national one, just a small, locally owned store. She liked that but doubted she would go in. It was close to the lake and the less people that knew she was here, the better. She made her way down the road, then turned right onto the lane that would take her through the woods to the few houses on this part of the lake.

Lindsay felt relief as she pulled into the driveway of the lake house. It was still raining, but at least it wasn't heavy. She grabbed one of the suitcases along with the backpack and headed for the garage, attached to the side of the house. When Ava left, Lindsay had asked her to keep the utilities on and everything in working order. She knew an older gentleman who lived nearby had kept on eye on things for Ava while she was gone.

Lindsay had considered renting the place out while no one was living there but decided against it. She didn't want to worry about anyone damaging things or being there if and when she needed it. Like now. She made her way to the garage side door. She stopped just inside the door waiting for her eyes to adjust and at the same time, reached for the light switch. She wasn't surprised the lights didn't come on when she moved the switch. With no light, the garage was pitch black. It wasn't much better outside in the rain, still before dawn. She set her suitcase down and pulled her phone out. Turning on the flashlight function, she made her way around Ava's car that was still parked here and entered the house. She tried several switches, and when none turned on the lights, Lindsay headed toward the kitchen pantry where she knew there would be candles. She and Ava both loved scented candles and the electricity was known to go out here at the lake during storms.

After lighting several candles in almost every room in the house, Lindsay brought in her other suitcase and bag and put everything away. She roamed around the house to check things out. Once she was satisfied everything was all right, she took a shower. Out of habit, she walked through the house again, taking everything in more closely. She had fallen in love with the house the moment she had seen it on-line, although it had been a little bigger than what she was looking for. Four thousand square feet was more than she had intended. She had flown out here and immediately bought the house, paying cash. She loved the second-floor balcony that overlooked the living room below and the lake beyond through the windows in the back of the house. The windows spanned the entire two stories of the living room.

The balcony that she was standing on only led to the master bedroom then another door that led to the laundry room. Her bedroom faced the lake as did the other two bedrooms on this level but those had to be accessed from the other staircase in the back of the house or by going through the laundry room from here. From her bedroom, she could come here to go downstairs or she could go out the backside of her bedroom to the hallway on the other side of the laundry room. The floorplan made a circle by going from this balcony through her bedroom, out the back hallway then coming back through the laundry room to here. Multiple exit options where important in houses as well as everywhere else.

Lindsay settled into a chair on the balcony with her laptop. Pulling up the tracker for Derek's and Sam's locations, she was wary to see that they were both in Philadelphia at the boss's house, or her father's house or office or whatever it was. She knew Sam must be worried sick about her. More so after finding Tall One tied up in her laundry room. She could only imagine what he was thinking. She wondered what the boss, her newfound father, was thinking. She made herself a promise right then, she would not worry or think about what they were going through. She was here to figure out her life and it didn't matter what either of them were thinking. Because, what she had been thinking her whole life was a lie. She was here to figure her life out and they didn't matter.

16

"What in the hell is she thinking?" It was just after five in the morning and Sam nor Robert Langston could sleep. Robert asked this question for the third time.

Sam hadn't answered the fist two times but now he did. "What do you mean what is she thinking? We don't know if she was taken and is hurt. Or even......." Sam wouldn't say it. "You're still thinking she's gone off on her own?"

Robert was mad now. "Say it Sam. Dead. Lindsay could be dead. Or faking it since we both did."

"She isn't de….that and isn't faking anything. Her worst is still better than our best combined. We would both deserve it if she disappeared from our lives, one way or the other. I refuse to think like you. I will not stop hunting for her until I have her body. Either way." Sam felt that queasiness coming back. Every time he thought of anything bad happening to Lindsay, it was a gut punch. "Listen, we need to focus on finding her regardless of what we find. Have they gotten anything out of Tall One yet?" They had all called Rob "Tall One" since he worked for the agency and Lindsay, as Kendall, had given him that name the first time he walked into the office upon introduction.

Before Robert could answer, Joe walked in. "I can answer that. You won't like it. Tall One's sticking to the same story he originally told us. Says he was there to talk to Lindsay because he missed her. He swears Jack didn't send him. He said she was acting crazy and stabbed him with her little potion before he could convince her he just wanted to talk. Jack is still saying he didn't hire Tall One to go after Lindsay."

Sam just shook his head. They all knew there was more to that BS. How to get it out of him? Sam looked at Robert. "Hey, Robert, has any information came back on Tall One yet?"

Robert looked thoughtful for a moment. "I'll make a call."

Robert left the room. Joe followed him out, saying he was going to get them coffee. Sam asked himself why Robert would leave? This was his office. Sam walked over to Robert's desk. It was meticulous. Sam guessed when one faked their own death and then ran an international secret ops organization, nothing less should be expected. Sam and Robert never really had a working relationship because most things came through Derek. Since Sam's faked death, they started working a little more closely together but Sam didn't really know much about him. He figured since Derek worked for him, he had checked Robert out. Sam stood behind Robert's desk, staring at it but not seeing it because he was so lost in thought. Wondering to himself, but out loud asked, "What am I missing?"

Joe walked back in just in time to hear the question. "Lots. We are all missing lots. You know her better than the rest of us. Would she disappear on her own? I know they've asked, but not sure if you thought more about it." Joe set the mug of coffee down on the table in front of the chairs. Away from Robert's desk. "I wish I had an answer for you. As you know, Lindsay has been through a lot. I would like to think she would talk to me but part of me is thinking she did leave on her own. She said she needed time. She would go through extremes because she knew we were all protecting her or 'watching' her as she said. She wasn't happy about that. What bothers me is that Tall One was tied up after she drugged him. Why would she tie him up and leave? Why tie him up? He could have just left on his own once he woke up. Did she want us to find him? Is there something she knows that we don't? Did someone else tie him up and follow Lindsay to the ranch and take her from there? She couldn't disappear into thin air." Sam slammed his fist on Robert's desk. Sam didn't need Joe to answer. They both knew she could.

Joe felt Sam's anger. Joe knew more than Sam did about Robert and his enemies and some of the things that Robert had wanted to talk to Lindsay about. There were things that Robert needed to handle with Lindsay and things that he needed to tell her. Joe would never tell Robert's secrets nor would he worry Sam any more than Sam already was. But this wasn't good. Joe was worried.

"Where did Robert go?" Sam didn't look up. He was more talking to himself than Joe.

Joe answered anyway. "Coffee's over here. Let me go check on him." Joe left Robert's office and headed upstairs where Robert was on the phone behind a closed door. With Joe's overly sensitive hearing, he heard Robert say, "Where are Charlie and Casey?" Then a pause. "I asked you to find them three days ago. What's taking so long?" Another pause. "I want them here now!" Joe almost didn't knock as he knew Robert was furious, but he did and didn't wait for an invitation to open the door. He walked in just in time to see Robert throw his phone across the room.

Joe looked at Robert with optimism. "They'll turn up."

Robert stared at the wall thoughtfully for a moment before saying, "Why didn't I tell Lindsay immediately? She needed to know. Damn it!" Robert wanted to punch something but thought better of it. Joe knew it was a rhetorical question.

"Are you going to tell Sam and Derek?" Joe knew the answer but needed Robert's confirmation.

"No." Robert's simple answer spoke volumes.

17

"I know Lindsay is at her house on Lake Dare in North Carolina. I could only hope she would go there, as opposed to some of her other properties. She's an easy target now. All alone. I doubt anyone else knows about it." She tapped her fingernail on the table in front of her. He knew she was calculating her next move.

"How did you ever find out about that lake house?" He watched her tap her long, manicured fingernail on the table. It grated on his nerves. Just like she did. For all outward appearances, she was classy, in excellent shape and beautiful. She had stunning, unique green eyes. She was cunning and smart. She was also one of the most evil people he had the displeasure of knowing. He found everything about her to be repulsive.

"I know things about Lindsay Phillips/Kendall Thomas that she doesn't know about herself. I have hoped this day would never come, but now that it's here, let's do this." He could see the spark in her eyes. He saw no remorse for this day coming and was doubtful she had hoped it would never come. In fact, she had most likely waited for it.

"What exactly is this?"

"This is why you are here." She glared at him to make sure he understood.

"Is that what you are telling yourself? Funny, I don't see it that way." He glared back at her but was first to break eye contact.

"There's nothing funny about this situation. I had hoped she would die long before she ever found out the truth. Jack should have stopped her a long time ago. He's never failed at anything until Lindsay. I should have run her over on her graduation night when I had her alone on the road to the lake in that small town she lived in. Damn her luck." He could see her eyes glaze over as she flashed back.

"I doubt it's luck. Lindsay has worked hard to get where she is. She is talented and spent her whole life having to prove herself. Or at least as Kendall." He didn't know anything about her as Lindsay, but he did know a little about Kendall. He had never met her, but she was somewhat legend-ary in her world.

"Since when did you become the Lindsay/ Kendall expert and stop sounding like her biggest fan. It pisses me off even more."

"I don't really understand why you are filled with so much hate for her. What did she ever do to you, anyway?"

"That's not for you to understand. I don't care either way if you or anyone else understands. This is about me."

"It always is. So, leave her out of it and go live your life." He had been leaning with his back against the wall, arms down at his sides, but now he crossed his arms and relaxed his right leg.

"I was doing just fine until…..never mind. I'm not having this conversation with you of all people. Don't forget, you work for me. I call the shots. You'll do as I tell you." He could see her seething behind her cool exterior.

Now he was seething even more than she. "Let's be clear, Princess, I do not work for you." He hadn't moved a muscle and barely moved his lips.

She didn't miss a beat. "Let's be clear, Mr. Macho, you are now. Do as I tell you and you can have your life back, free and clear. If not, I'll make every day of the rest of your life a living hell." She smiled at the thought. The woman was indeed evil.

"Like this isn't? Being associated with you is a living hell let alone doing anything for you. Being in the same room…."

She held her hand up and cut him off. "Hence why I didn't give you a choice. You don't have to like me; you just have to follow my directions where Lindsay is concerned." She was vehement, but changed to sultry quickly. "It's a shame really, that you have such distaste for me. We were excellent together. We are very similar, you and I. You're not only intelligent and clever but you are as sexy as I've seen." Then, just as quickly, she changed back to vehement. "And speaking of clever, don't try to out clever me. I'll win. Your life as you know it will be over, just like Lindsay's."

"Excellent together? Don't fool yourself. When the truth comes out, and it will, your life as you know it will be over. You won't be protected anymore. You'll be done, Princess. And let's be clear, we are nothing alike." Now he glared at her, disgusted and refusing to break eye contact.

She all but spit at him as she stated, "Let's be clear. I don't lose. Ever. And stop calling me Princess." She glared back and was seething again.

18

Lindsay kept herself busy the next few days. She dyed her hair dark brown, put brown colored contacts in her eyes, and went into town to the grocery store. She was thankful the store was mostly empty. The clerk looked at her a little funny when Lindsay put the three weeks of groceries on the grocery belt, but fortunately, didn't ask any questions other than if she was camping nearby. Lindsay just smiled at her and started bagging her own items. She made it out of town and back to the lake without incident.

On her second day at Lake Dare, Lindsay was sitting on the front deck, looking out over the lake pondering the last few years, when she heard something in the bushes. She glanced over and even though it was daylight, she put her hand on her gun, which was hidden in her waistband. She was not completely comfortable here yet. An older gentleman stepped into the yard on the side of the house, but didn't seem to be surprised to see Lindsay.

"Hello young lady! I'm Mr. Williams, the neighbor. How are you today?" He approached the deck but didn't step onto it.

"Hello, Mr. Williams. I'm fine thank you. Hope you are well?"

"Yes, yes dear, I am. Not bad for an old man. I keep a lookout on this place for Ava. She didn't tell me to expect anyone. May I ask who you are?"

"You certainly may ask. I'm Ava's niece, Kendall James." Lindsay stepped off the deck into the yard, closer to Mr. Williams and put her hand out to shake his, although she usually avoided shaking hands. "Thank you for keeping an eye on the place. Aunt Ava and I both truly appreciate it. I'm sorry I didn't warn you or her, but it was a spur of the moment trip and well, here I am."

"It's a pleasure to finally meet you Miss James. I've heard wonderful things about you. Everything has been good around here. No problems, except as I'm sure you know, electricity goes out a lot."

"Yes, I have heard that. I'm glad there have been no problems. One of the great features about this lake life, huh?"

"That's true. Pretty quiet around here. Most homes are locally owned and the only tourists are the campers about five miles on the other side of town. Once in a while, some will end up over here. We've been trying to get the town to close the open access to the boat launch and picnic area but so far, they haven't been willing to do that. Most townspeople think it brings in business and money, but the lake owners don't care for public access and it would make it more of a private lake. The lake is big enough for more traffic but that's not our point. Well, I've taken up enough of your time. If you need anything, I'm only two houses over." He pointed back behind him.

"Thank you again for keeping an eye on the place and thank you for your kind offer. Can you tell me who owns the two houses on each side of me?"

"Of course. The house between us was sold

to a gentleman, Mike Smith, about the time you bought this one. He paid way too much for it if you ask me, but that's none of my business. Never seen him, never met him. He rents it out occasionally, but it sits empty most of the time. I look after that one too when I check in on yours. The house over there is Mrs. Wigley. She has been widowed for many years. She's somewhat of a recluse. Rarely ever see her. I think she should sell, but I guess she has been here so long, it's home to her. I used to check on her but she got mad at me and told me never to come back. Her grandson checks on her weekly now. I keep my ears open, but if I get too close, she howls and threatens me. Crazy old bat if you ask me but that's none of my business. Nice to finally meet you Miss James. You take care."

"Bye Mr. Williams. Thanks again." Lindsay watched him walk off in the direction that he came. She was thankful that the house beside her was empty and the other was a recluse. She was looking forward to the peace and quiet and just what she was hoping for coming here. The houses all had a strip of trees between them, just thick enough that you couldn't see through them, for the most part.

Early the next morning, Lindsay called Ava to let her know she was at the lake and to check in on her. Lindsay asked if Mr. Williams is the older gentleman who watched the house while it was empty. Ava confirmed that was him and he had already called Ava to let her know "Kendall James, her niece had arrived safely." So, Ava already knew she was here and had been waiting for her to call. Ava was doing well and was considering stopping by the lake house over the summer during their US travels. Lindsay told her she would love to see her and her husband and to let her know when she was coming. Lindsay told her that she would be there for about three months, if all went well.

Ava was concerned since Lindsay had never visited the lake house during the years she had lived there. "Lindsay, are you okay? I know you aren't. What's going on? Tell me right now. Do I need to come back there? I called you several times yesterday but got no answer."

"Ava, relax. There is a lot going on but I'm fine. I'm safe and no one knows I'm here, except you and Mr. Williams, of course. I am hiding out. The boys are safe but don't know about this place. All is well. I just need to do some serious thinking. Stop worrying. Please come visit when you can. Also, do you have a pen? I need to give you some new cell phone numbers to reach me."

Ava promised to call before she came, mostly to avoid Lindsay shooting her should it be during the middle of the night.

The next week passed quietly and Lindsay was enjoying her solitude. Until she wasn't.

19

Lindsay was sleeping soundly. She had gone to bed about 1:00 a.m. and was in the middle of a vivid dream about Sam when she sat straight up in bed. She slept deeply, but could wake up instantly and be alert.

She listened intently. It was too quiet. The hair on the back of her neck stood up. Looking at the clock, she realized she had only been asleep about forty-five minutes. Silently slipping out of bed, she put on sweatpants and grabbed her gun. Like a ghost, she moved toward the bedroom door leading to the second story balcony. Opening the door, she eased to the edge of the balcony and listened again. Still too quiet. Her eyes had adjusted to the darkness quickly. She intentionally kept all the lights off when she went to bed. She knew the layout and anyone else breaking in wouldn't. She and Ava had talked about putting a security system in, but it wasn't needed here. Drama Llama had taught Ava how to shoot and security alarms could be disabled or bypassed, and typically provided a false sense of security.

Lindsay soundlessly made her way downstairs. She silently walked through each room and into the kitchen. As she entered the kitchen, she saw someone at the door. She stopped and watched for a moment. They appeared to be trying to pick the lock. She watched for a moment more when she heard a female voice swearing. She eased closer to the door, watching the figure the whole time.

As Lindsay stood there, the female voice became more and more agitated and louder. Finally, Lindsay couldn't stand it anymore. She whisked the door open and stood with her gun aimed at the woman.

"What the hell are you doing in my house? Get out of my house! Why did you lock me out, you fool! Who are you?" The furious lady was about seventy, and now standing in Lindsay's kitchen in a long nightgown.

Lindsay had backed away from the delusional lady but kept her gun pointed. She wasn't sure if the lady even noticed it because she was so mad. "Ma'am, you have the wrong house, I'm afraid. Are you Mrs. Wigley?"

The lady looked at her, and started screaming again for Lindsay to get out of her house. She threatened to call 911 if Lindsay didn't leave immediately. Lindsay tried for a few minutes to calm her down, holding firmly to her gun, but not pointing it at her any longer.

Not sure what to do with this lady, Lindsay tried to convince her to walk next door with her. Lindsay thought once she saw her own house, she would realize her mistake, if she were Mrs. Wigley. The lady wasn't budging. Lindsay had considered calling the police but didn't want to involve them. Before Lindsay could figure out what to do with her, a car pulled into the driveway. A police car. Lindsay was not impressed.

Putting her gun in the waistband of her sweatpants, Lindsay watched the lady in the middle of her kitchen, screaming at her to get out, and doing some twirly dance-like thing. She was certifiably crazy. The door was still open as neither Lindsay nor the lady had closed it. Lindsay watched as a uniformed officer walked up to the open door.

He looked at Lindsay, then at the crazy lady, who was now making a very strange sound, completely indiscernible and still doing her twirly dance.

Looking back at Lindsay, he nodded and said, "Officer Becker, Ma'am. May I come in?"

"Please do." Lindsay waived her hand with a swoop and pointed at the crazy lady.

"Mrs. Wigley, I'm Officer Becker. Will you please come with me? You are in the wrong house. C'mon, I'll take you home."

Mrs. Wigley stopped her strange sound and movement and looked at the officer. She started screaming at him to get out and take the lady with him. Officer Becker asked Lindsay to step outside. Lindsay shook her head no.

Officer Becker turned his head and spoke into the mic on his shoulder. "She won't leave." Lindsay instantly recognized his side profile but wasn't expecting him to be an officer. The response back was, "OK." Almost immediately, another police car pulled into the driveway. This was a little weird and Lindsay moved back to the doorway going out of the kitchen. She wasn't sure if the officer was referring to her or Mrs. Wigley.

Mrs. Wigley in the meantime had wondered over to the coffee pot and was making coffee as if she were in her own kitchen. Lindsay couldn't believe this was happening. Mr. Williams hadn't said Mrs. Wigley was full on delusional.

The second Officer appeared in the doorway and asked Lindsay if he could come in. She nodded and again did the swoop with her hand. The Officer cautiously approached Mrs. Wigley and said, "Mrs. Wigley, your grandson, Zackary, asked me to bring you back home. Would that be okay with you?"

Mrs. Wigley stopped abruptly and spun around. "Oh, Officer, of course you can! I'm sorry, I didn't mean to overstay my welcome or make myself at home. Please excuse me, dear." Looking over at Lindsay, she smiled meekly and headed for the door.

While the second Officer walked Mrs. Wigley next door, Officer Becker looked at Lindsay and again introduced himself. "I'm Officer Lance Becker as a I mentioned. Sorry for the disturbance tonight." He stuck his hand out to shake Lindsay's hand.

Lindsay politely smiled but didn't put her hand up to shake his. "I'm sorry, I don't shake hands. Germaphobe. I'm Kendall James. We've met. Kind of. So that's Mrs. Wigley?"

"Apparently. I've not met her until tonight, although I've heard of her. This isn't the first time she's left home in the middle of the night. We were alerted by her grandson she had left and he asked us to check on her. I was driving by slowly when I heard the shouting and figured she might be here. The other officer was close because we both started at her house, next door. Yes, we have 'kind of' met. Sorry about that."

"I should apologize to you. It's always a downpour when I get a flat. Are you always so friendly off duty and always so hard headed?" Lindsay wouldn't forget his side profile, but at least now it was dry. She smiled but it didn't reach her eyes.

"Hard headed. Me? I was actually just coming into town and running extremely late. I had hit more traffic than I had anticipated on the way here and I hadn't had enough coffee. Sorry, those aren't excuses for not courting you properly before I tried to assist you, in a torrential downpour."

Lindsay may have actually blushed at that sarcasm or unnecessary inuendo. Not only was Officer Becker sarcastic but he was a ruggedly good-looking man, with an obviously athletic build. She was sure he had women dropping at his feet and had no problem getting one. She didn't see a ring on his finger, but that didn't mean anything and she wasn't interested. "Well, whatever it is you find necessary to do to the women in your path, personally or professionally, it's none of my business. Thank you for your help. I did, do, appreciate it. If you will excuse me, I would like to get some more sleep. Thank you for your help with the tire and Mrs. Wigley. Good night."

Lindsay had started to move toward the door hoping he would move that way also. He didn't. "Maybe it's the time of day, or night, we keep meeting that brings out the best in you." He grinned but she wasn't going to take the bait, nor look him in his charming face. Although she could appreciate his sarcasm.

"Goodnight, Officer Becker." Now she was at the door and holding it with one hand.

He made his way toward the door. "Third times a charm?" He stopped just in front of her.

"Maybe if your attitude improves and it's not the middle of the night." She looked directly into his eyes. She was startled by what she saw in them. They were a unique blue. Almost like a beautiful afternoon sky-blue with a lighter blue around the edges. That wasn't what startled her about them. They had a story, a very in-depth story.

"I do my best work at night." With that, he was gone.

20

Lindsay was not impressed with Officer Becker. Maybe she should take him some coffee. Maybe she should research him too, after she finishes with Robert Langston, Jack Cooper and Sam Stone. So many men messing with her life. The last thing she needed was another. She crawled back into bed since it was now a ridiculous hour but was unable to sleep. She had been sleeping a lot the last week.

She decided to start her research then, since she was wide awake. For some reason, she started with Sam. Maybe it was because she remembered the dream she was having before she was rudely woken up by crazy Mrs. Wigley. Sam was in front of her but he was in a fog and Lindsay couldn't see him clearly. He was trying to tell her something but she couldn't hear him.

She was not able to find a lot on Sam once she started researching. It appeared everything she was finding was everything he had told her and the other things she had already known from her prior research. Everyone had secrets and she doubted Sam was any different. She would keep digging.

Lindsay finally gave up after about five hours and headed to the kitchen to make coffee. She loved her coffee and enjoyed multiple cups on the deck every morning this week. She could drink a full pot on her own.

She had settled nicely into her lounge chair on the deck with a new book she found in Ava's room. She did enjoy the quietness of the lake house. She had just taken a sip of coffee when all of a sudden, a dog bolted into view on the edge of her lawn. He was running at full speed and right into the lake. She watched, entertained for a few moments, then picked up her book to start reading, losing interest in the dog. Before Lindsay realized it, the dog was running up the steps of her deck right to her. Wet. He all but jumped on her, then shook the water off himself. He was obviously very friendly. His tail never stopped wagging.

Lindsay wasn't impressed with water everywhere but when she told the dog to sit, he did. She tried checking the tag on his collar but he kept play nipping at her and she couldn't get to it.

"I think he likes you better than he likes me. Hi. I'm so sorry. I'm Zachery, Mrs. Wigley's grandson, and this is Mrs. Wigley."

When Lindsay looked up, she recognized Mrs. Wigley immediately, although her hair was now perfect as were her clothes. She introduced herself, "Hi, Mrs. Wigley, it's a pleasure to meet you. I'm Kendall James. Hi Zachery."

"Pleased to meet you Ms. James. I'll try to keep Lucky next door. He's only here occasionally so hopefully he won't ruin your peace and quiet too often." Mrs. Wigley was very calm now but she was wringing her hands.

"Please, call me Kendall. I'm sorry to hear Lucky is a part-timer. Are you dog sitting?"

"Yes, well, I guess you could call it that. My grandson here thinks the dog will be good for me to have as company, but I'm not so sure that I can take care of a dog. I can barely take care of my-self."

"Well, Mrs. Wigley, if you need help, please let me know. I'll be here for a few months and would be happy to help any way I can."

"I simply couldn't impose on you, dear." Mrs. Wigley continued wringing her hands.

During the exchange, Zachery hadn't said anymore, instead, he stood staring at Kendall. Suddenly, he blurted out, "I don't mean to stare, but you are beautiful." He instantly blushed.

Lindsay took the compliment in stride, as out of the blue as it was, and didn't skip a beat, "Thank you, Zachery. That's a nice compliment. Seriously, if I can help, please let me know. I don't mean to be inhospitable, but I do need to check on something inside. It was very nice meeting both of you. Will you please excuse me?" Lindsay was hoping they would take this as a reason to leave. Fortunately, they turned and left with Lucky on a leash and Zachery chiding his grandmother for not having the dog on a leash and how he will run if he's not.

From the second-floor balcony, Lindsay watched them leave. Mrs. Wigley obviously had mental issues. Zachery just gave her the creeps.

Lindsay had come here for peace and quiet. She needed the escape and the opportunity do her research. So far, nothing was going as she planned and that was a problem. She hoped Mrs. Wigley wasn't going to go crazy every night now and be prim and proper during the day. She was a little off even in her meeker state of mind.

Resigned, Lindsay went back to researching on the balcony.

21

The next few days were peaceful and Lindsay was hopeful things would stay this way. She had booked a flight from Atlanta, Georgia into Denver, Colorado. She would be driving the few hours to Atlanta in the early morning so she could make her flight at 8 am. She had everything ready for the upcoming trip in two days except her other fake identity documents. Those would be kept secure in her safe until just before her departure in the wee hours.

Lindsay was getting frustrated with the little information she was finding on Robert Langston and Sam Stone. She hadn't found out anything new and this bothered her. They weren't ghosts. Robert apparently avoided anything that would draw attention to him. Sam seemed to lead an ordinary life.

Late that evening, as Lindsay was preparing her coffee for the next morning, she heard a shrill scream. Looking out the kitchen window, she expected to see Mrs. Wigley. What she saw surprised her. There was a woman running through her backyard toward the lane. She grabbed her gun and hastily put on her sneakers. As she ran into the yard, opposite of the lake, the woman was nowhere to be found. She had thought of turning off the outside lights, but usually kept them all on until she went to bed. She kept them on. Lindsay cautiously made her way to the lane. She was thankful for the street lights. They were perfectly spaced so that they shone light evenly down the lane.

Lindsay stopped by the edge of the trees and listened. For a few moments, she didn't hear anything. As she turned to go back toward her house, she heard rustling in the trees between her house and the empty house next door. She silently made her way through the trees separating her yard from the neighbor's. She couldn't help wonder if the woman was hurt or hiding.

She stopped at the edge of the trees leading into the backyard of the neighbor's house. There were no lights on inside and everything was eerily quiet. She stood still, barely breathing.

After several more moments of listening and hearing nothing, she made her way through the thin strip of trees back to her yard. As she made her way across the yard, she heard something behind her. She turned suddenly, but kept moving toward her house. Not seeing anything behind her, she turned back toward her house. Her blood turned to ice when she realized someone was standing between her and the door. He had a gun pointed directly at her. Her natural instincts kicked in. She sidestepped, rolled prone. She was able to get one quick shot off, but so did he.

Lindsay, now in a kneeling position with her gun pointed directly at his head, noticed he was on the ground but starting to get up. "Do not move. I will blow your head off! Throw your gun toward your right."

He stayed down and threw his gun as she told him. She wasn't sure what to make of his first words since they were said so casually. "Damn it, that's gonna leave a mark." Then to her surprise, he continued, louder and less casually, "Kendall, I wasn't shooting at you, but the coyote behind you. Look at the spot where you came out of the trees."

Still having her gun pointed at his head, she didn't look back and still hadn't moved. Lindsay didn't recognize him or his voice. That didn't mean anything. She was well prepared to shoot someone who knew her name. Her first thought was, which Kendall did he think he was talking too? Kendall Thomas, the secret agent or Kendall James, the author who owned this house? Either way, she didn't recognize him. With her memory, she would remember him.

"Put your hands above your head, now! Don't move. Who are you and how do you know my name?" Lindsay noticed he was bleeding.

"I'm Grayson Tyler, your neighbor. Mr. Williams, who lives on the other side of me told me you were here."

"Mr. Williams never mentioned you." Lindsay couldn't help but notice his shirtless, well-defined, muscled body now that he was in full sitting position with his arms over his head.

"I just got in yesterday morning. Look, I happen to be making coffee for tomorrow when I looked out the window and saw the coyote cut through the yard. I came out to see where he was going and how many of them there are."

"Then explain to me how you ended up at my door with a gun. And explain to me why there are no lights on at your house."

"You can put the gun down now. You did the damage. There usually are more than one coyote. I last saw him go through the trees between our houses. I just checked your trash by the garage. Put that down before you hurt me again. I don't use a lot of light. The living room lights are on facing the lake."

Lindsay was reluctant. "How bad is it?"

Grayson looked at her, then at his arm. "It's not bad, but you probably need to get the bullet out."

"What makes you think I can get the bullet out? I'll call the town doctor and send him to your house." She still hadn't checked the edge of the trees but wanted to see his reaction.

"I can walk you through it. Do you need to involve everyone?"

"Who are you hiding from?"

"I could ask you the same thing."

Lindsay just looked at him, kept her gun pointed on him and walked over to pick up his gun. She looked over to the edge of the trees and could see something lying still, whether it was a coyote or a dog, she wasn't sure. She decided she would walk over to be sure. While walking backwards toward the trees, she asked Grayson if he had seen a woman anywhere.

"Only you but I'm not sure you are a woman. Few women shoot and move like you did."

Lindsay was still looking at him and kept her face expressionless. He wasn't getting a response. He had seen too much; the shot that she got off after she started the sidestep and her professionally executed roll to prone. She looked down at the animal and confirmed it was a coyote.

She made her way back to him and swiftly knelt down behind him, feeling his back pockets, then his front pockets, then down both legs. At first, he didn't say anything but then, "What the hell are you doing? I can just take them off if it makes you feel more comfortable."

She was too close for her own comfort but there was no choice. "That's a great idea. Take them off. You do have underwear on, right?"

"Maybe." He looked at her and actually grinned!

She was standing in front of him now. With her gun in hand, she flicked it downward and commanded, "Hurry up and get them off. Don't do anything stupid."

"Can I stand?" He was enjoying this entirely too much.

"No, and hurry up before you bleed to death."

"I'm only going to bleed to death laying down and taking them off with one arm. I'm standing up now." As he stood, he kept eye contact with Lindsay and without looking at any other part of her body, casually said, "If you take my bullet out, I'll clean your wound."

Lindsay started to feel the burn in her upper arm just as he said that. Lindsay hadn't realized the bullet had grazed her arm until he said something. She really didn't have time for a shoot out with a neighbor who was not supposed to be there.

"Throw your jeans over by the side of the house and walk slowly inside." Once inside, she directed him to one of the dining room chairs. She went into the adjoining living room, grabbed her laptop and opened her favorite program to check people out. Grayson Tyler. As Lindsay typed his name in, she thought to herself, "He probably wouldn't bleed out if I take a minute longer than necessary." She scanned the list of Grayson Tylers that popped up and there weren't many of them.

Of all the possible matches, she guessed he was the Photographer by his picture. Then said under her breath, "Really, just what I needed. Also, professional diver. Obviously more to his story but there seemed to be no criminals with his name."

Lindsay went outside, grabbed Grayson's jeans, then went to the kitchen and gathered supplies. As she went back to the dining room, she noticed Grayson had moved his chair against the far wall and looked to be taking a nap. Lindsay knelt beside him and, without saying anything, tried to move his hand off the wound. He let her move his hand and then whispered, "Be gentle."

"Are you always like this after you get shot? You're amazingly calm?" Before he could answer, a car pulled up the driveway. Lindsay got up to see who was outside. Seeing Officer Becker step out of the car, she looked back to Grayson, "Want an ambulance?"

Grayson looked at her and quietly said, "No. I would prefer you take it out and I be on my merry way."

"What makes you think I can operate on your arm?"

Before he could answer, Officer Becker was knocking on the door. Lindsay opened the door with what she hoped was a sleepy look. She also had her hand over her own wound. "Good evening Miss James. May I come in?"

There was no reason for him to come in and every reason for him to stay outside. Lindsay slowly responded, "I was just on my way to bed. What can I do for you?" As soon as it was out of her mouth, she regretted it.

Officer Becker lifted an eyebrow. He must

have thought better of saying what they were both now thinking. He opened his mouth then shut it. When he opened it again, he simply asked, "Everything okay here? We received reports of gunshots and I happen to be close by. Did you hear or see anything?"

Lindsay gave him a surprised look and stated, "I had been playing music in my earphones so I haven't heard anything." She wasn't sure why she was lying to him and on behalf of a complete stranger in her dining room who needed her attention. Other than the fact that she wanted him out of there as quickly as possible. He didn't need to know about her gun. She didn't want anything pulled up in any systems.

"Well, then, I'm sorry to have bothered you. Good evening Miss James." He looked at her with some doubt in his eyes, but only hesitated a moment before turning and heading back to his car. Lindsay remembered the coyote in the yard and hoped he didn't see it. Apparently, luck was with her as he backed out of the driveway.

Lindsay wasn't sure what to make of the tension between them. Maybe they had gotten off to a rocky start. He was amazingly good looking, but she wasn't attracted to him. There was tension though, that she didn't know how to classify. Something else to figure out. Later though. Right now, she needed to get this Grayson Tyler person out of her dining room.

22

Lindsay turned and headed back toward the dining room, hoping her visitor wasn't bleeding out. She found him picking at the bullet wound. "At least you're still upright. I'll gather some towels and gauze." While she was collecting what she needed, she cleaned and covered her wound. It was just a scrape with a burn around the edges. She would put ice on it later. She had taken the bloody shirt off and had replaced it with a tank top.

As she walked back into the dining room, she made eye contact with Grayson. She found his intense stare disconcerting. She should have put more on than a tank top. She should have him put his jeans back on. He had taken his shirt off and was now sitting in nothing but boxers, or whatever those were. "How many bullets have you removed?" There was no amusement in his eyes this time.

"It doesn't matter if you aren't going to the ER. How many have you removed? I count four prior shots." Lindsay was trying desperately not to let her eyes roam freely about his body.

"Let's get this over with so I can take care of yours."

"I already did. It's just a scrape." Lindsay avoided making eye contact with him.

"You can't put a Band-Aid on a bullet hole." At that moment their eyes met. Grayson saw the bullet hole, not on her, but in her.

"Fortunately, I don't have a bullet hole. Okay, tell me what to do and let's get this over with." Lindsay moved a chair beside Grayson to get the best access to his arm.

Grayson proceeded to walk Lindsay through the steps. Each one only speaking when necessary. Finally, Lindsay rolled the final dressing around his arm. The amusement was back in Grayson's eyes. Lindsay was too close for her own comfort and couldn't wait to be done with this task.

"Well, at least you won't bleed out. Do you have pain meds hanging around next door? You're probably going to need them soon." Lindsay moved away quickly and began cleaning up the bloody towels along with the instruments she had used.

Grayson ignored her question, "How does an author know to move and shoot like you did back there?"

"Research. I'm a ghost writer and write for different genres. How does a photographer get shot up so much? Surely, it's not by neighborhood women? Or their husbands, maybe?"

Grayson roared with laughter. He liked her sense of humor. "You're the first neighbor and not even for good reason. Two of those are from taking photos in Chicago during a riot years ago. One is from a photo op in Iraq and the other is from my brother during a hunting trip in Africa. That makes you the first to shoot me for no good reason."

"You were standing at my door with your gun aimed at me. What did you expect?"

"It was aimed at the coyote." He looked at her with amusement again. "Maybe you shouldn't have that gun if you are going to let loose on every little thing. Were you taught to shoot first, ask questions later, because that is exactly what you did?"

Lindsay looked at him, not sure what to say because it would either be sarcastic or give too much away. Let him think she was an airhead. What did she care? To change the subject, she asked, "How long are you going to be next door, permanently?"

As Grayson answered, "Not sure." Lindsay got up and started to move away from him.

Grayson reached up and grabbed her good arm. "Let me take a look at that."

Lindsay looked down at him and shook her head no, while pulling her arm away. "It's fine. You can go now. By the way, you didn't see a woman before you shot the coyote?"

"No, you asked me that already. Did you see someone? Why did you go out with a gun?"

"It must have been my imagination. Being a writer, it tends to get away from me sometimes. I'm sorry about all this. I'll see you out." Lindsay didn't look at him because she knew how seriously feeble her story was.

Grayson looked at her, amused again. He stood up, picked up his clothes and instead of putting them on, headed toward the kitchen door where he came in.

Lindsay had kept her eyes averted. When she heard him making his way past her toward the door, she knew it was too quick for him to have put his clothes back on. She held her stare at the back of his head while she followed him out.

Once he reached the door, he opened it and paused without turning around. "I'll take care of the coyote. Thanks for operating." Then he was gone.

Lindsay walked to the kitchen window facing the side yard and watched Grayson walk across toward the coyote. As he got to it, he put his jeans on and with his uninjured arm lifted the coyote by its back legs and dragged it into the thin line of trees separating their houses.

She told herself she watched him to make sure he went the direction of his house. She turned and leaned on the counter. She pondered the last hour. Once her anger had worn off from their unconventional meeting, and she had started working on Grayson's wound, she realized that she had a physical reaction to him that she did not like. It had taken all her willpower to stay poised and focused. There was definitely more to this man than met the eye. She wasn't going to find out, either. She already had enough male puzzles to figure out. She would keep her distance. She went to bed, but tonight sleep didn't come quickly enough.

23

Lindsay woke later than usual, having not fallen asleep until the wee hours of the morning. She liked her new daily pattern. Until today. As she made her coffee, which she had forgotten to set the night before, she was instantly drawn to the backyard. Thoughts of last night flooded her.

Trying to push them back, she showered and dressed while she waited on her coffee. Having to manually start the coffee in the morning was never a good start in Lindsay's book. Feeling more refreshed and alert after the shower and first sip of coffee, she took her laptop to the deck overlooking the lake.

Lindsay had been reaching dead-ends on her research of Robert Langston, Sam Stone and Jack Cooper. She had looked into Derek and Joe also. Examining all of Robert's companies didn't turn up anything she hadn't already seen. She was frustrated with the scarcity of information but once she thought about it, it made sense. She asked herself repeatedly what she expected to find. They were the best at what they did. She had gone to the Dark Web but came up empty handed.

Lindsay needed to get deeper than the Dark Web. She needed to access the Deep Web but without the specific browser, TOR, it was impossible. She had a contact, Casey, who at one time was part of ShadowCrew, before they were busted. He had access Lindsay couldn't get, unless she reached out to an old FBI friend. That she did not want to do seeing as no one was safe from working for Robert Langston. She decided it was time to reach out to Casey. He didn't know her real identity, just as she didn't know his. She suspected he went with a name like Casey because it was such an innocent name. They had crossed paths long ago when Lindsay had done some work with the Secret Service regarding ShadowCrew, and a friendship was born. They had stayed in touch through the Dark Web, but now it was time to bring him in. Lindsay decided she would wait until she was in Denver. Today she was going to read a good book and relax.

Doing just that, she was completely lost in her book when something caught the corner of her eye. She looked up to see Mrs. Wigley and Zachery chasing Lucky toward the lake. She watched them in amusement for a few moments wondering if she were truly going to have any peace here.

She may have asked herself that too soon. Feeling like someone was watching her, she turned to see Officer Becker standing at the bottom of the deck steps. She hid her surprise well and asked, "What brings you by this time?" She didn't hide her sarcasm well though.

Officer Becker studied her for a moment with those gorgeous, sharp blue eyes of his. "Please, call me Lance. I was in the neighborhood and thought I would check on you. You seemed 'weird' last night."

"I doubt you know me well enough to know my 'weird'. I was tired, though. Did you find what you were looking for last night?"

"No, nothing. Are you sure you didn't hear

anything?"

"I'm sure. Everything was fine here as far as I knew. I see Mrs. Wigley is also fine. Thank you for stopping by." She didn't know what it was about him that bothered her.

"Listen, I would like to make up for any slight…" Lance stopped midsentence, looking past Lindsay, and through the window into the house. "I'm sorry, I didn't realize you had company."

Lindsay turned to look through the window Lance was intent on and, at the same time, said, "I don't." Lindsay didn't see anyone. She looked toward Mrs. Wigley and saw that it was only her and Lucky now outside. Mrs. Wigley wasn't in her house and the kitchen door was still locked from last night.

"I'm positive I just saw someone inside. Stay here while I check it out." With that he drew his gun and proceeded to go inside, gun at the ready.

Lindsay followed him into the house, saying, "I'm sure it was a shadow or something. No one would be in my house in the broad daylight."

Lance told her again to stay put as he made his way up the stairs to the balcony outside Lindsay's bedroom. Lindsay followed him up the stairs. Her gun was usually not far from her, but today she had left it in the bedroom. There were a few others around the house, but she didn't feel the need to get one. She also thought Lance was seeing things so she wasn't concerned.

Lindsay followed him as he made his way around the second level then proceeded to go down the back stairs. As they reached the kitchen, Lindsay noticed the door was open. She knew for certain it had been locked last night and she hadn't opened it this morning.

She didn't feel the need to inform Lance. She would deal with this. "Okay, we're good. Nobody's here. I'm sure it was a shadow. Thanks again for stopping by."

"Kendall, the door was not open when I got here. I knocked on a closed door. When you didn't answer, I made my way around the house to check everything out and thought you might be on the deck. Are you trying to get rid of me?"

"Good grief, no. Why would I do that if I thought there was something amiss?" She looked at him with wide eyes.

"I don't know, why don't you tell me?" He didn't get an answer, nor did he suspect he would.

"It's broad daylight and I'm just an author. What could anyone possibly want with me? If they wanted to steal something, I doubt they would do it in broad daylight." She looked at him with one eyebrow raised, waiting for an answer. She threw in her most innocent look.

Lance thought to himself that she should have been an actress. "Do you have cameras?"

"No, I never had a need for them, nor did Aunt Ava. We've never had a problem here. By the way, I thought you were a game warden. Why do you do the Sheriff's job?"

"Because for some reason, where you are concerned, I keep getting drug into that role. Alright, I'm going next door to check on Mrs. Wigley and her grandson." He looked at her expecting a question.

"Ok, thanks for stopping by." Lindsay held the door open and waited for him to leave. She would push him out the door if he didn't go this time.

Lance stared deep into her eyes like he was trying to see beyond the murk in a deep pond. He didn't say anymore, but turned and walked out the door. Lindsay shut it behind him.

Leaning her back against the door, Lindsay let out a deep breath and realized what bothered her about him was that she didn't like the way she felt around him. Although he wasn't her usual type, there was something about his eyes. She was deeply drawn into them. Like a non-swimmer on a diving board. She knew it was a bad place to be. She also didn't need any more men in her life, attraction or not. This pull was only physical, mentally, she was done. She had to ask herself, why she seemed to be attracted to the two newest men in her life. Was she losing her mind? That was the last thing she wanted, or needed. Was she trying to replace the two she was most mad at with two others? She decided she was unconsciously trying to distract herself from the real issues. Speaking of issues, both of those men probably had more issues than the New York Times. She needed none of that. She had her own subscription to worry about.

Obviously, reading wasn't going to work as her mind went into overdrive and she couldn't focus. She realized she had read the same page a dozen times and still had no idea what it said. She needed a distraction and not the male kind. Something that would take her mind off of everything. She hated cooking and found it to be a chore. She only cooked when absolutely necessary to feed the boys or when she needed to remove herself from her overactive mind. Making lasagna was the perfect distraction.

24

Lindsay put the lasagna in the oven and headed upstairs to check that she had everything for her trip tomorrow. She considered putting cameras in but wouldn't have time before she left in the morning. She did have another idea that she would do before she went to bed.

An hour later, as she pulled the lasagna out of the oven, she realized it hadn't been the smartest time to make the dish. She wouldn't have to eat it all because her trip was going to take a few days, at least. Not for the first time today, she wondered how Grayson was doing. Earlier thoughts of checking on him were nixed, but now she had an excuse.

Lindsay scooped out the amount she would eat, wrapped the rest to take with her and headed out the door. She decided against taking a shortcut through the trees and walked down the lane. She should take up jogging again. This was the perfect place to jog and not worry about traffic or anything else. The exercise did clear her head.

She knocked on Grayson's door. He hollered, "Hold on a minute." Lindsay was having doubts about this when he opened the door, standing there sweaty and with only well-worn jeans on. She wasn't sure why this had an attack to her equilibrium. She had seen lots of beautiful, fit male bodies in her life and she had seen his last night. It took her a second to recover, then she held up the lasagna to him. "I made too much and didn't want to waste it."

Grayson eyed her suspiciously, not sure what to make of this. He moved aside and let her in. "I wouldn't have taken you for Rachel Ray."

"I'm not. Don't expect it again."

"Peace offering or poison?" He did smirk with that comeback.

"Why would I need a peace offering? Anyone standing in my yard with a gun pointed at me is bound to get themselves shot. You are no exception. I made too much and I wanted to make sure you didn't die in your sleep from infection. How's the wound?"

"It's a wound. Not the first, not the last."

"Never thought of photography bing dangerous. One should get hazard pay." She smirked back at him. "So, it's good? Did you clean it this morning? Do you need me to do it?" What was wrong with her? She never rambled.

"It's all good. How is yours? Want me to look at it? Did you clean it today? Do you need me to do that?" He gently took her good arm and pulled her into the living room and sat her on the couch. Releasing her arm, he sat down beside her. "Take off your shirt and let me see it." The last statement wasn't a question.

Lindsay jumped up and started to head for the door, but he caught her and swung her around. The force of her trying to escape and him pulling her back, caused her to be chest to chest with him. "It's just a skim and fine. Nothing compared to yours and yours needs more attention than mine. Since you said yours is okay and I see you haven't died from infection, I'll be going. Enjoy the lasagna. And no, it's not poisoned." She needed air. What was wrong with her. Where had her cool exterior gone? She was a rambling mess. Maybe she needed to work, as Kendall Thomas. This sitting around doing research and trying to relax must be getting to her. She backed away and headed for the door again.

Grayson didn't stop her this time.

25

Lindsay hightailed it back to her house and got busy with setting up traps. She didn't have cameras but she had other resources. She doubted anyone had been in her house earlier in the day when Lance thought he saw someone. But one could never be too careful. She would consider cameras if anything appeared to have been moved when she returned.

The first thing she did was put fishing line six inches off the second to top step on the back stairs. She would do the same when she left in the morning on the front stairs. If anyone hit it going up, they would either not notice, but it would be disconnected, or trip and fall back down the stairs, depending on shoes, strength and quickness of movement.

The second thing she did was put tape on the inside of the all the closet doors. She was able to reach her hand under the doors enough to attach the tape so that if the door was opened, the tape would not stay attached to the interior door trim, but would stay on the door itself.

Next, she left each interior door partially opened and measured each two, four or six inches open.

Next, Lindsay made sure all drawers were shut tightly, except the random ones she pulled out a fraction of an inch so that when looking at them, one could not tell.

Lindsay wasn't sure she wanted to keep the fishing line on the stairs so she decided to sleep on it. She walked around the house looking for things to "booby trap" and when she was satisfied, she headed to bed. It was the only place to shut her mind off. She didn't like having these "feelings" and attractions to the other half of the species. She told herself she was just bored from too much inactivity. She should have known this would happen. Even though she was still furious with Sam, she missed him.

* * * * *

Lindsay took off early the next morning for Atlanta, before most would be awake. She had decided to leave the fishing line across the stairs. So what if someone got hurt. They had no right to be in her house.

Although she had been vigilant in making sure she was not followed, creature of habit that she was, she stayed in the car for a full ten minutes, watching everything and everyone. She double checked her ID, unloaded her gun and gathered her small overnight suitcase. She only checked baggage because she wasn't going on this trip, or anywhere for that matter, without her gun. She put her gun and ammo in the suitcase, and headed inside the airport.

With perfect timing, Lindsay was seated on the plane just minutes before takeoff. She had avoided cameras where she could. She left her hair brown to blend in with the average hair color. She also had on a business suit with flats, since it was a weekday. Anyone looking for her would be less likely to pick out a female in a business suit.

Landing in Denver a few hours later, Lindsay was quick getting her suitcase and heading over to the Uber area. She was able to get an Uber immediately. She had the driver drop her off at a fastfood restaurant, then called for another Uber. She had this one drive her to a rental car store where she picked up her vehicle for the weekend. Once comfortable with the new wheels, she was off for a forty-five-minute drive to the hotel she booked.

Lindsay was finally tucked safely into her room. Naturally, she had booked two adjoining rooms. The first thing she did was call the boys from the first burner phone. Their energetic conversation was just what she needed. Knowing that her boys were having a ton of fun with their dad gave her a great sense of relief. They were looking forward to getting to the ranch. She reminded the boys to use the second phone number they were given if they needed to call her.

After talking to the boys, she stopped at the store and bought a laptop, then had dinner. It was late Friday night by the time she got back to her room. It was the perfect time to try to reach Casey.

She set up the laptop, connected her scrambler and dove in. He responded about 3 hours later. She had almost fallen asleep by the time she heard the ding of the notification.

Hey my friend! How are you?

Casey! Damn, I thought you may be off on a tropical island and unreachable. It never takes you so long to respond. Don't you live on your computer?

My dear, I could be on the moon and still get you. I do only have a few minutes. What can I do for you sweetness?

Always the charmer. Lindsay hoped she wouldn't regret this. She would play it like it was no big deal. He already knew everything between them was top secret. Just in case, she started small. *I need ALL information on Sam Stone and Derek Stevens.*

Gimme a minute.

Lindsay went into the bathroom, splashed water on her face, looked at herself in the mirror and hoped Sam and Derek were clean. She wasn't sure now if she really wanted to know if they were truly hiding anything. She was convinced she was now officially an idiot. Isn't this what this whole ghosting thing was about? Figuring out who they all are so she could figure out who she is. Yes, she wanted to know. But it was more than that, she hoped they were who they said they were. Ding.

Got it sweet thang. Where would you like it sent? Here?

Yes please. The information popped up on her screen and she put a thumb drive into the side of the laptop and saved it. Casey's screen would blank it out in three minutes. *Thanks my friend. Are you around tomorrow?*

No. I am off the grid for a few days. Do you need more?

Lindsay hesitated. She wanted the rest while she was in Denver. Even with the scrambler, there was no guarantee Casey or someone else couldn't trace her. It was now or in a few weeks when she traveled to call the boys again. *Yes, two more please. Robert Langston. Jack Cooper.*

Lindsay held her breath.

Two full minutes went by. Ding. *Darlin' I have to run and got nothing yet. I'll ping ya when I get it. Tally Ho.*

Lindsay dropped down on the bed. That was

strange coming from Casey. It wasn't strange that he used various dialect or slang terms. It was part of his charm and secrecy. What was strange was that he had never, ever, put her off.

She closed out and pulled up the information on Sam and Derek from her thumb drive.

There wasn't anything that she hadn't already known, except Sam's ex-wife wasn't living in Texas as he had told her. She was remarried and apparently, to a Congressman, living in Tennessee. Maybe Sam didn't know. It wasn't anything to lie about.

The only information on Derek was all basic, where he grew up, siblings, where he went to school, graduating top of his class. There was no mention of Special Forces, but she did see his military service. She already had this information.

Either there was no story other than what she already knew or Casey wasn't telling her everything. But he had no reason not to. He didn't know her real identity and she couldn't be tied to anyone or anything.

Lindsay was uneasy about Casey. Maybe it was because of all the things that had transpired in the last month. Her time at the lake house was supposed to be quiet. Her chaotic time there was not what she had in mind. She needed peace and to relax to think things through. And she just wasn't getting it.

26

Robert scrubbed his eyes with the palms of his hands. He was tired. He slammed his fist on his desk. "No one has anything to report?" It was obvious he was also furious. He looked at each one of them with his steely stare.

Sam watched Jack closely. Jack appeared to be the only one not uncomfortable with Robert's outburst. Derek and Joe both shifted in their seats.

Sam looked at Jack. "Jack, you taught her everything she knows. You can't guess at something? No clues where she would disappear to? There has to be some place that she's mentioned. Someone that she can trust. You were closest to her."

"Sam, we've been through all this a dozen times. I have nothing. Tall One may have been someone that she would have tried to contact for help, but we see where that went." Jack checked his watch as though he had some where to be.

Dereck let out a deep breath. "Sam, I know we've been through this but have you thought of any place that she's ever mentioned she wanted to go?"

"No. Wherever she is, she doesn't have the boys with her so it's not like she's off on vacation. She is intentional in whatever she is doing. Or wherever she is."

"You guys are the best of the best. I've brought others in. I can't believe no one has anything. How did we not prepare for this?" Robert thought for a moment. "We've all got our secret places, I guess. Jack, had you ever advised Lindsay to have one?"

Before Jack could answer, Sam looked at Robert with disbelief. "Had you handled this whole thing differently, none of us would be in this position!"

"Sam, we've been through this. No one could have prepared for Lindsay to get pissed off and disappear into thin air. I might point out, yet again, that I had the best of you following her. Do you really want to play the blame game right now? I know you are frustrated, we all are." Robert had been sitting with his arms crossed. Now he unfolded them to appear open to all of their frustrations.

Jack shook his head. "I don't ever recall advising her. She may have gotten the idea from watching us with our 'secret place' here in Philadelphia. She never knew we had anything here and look at us. Our whole operation and our homes are here. She never knew until she followed me."

Joe, always the calm one, "This isn't productive. Maybe we should meet again tomorrow. I've got some people I need to check in with."

Robert and Sam were again staring each other down. They couldn't be in the same room for long before this contest of wills would start between them. Derek stood up, "Let's go, Sam."

Joe held up his hand. "Robert, Casey is here." Joe couldn't contain his excitement.

"Who is Casey?" Sam could feel the atmosphere change in the room.

Robert nodded to Joe and Joe couldn't jump up and get out the door fast enough. Robert looking less stressed all of a sudden answered Sam, "With any luck, he's our lucky break."

Joe came back ushering a guy in who looked like he hadn't hit puberty yet. He was tall, lanky and looked like he had just been blown through a wind storm. Sam didn't care what he looked like though. He wanted to know more about this guy, and quickly.

"Casey, what do you have and don't hold back."

Casey looked uncomfortable. "Well, don't get your hopes up Mr. Langston. Since the last time you summoned me, I've had several requests for you and/or Jack, which is typical as we get those often. I had all requests for any of the names that you had given me transferred to me. One came in that was a little different. The first request was for Sam Stone and Derek Stevens. I sent out basic info as requested. Then a few minutes later, the same person requested info on you and Jack. Oddly enough, the request didn't come in a transfer, but from someone I've built a relationship with over the years. I don't know her real identity because we had worked together on an undercover project years ago. I assumed she was law enforcement of some kind. I feel horrible about telling you."

"Casey, I'm losing patience. What is her name and what did you give her on us?" Robert's expression was guarded, although he trusted Casey and he paid him more than anyone else ever could. Only the best for the Langstons.

"I didn't give her anything. And I don't know her name. Her real name. Everything on her came up bogus. I do know that she is at a hotel outside Denver. I wrote it down." He handed a piece of paper to Robert. "It took a little while to track her location. She had the location off and a scrambler connected. But I got it."

Robert glanced at the paper. "Casey, have you ever had a request for the four of us from the same person?"

"No, that was part of what struck me odd. When we get requests on you guys, it's usually from different people, different locations. She was asking about all four of you."

"Joe, it's all we have so far and it may be a long shot. Get the plane fired up now and the guys on it. Derek go." He took a photo of the address and texted it to Joe and Derek.

"I'm on that plane, Robert." Sam was already standing and started to follow Derek out the door.

"Sam, you are too close to this. You could blow it."

"I'm not sitting around here waiting when I could be there if it's her. And please tell me who else in this room isn't too close to this?"

Derek knew there was no way Sam wasn't getting on the plane. "Boss, I've got 'im." They bolted from the room. Sam only had a moment of hesitation wondering if he should stay close to Robert for more information and to watch him.

Robert immediately started barking orders at Joe. "I want a list of all guests in that hotel. I want camera feeds. I want license plate numbers."

Casey cleared his throat, "I have the guests list of the hotel along with their vehicle information."

Robert stuck his hand out. "Where is it?"

"It's printing now to the Cannon printer, where ever that is." Casey never took his eyes off his laptop.

Robert didn't have to tell Joe; he was already out the door to the printer in the meeting room.

"Mr. Langston, I can't get the camera feeds just yet, except for the live ones. I mean, I can't rewind their system. Since I have no idea who you are looking for, it wouldn't do me any good to watch the cameras. Do you have someone who knows who you are looking for?"

"Yes, Joe can watch. I should have kept Sam here." Robert started pacing. He checked his watch every thirty seconds. Casey kept watching the screen of cameras, although he had no idea who he was looking for.

Jack, who had been sitting idly by, moved over behind Casey. Robert looked at Jack with a raised eyebrow. "Joe can watch the cameras."

Joe came back in just in time to hear that and moved in beside Jack, behind Casey, at the same time handing the hotel guests list to Robert. Casey moved and let Joe in front of the screen. Jack took his seat again by the window.

"Robert, we are going to need to talk about where we all stand regarding…." Jack trailed off because he didn't want to say Kendall's name in front of Casey.

Robert glared at him. "We all stand together in this until it's done. No questions asked. Am I clear? See if any names stand out." Robert handed Jack the guest list from the hotel since he had scanned it and no names jumped out at him.

Jack nodded and looked through the guests list. "None. I'll scan and send it to Sam and the guys." Jack could have had Casey send it directly, but they didn't want anyone else having Casey's contact and Jack needed something to do.

Casey was still on his computer. Jack was busy scanning and texting to Sam. Joe watched the hotel cameras. Robert sat at his desk, staring at the bookshelves.

"Has anyone heard from Charlie?" Robert waited a moment and, not getting a response, he looked at the ceiling. "Casey, any luck on finding Charlie?" Casey shook his head in the negative.

Robert looked at Jack. He hated to think he couldn't trust him, but he was just no longer sure. They tried to talk about the situation with Lindsay, but one would end up mad and the conversation would stop. Neither wanted to damage their relationship any more than it already was since the meeting in Jack's office between him and Lindsay where he ended up shot. Robert hated to think about what would have happened had Derek and Sam not shown up. Thank God Lindsay called his number.

"Casey, can you use another laptop and pull up cameras from around the hotel, street cameras?"

"I can see if there are any around there." Jack left the office and was back in a minute with two more laptops. Casey worked as fast as he could seeing if there were any nearby. "Yes! I have three nearby. I can break into them but the police will get notice. Do you want to set off any alarms yet?"

"No, we will wait until the boys get to Denver and if they don't have any luck, then we'll try that route. Run the IDs for the list of names from the hotel and see if there is a match to anyone who is female and 5'9" and maybe blonde hair, but she could have changed it. Start with single occupants first. If there is nothing, then move onto more than single occupants. We don't know if she is alone."

A few minutes later, Casey informed them the closest to that description was a single female, 5'8", brown hair. Jack asked what color eyes. Casey answered him that according to the ID, they were brown.

Jack grinned. "Do you have the photo up? Let me see it."

Jack and Robert both moved over to Casey's laptop screen and studied the picture ID. "It's hard to say with it being a DMV photo and not really clear. Casey, can you do anything with that photo?"

"Probably not but let me try." Casey began making clicks on the keyboard and changing the picture. Finally, after a few more moments, "This is the best I can do."

Robert and Jack both looked at the picture. It was Lindsay. "Joe, come look at this." Joe moved over to where they were and after only a moment, stated, "That's a pretty good job. Hair color change, shorter style, contacts, slight variance in height and weight. I would say that's our girl."

"Print that out. Get me the tag number of the vehicle she is driving and Jack get that license address up on satellite. Joe don't take your eyes off those hotel cameras. What room is she in so Joe can watch that camera?"

Everyone went from flat line to adrenaline rush in five seconds.

Casey was the best at what he did in the Deep Web and the Dark Web, but Robert was finding out he did much more than he knew of. It didn't take Casey long to say, "The car registered to her at the hotel is a rental."

"Get the location of the rental agency and we'll trace it backwards. We need more heads in here."

"Satellite's up on address but I doubt she lives there. Or that she has ever been to that address. It's a cabin in the middle of no freaking where, Colorado. She hates the woods and she doesn't like the cold, unless she's skiing." Jack thought for a moment. "I'm going to bet it's as fake as the hair and eyes on that picture. Also, being in that part of Colorado, three and a half hours from Denver, in the Rocky Mountains, it's definitely not her dream home, or even ideal home. She would probably be homeless before she would live there. She may take a few days to ski but wouldn't last in the cold any longer than that. Most importantly, it's too desolate for our city girl." Jack looked at the picture on the satellite, scowling the whole time.

"I don't care, get property records and if the name on the ID matches, get someone out there and check things out. Quietly."

"Got it." Jack would love to be the one to find Lindsay and prove to the rest of these guys, he really is on her side. He feels kind of bad now that he realizes Lindsay isn't out to destroy the organization. Then it hits him and he stops in his tracks. Is that what this disappearing act is all about. No, no, no. He has to find her first. She might be able to disappear into thin air, but he would be damned if she would destroy the organization. Did she have it in her? Jack wished he were on that plane to Denver himself.

27

Lindsay woke at dawn after falling asleep thinking about how much chaos was surrounding her. All she really wanted was peace. And a little information, which she was in the business of getting. She would love to blame Kendall for opening the can of worms with the Boss, her father, but that would be weird, even to her. She is Kendall. Leading a double life since becoming an adult was getting to her.

She put some coffee on, checked the laptop, nothing new from Casey, and then jumped in the shower. Casey had never failed to answer a request right away. This bothered her last night but she blew it off as being paranoid. Now, she was re-thinking that. Of all the people she has requested information on over the years, none were as powerful as Robert Langston, at least in this country. She had to ask herself if she had made a mistake.

She jumped out of the shower and quickly toweled off. She effortlessly put her hair up in a messy bun. She pulled the baggy shirt over her head and yanked her jeans up. She couldn't pull her personal laptop out fast enough. She opened the tracker to check Sam and Derek's trucks. Sam's was at Robert's office but Derek's was at the airstrip she had flown into during her one trip to Philadelphia with the guys. This was not good. She stopped for a moment and gathered her thoughts. Could Derek be on a job? Yes, the job of finding her. She knew everything else had come to a halt. Damn Casey.

She packed everything up and was ready to head out the door but turned back to the window. Pulling the thick curtain back just enough to see her rental car, she watched the surrounding area for a few minutes. There was nothing out of the ordinary. She had considered leaving the rental and calling an Uber, but driving herself would be the fastest right now. She had considered calling room service and leaving by way of cart or laundry service, but if anyone were watching, they would expect that. It was somewhat cliché.

She walked back to the door and peered out the peep hole. Not seeing anyone, she whisked open the door and walked toward the stairs, keeping her head down. She was three floors up and would rather get the exercise than get stuck in the elevator. She made her way out to the rental car, jumped in and drove off.

Lindsay drove back into Denver, making sure she was not being followed. She was starving and had a few hours to kill before her flight left. She pulled into the drive through of a fast-food restaurant and grabbed a quick bite.

She needed to dump this rental and get to the airport. She had no idea if Derek was hot on her trail but she would rather not wait and see. She drove to a convenience store a mile from the rental agency.

Lindsay got out and approached a lady coming out of the store. "Hi, I'm sorry to bother you but I was wondering if you have a cell phone I could use to call the car rental place. My rental is acting strange and I don't want to break down if I drive it any further."

The caring lady took her cell phone out and handed it to Lindsay. "Poor thing, I know the feeling with my old clunker. Hate to have a rental that leaves you stranded."

Lindsay smiled, thanked her and called the rental car company, turning away from the lady but not walking away. "I know this is going to sound a little odd, but I'm being followed. Nothing dangerous, just an over zealous ex-husband. I was wondering if there is someone there who can meet me at this convenience store and pick this car up?" After a brief pause, Lindsay thanked them and hung up. Giving the phone back to the lady, she thanked her again. The lady asked her if she would be okay until they got there. Lindsay assured her they were on their way.

Five minutes later, a car pulled up and a heavy-set man got out of the passenger side and walked to Lindsay's window, "Hi. I'm Dan Mills, the manager of the car rental company. Are you okay?"

Lindsay looked at him. She had already been on the website and checked out the employees, including the two managers of the company. He was who he claimed to be, as well as the other guy with him. They were both listed on the website.

Lindsay smiled a sweet, innocent smile. "Thank you for coming so quickly. I truly appreciate it. I hate to ask, but is there any way that you could take me to the airport? I will pay you $1,000 cash, but if anyone comes in asking for me, you have to say that you don't know me. Also, you can't tell them I was dropped off at the airport."

The manager looked a little skeptical. "An ex-husband, huh? Is he really tall, medium to long length brown hair and well built?"

Lindsay was impressed. Derek was good. Giving him a scared look, she used her best defeated voice, "Yes. I am going to assume he already came in looking for me? Did he ask for me by name?"

"He did, about ten minutes before you called. I didn't tell him anything except we don't give out customer information. Couldn't figure out how he knew you rented a car there, though. That baffled me."

"He has friends in the criminal world. One of the many reasons I need to get away from him." Lindsay was impressed. She was under an alias. So somehow Casey tracked her and he, apparently, was associated with Robert Langston, of course.

The manager still looked skeptical, "What the hell, it's just a trip to the airport. I'll take you as long as you promise you aren't the crazy one." With that, he smirked.

"I'm only crazy for getting involved with him." Lindsay gave him another sad look.

The manager let out a breath he seemed to be holding. "Ok, I hope I don't regret this. Let's go." Lindsay got out of the driver seat and went around to get in the passenger side.

Neither of them spoke during the drive. Lindsay was grateful he wasn't asking a bunch of questions. She hated lying and had already done enough of it for one day. She was busy watching behind them to make sure they weren't being followed. When they reached the airport, Lindsay had him drop her off at a terminal she wasn't flying out of, thanked him, handed him the cash she promised and warned him that the tall guy would probably be back.

Once the manager was out of sight with the rental car, Lindsay grabbed a taxi, because she didn't want to use the Uber app. She had the driver drop her off right outside the airport at a Hilton.

Lindsay went inside, ordered a coffee and sat down in the hotel restaurant. They had managed to find her through Casey. She thought about her options. She could get on this flight and get back to Atlanta. She could grab a flight to somewhere else and rent a car and drive back to the lake house. She would eventually need new IDs since the one she used at the hotel was obviously blown, thanks to Casey. She was furious. Was there no one who didn't work for her father?

Lindsay pulled out the phone she had used to call the boys. She called Drama Llama. He answered on the first ring.

"Hey, thank God you are okay." He sounded panicky.

"Is there a reason I wouldn't be? Please tell me no one has been by."

"No, but I expected to hear from you before now."

"I never told you when I would be in touch. Quit worrying. You are worse than a little old lady. I need a few new IDs. Got a pen to write the descriptions down along with a few names I like. I don't have to tell you to research the names first. Grandmotherly reports only. Use some of the photos I left with you. Ready?"

"Yup, go ahead. I know the drill." Drama Llama knew more about Lindsay's fake ID requirements than he did about the real Lindsay Phillips.

Lindsay gave him the information. "Now I need you to do one more thing. Listen closely.

It has to be pristine. You can't be late." She gave Drama Llama the rest of the directions. "Are you clear?"

"Yes, but you know you make no sense."

"Did I ever. I'm tired of telling you to stop analyzing me. Gotta run." She hung up before he could start with any questions.

She decided she would be on the flight back to Atlanta. If they found her, she would send them all away. It wasn't like anyone was out to kill her so, what was the worst that could happen?

28

Joe had been studying the hotel cameras when he spotted Lindsay coming out of her room and walking down the hall. He informed Robert and Jack she was on the move.

Robert had told Casey to get eyes on the car. Casey reminded him that he would need approval from the police department. Their street cams were almost impossible to get into without setting off red flags to the cops. Jack suggested Derek and Sam head to the car rental place in Denver and see what they could find there. Lindsay had to return the car at some point. In the meantime, Robert had Casey getting into their system.

Jack studied Robert. He could almost hear his thoughts; they had been together so long. "Robert, we'll get to her first."

Robert looked at Jack for a minute. "Who? You and me? Or you and someone else?"

"I know it's going to…" Jack shook his head. There was no need to do this now. Finding Lindsay was everyone's first priority. Jack was sorry that their relationship was damaged and hoped it wasn't going to be irreparable by the time someone found Lindsay. "She is going to be fine."

Robert's cell phone rang at that moment. "Please tell me you have her."

"No, sir. We went straight to the car rental place, but she hasn't returned the car yet. They won't tell us when it's due back. Can Casey get that info?" Derek didn't try to hide his disappointment and Robert could hear it, loud and clear.

"He's working on it. Look, I doubt she is staying in Denver. We found a property in the name of her fake ID but doubt she's there. We have people checking on it. She left the hotel. We are checking flights in the fake name. Nothing yet. Hang out near the car rental place for now. The airport is too big and if she hasn't returned the car, she's still in Denver. Any idea why? Ask Sam if she's ever mentioned Denver." Derek could hear the tension in Robert's voice. It surprised him because he had never heard or seen Robert anything but calm, cool and collected.

"I've already discussed Denver with Sam. She's never mentioned it to him. I don't think she's staying here. There is no connection that any of us know of. I think we would be best at the airport. There are sixteen hundred flights a day out of Denver, and it's busy but there is really only one way in, whether by car, taxi, Uber or bus. I doubt she's leaving the rental car at the airport in case it's traced. She too cautious. I'll leave one of the guys here and the rest of us can head over by the airport, if that's okay with you?"

"Yeah, that's fine. Humans typically lack the ability to be random. I don't think any of us are typical and we're talking about Lindsay, who has already shown us what she's capable of. Be in touch." With that Robert hung up. Looking at Joe, he said, "If you were trying to disappear, would you contact someone from the Dark Web from the place you were hiding out or would you move around?"

"I, as well as you, Jack, and any others here,

would move around. She has a fake ID. She has a rental. She is definitely hiding. But from who, and why? I'll call Deacon. He'll clear me on the airport cameras."

"I don't want this out to anyone for any reason. Not even Deacon. Can you do it?"

"I hate to lie to him, but.....I'll make an exception."

"Casey, you have her name and description, start running those through the airlines. Single passengers first since she left the hotel by herself. If no name matches, run descriptions per ID."

Casey looked at him like a deer looking into headlights. "You know there are sixteen hundred flights a day out of Denver, that's approximately one hundred ninety-two thousand people going in each day." Noticing, quickly, Robert's glare, Casey continued, "I have her fake name and will get started right now." As he sat down, he mumbled, "This may take longer than today to get through."

Robert looked at the ceiling. "Today the only thing I've learned is that there are sixteen hundred flights out of Denver a day. I couldn't care less. So thankful my team knows how to do research."

Joe hung up with Deacon and turned to Robert. "He's on it. Approval shouldn't take long. He asked if we needed his assistance with this case. I told him I didn't think so, but he would be a good one to have on our side and you know I trust him with my life. I know this hunt for her is unofficial, but they do have more resources with hunting someone nationally. It's just a thought. Deacon is in Atlanta but can be anywhere we need him quickly."

"No. But thanks. Someone needs to find Charlie and now. I would be more likely to use Deacon for that."

29

Lindsay walked out the front door of the Hilton and over to the airport shuttle. She liked these particular shuttles because they had the blackout windows. This was almost too easy. She knew she had to worry about her landing more than her takeoff. Even if they found her in Denver, she doubted they would find her at the airport. She used a new ID for this roundtrip flight and Denver was a decent size. This was one of the reasons she chose it. She thought about Los Angeles for her next flight but that might be too busy. At least it was summer and nowhere was really cold right now.

She had picked up a hat at the Hilton giftshop and now put it on. It was cute with the messy bun and sweatshirt, but this was not really normal attire for her. Lindsay just fit in more on the weekend than she would have in another business suit since she wasn't trying to stand out in a crowd. She got off the shuttle, grabbed her bag and headed inside.

Lindsay kept her head down and tried to blend in, not standing too close to anyone because of her height which sometimes gave her away. She liked being tall but it had its disadvantages. Like now. It occurred to her, she was the hunted instead of the hunter. It didn't sit well with her. She was trying to escape the very people that had lied to her so that she could have peace and quiet to think. Nothing had been peaceful about this and certainly not quiet. It was obviously too much to ask for the truth in her life, but now it appeared to be too much to ask for a little space to have time to herself.

She was on high alert going through Security. Watching everyone around her, but still keeping her head down. She couldn't' stop wondering why they couldn't just leave her alone. So what if she disappeared. She was a grown adult and didn't answer to anyone.

Lindsay reached the gate with three minutes to spare. She was glad she had stopped in the ladies' room to remove the hat and let her hair down. She had removed the baggy sweatshirt and now had a t-shirt on. The sweatshirt would be too much for Atlanta weather.

As she boarded the plane, she wondered if it would be possible to forget the fact her boss is her previously dead father. Could she forget Sam had "died" and lied and all of the pain that came with that mess. Could she let it go that she had been lied to her entire life? She had never been truly in control of anything. She wanted to go back to the time before she ever met Sam. Before she uncovered some of the truth she always craved.

During the flight, Lindsay actually shut her mind down and was able to sleep. She would have plenty of time to think once she got back to Lake Dare and the security of the lake house. If it was secure.

30

"C'mon Casey! We aren't looking for a needle in a haystack. I realize it's a lot but you are supposed to be the best. Joe, anything at all?"

Joe looked up at Robert and shook his head no.

They had been watching the Denver cameras for a while and Casey had been scanning the passenger list of every airline in Denver for a description fitting this woman. He still didn't know her real name. He had already searched her fake name and came up empty. "Sir, I can only search so fast with this list of 193,217 passengers." "I thought there were only 192,000 passengers a day out of Denver? Figures today would be busier than usual."

Casey started to answer, but Robert held his hand up. He didn't want to hear any more useless statistical information. He wanted to hear they found Lindsay.

For the next half hour, the office was completely silent. Finally, Joe shouted, "I think I got her!" about the same time as Casey stated he narrowed down his search to a few possible passengers.

Robert ran to the cameras and caught what could potentially be Lindsay. "Get the guys inside now!"

Jack called Derek and informed him to get

inside the airport immediately in Concourse C, Southwest Airlines and described what Lindsay could possibly be wearing.

Robert despised dealing with airlines. He had spent tons of money on airline tickets when following people. They usually had a name and could pull the manifest, but they didn't know the name Lindsay was using, nor did they know what flight or to where. Jack told Derek to buy a ticket from the first flight leaving Concourse C on Southwest Airlines, just to get him through security.

As Derek approached the ticket reservation area, he watched the flight to Atlanta disappear off the screen so he bought the next ticket out. To Las Vegas. He wished he were going there for fun, on a vacation. He hadn't had one of those in forever.

As he made his way through security, he kept his eyes peeled for Lindsay. Once cleared, he walked as fast as he could without bringing attention to himself, all while scanning quickly for a tall woman with a messy bun and a baggy sweatshirt. He made it to the Atlanta gate just as they closed the door to the ramp. He continued to the end of the concourse and had just turned around when Jack called him on his cell. Hopeful for an answer, Derek asked, "Where is she?"

"We think she took that flight to Atlanta. No match on the name, but on the cameras, it looked like we caught a glimpse of her. If you don't see her, there's a great chance she got on the flight to Atlanta. We'll check the Atlanta gate cameras but it may take a minute."

"They shut the ramp door as I got to the gate. We can't get there before she does. I'll keep looking. She may have gone into the ladies' room and even changed again. I'll get close to the Vegas flight before I leave here." Derek didn't miss anyone as he kept his eyes moving around the terminal during the conversation.

Robert could tell by Jack's demeanor Derek hadn't found her. "She obviously doesn't want to be found, but keep looking. You can't get to Atlanta before she does, so take your time there. We'll deal with Atlanta."

Jack turned to look at Robert. He knew Robert was already aware they had missed her if she got on that flight to Atlanta. Jack walked over to Casey and asked to see the IDs of the passengers on the Atlanta manifest matching Lindsay's description. After several minutes of flipping through them, there was one that might potentially be Lindsay, but the hair color and eye color were off, along with the weight. All easy to change and fluctuate. She could pull it off.

Joe watched Robert. He knew he was seething inside. They were so close, but that didn't count in this business. They had trained Lindsay and she was beating them at their own game. He knew Robert wasn't concerned that Lindsay was getting the better of them. It was that she could potentially be in trouble. "Want me to have Deacon check out the passengers on that plane? He's in Atlanta anyway. He did meet her recently, one time."

"See if he can spot her getting off the plane. Tell him not to approach her and stay out of sight. The most he could do is follow her, but that won't be easy. With her memory, she'll remember him."

"On it, boss." Joe walked out of the room to call Deacon.

"Robert, we can get to Atlanta before she

does. Even if we fly commercial, we can probably still beat her there from here." Jack wanted to be in Atlanta to meet Lindsay. He couldn't take any more risk. He had to know what her intentions were and why she was evading them. She was going to extremes for some reason. He wanted to know why.

"She doesn't want to be found. If that is her, and it's still slightly questionable if it is, she will be furious. I need a few minutes to think this through." He walked out leaving Jack with Casey.

Jack had considered making a run for the airport and flying to Atlanta himself. He knew Robert would never trust him again, thinking his intentions were bad. Instead, he sent Casey out to get lunch for everyone. Although Casey stated it wasn't his job, he went anyway. Jack pulled his cell phone out and made a call. He wasn't one for sitting idly by if there were something to be done within his power.

31

"Ladies and Gentlemen, please prepare for final approach to Hartsfield-Jackson Atlanta International Airport. Please put all tray tables in the upright, locked position, and secure personal belongings under the seat in front of you. We will be coming by shortly for any trash and to check your seat belts. Thank you for flying with Southwest Airlines. We hope you enjoy your stay in Atlanta, Georgia."

Lindsay awoke at the sound of the flight attendant's announcement. Her mind went into overdrive immediately. She knew there was no way Derek could make it to Atlanta from Denver faster than she had, but she didn't put it past them to have someone from the organization there. She was alert and ready.

Stepping off the plane, she again kept her head down but eyes constantly moving. She made her way to baggage claim. She was relieved to see her bag was one of the first ones on the conveyor belt. Lifting if off, she turned and bumped into Deacon, who had appeared out of thin air and was standing entirely too close. "Excuse me. I'm so sorry." She tried to pretend she didn't recognize him and started to move away as she mumbled her apologies.

"No problem, Kendall. It's good to see you again." Deacon had put his hands on her arms, pretending to steady her.

"Oh, Deacon! I'm sorry, I didn't recognize you." Lindsay gave him her best surprised look.

Deacon knew she was lying. He may only know her as Kendall and he was sure that wasn't her real name, but he knew about her photographic memory. She was after all, somewhat of a legend in the FBI world. Not everyone knew about her memory, but anyone who was somebody in the organization did.

"Kendall, do you have a minute to chat?"

Lindsay gave him her best smile, tilted her head up, and said, "Nope, not today. Maybe next time?" as she started to move away.

He had his hands still on her arms and didn't let go, but just gave her his best smile back.

Lindsay looked at his hand on her arm, "So, official business, huh? Not just a chance meeting?"

"Sorry, Kendall. Joe called me. Can we chat just for a moment?"

"Sure, but I need to hit the ladies' room first."

Deacon smiled and put his hand out as if to say, lead the way. They walked in silence. Lindsay went into the ladies' room, opened her bag, took her gun out and loaded it. She put her gun on her side. She put her electronics in her purse, leaving only clothes in the checked bag. She asked herself why they would send Deacon and how much did he know? Maybe he was here to stall her. Why not send Jack if he came from Philly, too. She didn't really care. She was out of here as quickly as the plan formed in her head.

Coming back out of the ladies' room, Deacon was immediately upon her. "May I carry your bag?"

"Nope, I've got it. Where to? I only have a

few minutes, though." Lindsay gave him her best smile again as she checked her watch.

"There is a coffee shop on the second floor." He gently put his hand on her arm as they started walking.

As they walked by a set of double doors, Lindsay gave Deacon a regretful smile. "Oh, look, my ride is here. I'm so sorry, but I hate to keep him waiting. Next time?" Lindsay didn't wait for an answer. She turned and bolted out the double doors and jumped into a car that was parked just outside. As she got in the car, she pulled her gun from the front of her jeans, pointed and said, "Drive."

The guy looked at her, startled. "Lady, you are in the wrong car." Then he noticed the gun. "Please don't shoot me. I'll take you anywhere you want to go."

"Drive now!" Lindsay looked out the car door to see Deacon standing there with his hands on his hips, frowning. She knew it was a matter of time before they would track this car.

As they pulled away, Lindsay spoke softly now, "Drive like you normally would." Lindsay had him take her to a bad section of Atlanta where she knew there were no street cams.

As she got out, she threw the guy an envelop of cash. "Don't tell anyone where you dropped me off. Forget you know me. Get out of here, now."

Within twenty minutes, a car pulled up. She ducked down to look in the window. "I'm driving." He got out and went to the passenger side and got in. "What took you so long?"

"I'm actually early but I almost missed my flight and had to get the rental car. Nothing like a last-minute trip to one of the busiest airports in the country. You couldn't pick a smaller one?"

"Nope. Quit whining. Do you have my IDs?"

"It's good to see you, too. What's up with the hair? I like the blonde better."

"We'll discuss that later. Listen, we need to get this done quickly. I need to move. I'm taking you to a hotel. You will go in the side door, walk through the hotel to the lobby. Catch the shuttle to the airport and get my car from this lot." She handed him a piece of paper. "Then drive back to where you just picked me up. Got it?"

"Yeah. Want to fill me in on all the secrecy? Or why you can't retrieve your own car? Lindsay, are you in trouble?"

"Drama Llama, always asking dumb questions and worrying like a little ole' grandma. Hey by the way, I'll need you to get that car in Frederick. I left it there. Check it too for any tracking devices. No one knows our connection, right? No one has come around asking questions? Are you staying out of the bar?"

"Okay, okay, no, no and yes." He gave her a silly grin. "And who worries too much?"

"You are the best. So how is the girlfriend? She still around?" Lindsay looked at him with her most innocent look.

"That face might work with others, but I know what you are doing. Yeah, she's around. Been busy with work so haven't seen much of her. When did you start asking multiple questions without out waiting for answers in between? Tells me you aren't yourself."

"I may put you to work for me yet."

"I already work for you. Doing IDs, delivering cars and clothes to strange locations and now retrieving cars. I don't know what you are up to but it's either tracking someone down, or being tracked down. Which is it?"

"You need to stop right there. Worrying about me as a friend is one thing. Trying to figure me out, is a whole different thing. Let it go. I swear, if you don't, it won't go well and will ruin our friendship."

"Okay, okay, relax. I'm just here if you need me." He put his hand on her arm and gave it a quick rub."

"Thank you." They drove the rest of the way to the hotel in silence. As Lindsay pulled up to the side door, she handed him the car keys and reminded him, "Make sure you aren't followed."

32

"I can't believe this. Lindsay lost Deacon at the Airport." Joe stood there shaking his head. He hated giving the boss any bad news.

"Did he at least get anything out of her? How did she look? Was she angry to see him? Was she alone?"

"Woah Robert. I realize you aren't really yourself, but one thing at a time. Deacon said she wasn't mad. Played dumb at first, then was sweet, then took off in a car with a stranger outside baggage claim after agreeing to meet with him. They are tracking the car now, but Deacon said by the look on the driver's face, she basically carjacked him."

"What! She really doesn't want to be found. What the hell is she doing besides beating us at our own game?"

Joe didn't say anything.

Robert paced for a few minutes. Joe hated seeing him like this, which he never had before. Robert wasn't taking this well. No one else would notice, except maybe Jack, because they had been working together for so long.

"Derek and Sam are on their way to Atlanta. Casey didn't find anymore?" Joe tried to change the subject as best as he could under the circumstances.

"No, I have him digging but nothing new. Sam isn't going to be happy about this at all. What is Deacon doing?"

"He's not doing anything more unless we ask or if the owner of the car files a police report. It's difficult to have him do much more without filling him in and bringing him up to speed. You know this is unofficial and Deacon is by the book. I could ask him as a favor and let him know that she's potentially in danger, but he will need to know from who and I'm not sure we would we want to disclose all your enemies, which would lead to more questions as to why Kendall is in danger because of your enemies."

"Sadly, it's not just my enemies that put her in danger." Robert said it barely above a whisper.

Joe's phone rang before he could respond. It was Derek calling on video.

"Hey Joe, anything more?"

"Yeah Derek. Deacon talked to her in Atlanta. But she lost him."

Sam looked at Joe on camera, "Who's Deacon and what did she say to him?"

Joe answered, "He's FBI, strait-laced and a great guy. I never would have thought Kendall would lose him of all people, but in all fairness, he didn't know anything more than he was to find her at the airport and see if he could get her to tell him what she was up to or to talk to one of us. He doesn't have a clue of what is going on. Had he known; it may have turned out differently. She didn't say anything. Hijacked a car and bolted out of there."

Sam looked thoughtful, then starting speaking slowly, "So, we know she is alone and she is doing whatever she is doing and she is where ever she wants to be and she doesn't want any of us involved. She's willing to commit a crime to escape us. Does that sum it up? Did I miss anything, because I need more than that!" Sam looked like he could punch a few people and his voice couldn't have gone many decibels higher.

No one said a word. Everyone looked down, lost in their own thoughts and not wanting to say the wrong thing to Sam, including he was right. That about summed it up from their perspective, too.

After several more minutes of complete silence, Sam asked, "Where's Jack?"

Joe didn't answer but they could see he was moving. Suddenly, he had a landline phone in his hand. Joe put the phone to his ear, then hung up without saying anything. A clear indication Jack was not answering.

Joe didn't have anything else so to get out of the conversation, quicky said, "We'll be in touch when we know something or call back when you land in Atlanta. It may be a waste of a trip for you. I think she's long gone." He disconnected before either of them could say more.

Robert sat down and put his finger up to his lip, taping it. Joe knew this sign. Robert was contemplating something. He rarely did this. Robert was usually quick on decisions and loaded with facts.

"This is like hunting a ghost. What the hell is she up too?" The question almost sounded rhetorical but Joe answered anyway.

"We know she wants more info on you, Sam, Derek, and Jack. Maybe she is just digging for the truth for her own knowledge."

"To what end?"

"To figure out the truth about her life. Seems

139

there have been lots of lies." Joe held his hand up. "I get that you were trying to protect her. But not only were there a lot of lies, there were a lot of deaths that were lies. Look at things from her perspective."

Robert didn't acknowledge that but simply shook his head. He paced again for about ten minutes. Finally, coming to a standstill, he shook his head again, looked at the ceiling and in almost a whisper, simply said, "Charlie, Charlie, Charlie."

33

Lindsay was glad to be back at the house on Lake Dare. She had left Atlanta well after dark to make sure she hadn't been followed. She had taken a few detours so the ride back took an hour longer, but she was certain she hadn't been followed.

Now to check the house to see if anything was out of order. At least the order she had left it in. Lindsay hoped everything was as she left it. She only had the energy for a shower and her bed.

Walking through the kitchen door, she knew things were not right. She let out a breath she hadn't realized she was holding.

She checked the kitchen drawers and doors. Someone had gone through them but with delicacy. Nothing was out of place but the drawers she hadn't left completely closed were now completely closed.

The fishing line on the back stairs was unhooked. Lindsay didn't need a list of how many inches she had left the doors open. She used her memory. Every door was moved. They appeared to be put back where she had them but they were all a few inches off, either way.

It didn't appear anything was taken. Apparently, someone was looking for something. Or just being extremely nosey. But who? If Mrs. Wigley had come in, things would be messed up. There is no way she could have come in here and not messed things up. It may be time to get cameras. Then again, Mrs. Wigley's grandson was an odd creature. Maybe he was just being nosey.

Lindsay would get cameras next time she went out of town to call the boys. For now, she would be careful. And distance herself from all the chaos of the neighbors. She checked all the exterior doors, windows and outside before heading off to bed. She was exhausted.

* * * * *

Lindsay woke up to someone banging on the door. At least it was daylight. Throwing on sweatpants and a t-shirt, she looked out her bedroom window. Seeing whose car was in the driveway, she considered not answering. Then thought better of it.

Opening the door, she gave Officer Becker a smile. "What brings you by this early in the day? Let me guess, you happen to be in the neighborhood?"

Lance smiled at her with that enchanting smile of his. Here we go, Lindsay thought. "No, actually, I'm on official business and it's not early in the day. It's noon. Sleep well?"

"What could a game warden need from me at any hour of the day?" Lindsay smiled back at him, but used her most innocent smile.

"Shoot any more coyotes lately or remove any more bullets?" Now he was serious.

"Huh?" Now Lindsay turned her confused look on him.

"Cut it out, Kendall. I know you shot a coyote in your yard the last time I came by and asked you if you had heard or seen anything. What I don't know is why you lied to me."

"Hmmmm, must have slipped my mind. It's not illegal to shoot one, right, Mr. Game Warden?"

"No, but it is illegal to shoot someone without reporting it. Why didn't you take Mr. Tyler to the emergency room after you shot him?"

"Well, you might want to ask him why he wouldn't go when I suggested it."

"I would if I could find him. After he left the doctor's office from getting antibiotics, he hasn't been seen since. So, you did shoot him?"

"I never said that. I simply said you needed to ask him why he didn't want to go to the ER after he was shot. And no, actually I was out of town for a few days, so I haven't seen him. Did he die? Have you checked his house?"

"We can't enter his house without a search warrant. You don't seem genuinely concerned that he may have died. Did you take him out of town with you?"

"No. I'm not concerned. He was on private property. I don't know him. It isn't like we're friends. If there is nothing else, thank you and have a nice day, Officer Becker."

"Kendall, are you okay?"

"Yes, I got in late last night from my trip. I haven't had coffee yet and I can't help you. You seem to know everything I know. Good day." With that she shut the door.

She had gotten half way across the kitchen when there was another knock. Lindsay went back to the door and swung it open. "Was there anything else, Officer Becker?"

"Yes, I asked you to call me Lance." He gave

her that smile again.

"Lance, remember how cranky you were when you didn't have your coffee? That's where I am. I also asked you to call me Miss James." She slammed the door this time, and locked it.

Making her way over to the coffee pot, she looked out the window to see the game warden leaving.

She wondered where Grayson had disappeared to. She had been gone a few days so, obviously, she hadn't seen him, except the night before she left, when she had taken food to him. He was fine then. If he were out of town, that eliminated him from breaking into her house. She needed to check the locks to see how who ever had come in, did it. The doors were all locked when she arrived.

34

"Nice nail color."

She looked at her nails like she was admiring fine art. "I'm surprised you noticed. Thank you. So, did you find anything of interest when you got in Lindsay's lake house?" He wasn't surprised when she flipped from sweet to all business.

"Not a thing. Boring as bird watching. She isn't stupid. I'm not sure what you expected me to find."

"Was there a computer or laptop, paperwork, guns?"

"Of course, there were guns. Why would you ask me that? Her not having guns is like you not having your weekly manicure. There was no computers or laptops or paperwork. It looks like any average single woman lives there."

"Oh, you want me to drag this out of you? I hate games, but I'll play. Are there any inside cameras? Security of any kind? I know there isn't anything outside. Did you get the internet password yet?"

"No. I am telling you, there isn't anything. If I hadn't seen her for myself, I would say just a regular, boring person lives there. There is no indication of her identity. Everything is in the name of Kendall James or Ava James. And by the way, you might want to consider staying away from the lake house. Actually, do whatever. Maybe you'll give yourself away. She'll bury you."

"She's good. But I'm better." She started that irritating tapping of her nails that he despised.

"What's your plan now, Princess?" He not only sounded bored, but looked it, too.

"I doubt you looked hard enough. I'm telling you, if you have info and don't give it up, you will pay for it. And from now on, every time you call me Princess, I will stick a nail in your coffin. Stop being an ass."

"Can we just get on with this? I have things to do."

"Like what? Get back on with your life? Ha! You'll only do that if you don't fail this deal."

"More like a mission. There is no deal. A deal I could decline. What's your plan?"

"Let's discuss it over a nice, friendly dinner? Shall we?" She lit up with her best smile.

"No. I'm not suffering through dinner with you. Get out and let me get back to my mission. The sooner this is over, the sooner you are out of my life."

"Now now, sweetheart. That isn't any way to behave when a lady such as myself offers you a scrumptious dinner. Whatever, your loss. Here is what I expect you to do next."

There it was again, sweet to evil in an instant. Like she had an internal switch.

35

Lindsay decided she was going to relax on the deck and read a good book. No researching. No thinking. A complete day of nothing but relaxation and unwinding. Now, if she could just keep the neighbors in their own yards.

She got lucky and was able to get lost in her book for about two hours. She put her book down and stared off at the lake. She could see a lone kayaker. He had great form.

She watched him a while. Her mind drifted off to better days of being on the Chesapeake Bay. She had a friend with a boat and loved to go out when the boys were with their father. One summer, she spent all her free time with him on the motorcycle, driving to the bay and taking the boat out. Some of the best fireworks she had ever seen were from that boat in Annapolis. She missed the simpler days and would love to have those back now.

Her mind had wondered so far off, she hadn't realized the kayaker was coming toward the front of her house. She kept watching him come closer and closer until she realized it was Grayson. It was too late to avoid him without being rude. She didn't move off the deck. She was hoping he would turn toward his house next door.

Grayson reached the edge of Lindsay's lawn.

He got out of the kayak, pulled it up on dry land and continued toward her until he was at the edge of her deck. "You're back." There was no smile.

Lindsay couldn't help but think he wasn't happy to see her. "Yes. I see you are, too."

"I didn't go anywhere. Guess the game warden was by already." It wasn't a question.

"Yes, before I rolled out of bed. What is that all about and why did he say you disappeared, yet, here you are?" Lindsay looked at him with a straight face, trying to keep her eyes on his and not his naked torso.

"Because I'm not answering the door. The wound got infected. I had no choice but to see the town doctor and get antibiotics. Apparently, Doc and the game warden chatted. The only thing I told the doc was that I accidently shot myself while cleaning the gun. Doubt he bought it, but it was all he was getting."

"Officer Becker asked me if I shot any more coyotes or removed any bullets lately."

"Interesting. I can only assume he threw something from left field and you caught it."

"To be that accurate? Doubtful. Are you sure you didn't throw me under the bus? Do you have outside cameras at your house that reach this way?"

"No, cameras give people a false sense of security." He looked at her with a raised eyebrow. "Think you need some?"

"False sense of security? No, my security has never been false. Had I had cameras though, I could have caught the woman on video that ran through my backyard that night and I could have stayed safely inside my house to see what other creatures passed through." Lindsay wasn't going to tell him that her whole security in who she was, was gone.

"Creatures? You worried about safety when you move and shoot like a pro? Hmmmm. Interesting." He raised his eyebrow again. "Why do you ask if I have cameras?"

This guy was no photographer. "Because I was thinking maybe the police or game warden hacked your cameras to see what really happened that night. That's too far left field to be a guess." Now she raised an eyebrow at him.

"About that security. People breaking into cameras. If the good guys can, so can the bad. They are a waste of time."

"Hiding from some bad guys or just the good guys?" She raised her eyebrow again.

"Not hiding from anyone. I shot the coyote, you shot me. Just trying to keep you out of trouble."

"Me? But you were…."

He turned away and started walking back toward his kayak while she was still talking. He stopped about half way down the yard, turned back toward Lindsay and said, "Oh by the way, dinner was excellent. Thank you." Then continued toward his kayak. Picking it up and putting it over his shoulder, he walked across the yard to his house.

Lindsay wasn't sure what all that was about, but something was definitely not right about Grayson Tyler. She didn't care. She would just stay away from him. She didn't need any more confusion, or liars, in her life.

36

An hour later, Lindsay was hungry. She walked through the house toward the kitchen. As she got closer, she heard something, but wasn't sure what it was. Probably Mrs. Wigley again. But Mrs. Wigley couldn't get in since the door was locked.

As Lindsay peeked around the door way into the kitchen, she let out a scream that could have woken the dead. On the kitchen counter was a raccoon and it was hissing at her. Lindsay was frozen in place. Where was her gun when she needed it?

While Lindsay stood completely still, trying to figure out what to do with this raccoon, Grayson came running through the house from the deck. As soon as he saw Lindsay, he moved up beside her but not in the kitchen doorway. He had his gun out and whispered to her, he was there. She spoke quietly but loud enough for him to hear, "There is a raccoon on my kitchen counter."

"Really? I thought someone was trying to murder you with that scream. Move toward me slowly." Once Lindsay was behind him, he asked her to get the keys to the kitchen door. Grayson moved into the doorway so he could keep an eye on the raccoon.

Once Lindsay returned, he asked her if she wanted to stay there with his gun or go around the outside and open the kitchen door so the raccoon could go out. She chose to go into the bathroom and shut the door while he got the raccoon out, what ever way worked best for him.

Five minutes later, Grayson announced the house was raccoon free and she could come out of hiding.

Lindsay tip-toed into the living room and stopped close to Grayson. "He's gone? How did you get him out?"

"You are terrified of them, aren't you?" He was amused but refrained from showing it.

"Yes." Lindsay didn't tell him she was afraid of the woods and everything in it. This made her question why she chose a lake house instead of a city condo. She knew the answer.

"He's gone. You're safe. But how did he get in?"

"Ummm, I think that is part of what terrified me. I wasn't expecting an animal that big to get inside. Completely unexpected."

"Do you want me to look around and see?" He could tell she was rattled and shaking.

"No, I will. Thank you. How did you get here so quickly?"

"I was going for a jog when I heard you scream. Want to go?" As Grayson said this, he looked down at his clothes. That was when Lindsay realized he was wearing jogging clothes.

"Uhhhhh, I should. I've been thinking about jogging again but just haven't taken the time to do it."

"Well, let's go."

"I'm not up for it right now, but thanks."

After Grayson left, Lindsay checked everywhere in the house. The doors, windows, closets, every single room. There was only one way for that thing to have gotten in; someone had to have put it there. But who and why? She would have to remember to ask Grayson if the door was locked. He came through the lake side though. Most people jogged on the lane. She needed to ask him if he was running on water, too. Nothing about it made sense.

37

Two days later, as the sun was beginning to rise over the lake, Lindsay sat straight up in bed. Someone was in her house. She reached over and pulled her gun from under the pillow beside her. She was wearing a t-shirt and underwear but wasn't taking the time to put on sweatpants. She could feel the closeness. Her bedroom door, leading to the balcony, was open. She always slept with it closed and was sure it had been when she went to bed. She silently checked her bathroom, then the closet. Both were empty. She peered through the open door out on to the balcony. It was empty. She quietly turned toward the stairs and thought she saw a figure moving stealthily in the direction of the back of the house. She ran to the back stairs. As she started down, she tripped on something and tumbled the entire length of the stairs.

She landed half way across the kitchen between the stairs and the backdoor. The fall must have knocked her out because the next thing she heard was someone banging on the door and yelling, "Kendall, Kendall!"

Lindsay glanced around, slightly confused. She slowly got up and looked at Grayson. He was on the other side of the door. She held up her hand and said, "Hold on" in a weak voice. She spotted her gun on the kitchen counter. She walked over to it and checked to see if it was still loaded. It was, but how it got on the counter was only one guess.

Someone had been in her house and put it there after she fell down the stairs.

Moving a bit unsteady, she opened the door, leaning on it and asked, "What?"

"What? That's all you can say? I thought you were dead and was about to bust the door down. What the hell happened?"

Lindsay looked at him, still slightly confused. "What do you want?"

"Did you usually sleep in the middle of the kitchen floor, half dressed?"

Lindsay looked down at her attire, or lack thereof, then back at Grayson. "I'm sure you aren't here to check out my sleeping arrangements nor what I sleep in. Why are you here at this hour?"

"I wanted to see if you wanted to go jogging with me, but it doesn't look like you are in any condition. What the hell happened?"

"Rough morning. Thanks for the offer but I'm not…."

Lindsay grabbed her stomach and that's when Grayson saw her arm. "I'm going to be sick!" She pushed the door closed and ran to the sink, barely making it when she vomited.

Out of the corner of her eye, she saw Grayson walking toward her. She held her hand up again as if to stop him. With her other hand, she grabbed her gun, keeping her head over the sink.

"Woah! Kendall, I know you are a great shot but finish puking before you worry about me." He stopped where he was.

After Lindsay finished, she turned and slid to the floor. With the gun in her hand still, she looked at Grayson like she was confused but didn't lift the gun to point at him.

"Now tell me why you are here again?"

"I wanted to see if you wanted to go jogging with me, but when I walked up to the door, I saw you spread out in the middle of the floor. I didn't see any blood but I thought you might be dead. Or maybe that you sleepwalk. That's a weird place to sleep, unless there's something seriously wrong with you. What the hell happened?"

"I tripped on the stairs this morning. Quite clumsy, huh? Thank you for your concern, but you can go now."

"I'm not leaving you alone. If you fell down the stairs and knocked yourself unconscious then puked, you need a doctor."

"You aren't a doctor so you can go." She looked like she barely had enough energy to say that much.

"Leave your gun down. I'm carrying you to the couch, ok?" Grayson moved slowly toward her as he said this.

Lindsay lifted the gun. "Stop."

Grayson stopped mid step. "What are you doing? If I wanted to harm you, I would have done it while you were out cold. Use your pretty little head, or at least what's left of it." Then he started toward her again and before she could do anything else, he picked her up and walked to the living room. He gently laid her on the couch. "Hold on to your gun if it makes you feel better." He disappeared into the bathroom and came back with a cold washcloth and laid it on her forehead.

"Obviously more happened than just you falling down the stairs. Care to share?"

Lindsay looked at him. That was her line most of her life. Seems no one really wanted to do that anymore. Probably because they were about to lie and didn't really want to. Who was she kidding, they had all perfected it. Lies were the story of her life. Grayson was probably a liar, too.

"No. Thanks for your help. You can go. I'll be fine."

"Kendall, what am I missing? You fall down the stairs, get knocked out cold, then wake up only to get sick. Your arm looks bad and your wrist is starting to swell. Sprain? And you won't let go of that gun. What really happened?"

Lindsay looked at him for a moment contemplating telling him. She was usually great at reading people. However, she was finding herself a little insecure in that department lately. How could she have been surrounding by a circle of liars and never saw through them.

"I thought I heard something. I got up to check and fell down the stairs. Simple as that." She watched his face. He didn't look convinced. She wondered if that was because he was the one in her house. But why would he be? She wasn't making any sense, even to herself.

"You didn't think to put more clothes on before checking, but you thought to get your gun? Interesting."

"What's interesting about that?"

"You obviously thought someone was here so you got your gun but not convinced enough to get dressed. How sure were you someone was here?" He let out a little chuckle.

Lindsay blushed. She had no response for that, except that she needed coffee since he wasn't going to let her go back to sleep.

"You rest and I'll make you some coffee. That

stuff is bad for you though. You should quit." He headed to the kitchen. How did he know she loved her coffee?

Lindsay wondered why he didn't offer to look around the house since she told him this started because she thought someone had been in here. They could still be there. Or he was now in her kitchen making coffee.

Lindsay got up and slowly headed to the door leading to the deck. It was unlocked. She was positive she had locked it before she went to bed. She walked to the stairs and looked up. She didn't see anything on them. She cautiously took the stairs one at a time, watching every step closely. Her body was starting to hurt from the fall. She realized she had left her gun on the table in the living room. She went into her bedroom and got another gun from the nightstand. She checked her room again. It was as she left it earlier.

She checked out the other rooms to find them all empty. As she closed the last door and turned, she almost bumped into Grayson. She immediately jumped back and raised her gun.

"What the hell is up with you, Kendall? Why are you so spooked?" He held both hands up, one gripping her gun, but he wasn't holding it like he was going to shoot.

"Lay the gun on the floor." She was now in a stance, ready to fire.

Lindsay could tell he was trying to read her, but she kept a look on her face that wouldn't give anything away. He laid the gun on the floor then started backing up slowly. For each step he took, she took one toward the gun. Once she was there, she picked it up.

"Okay, now that we are done playing 'who gets to keep the gun' can I be dismissed to the kitchen again?" Now he was smiling at her like he was in a dental commercial.

"What are you doing up here?"

"I came to find you because you weren't in the living room where I left you and because it dawned on me that someone might still be in the house. Although, I don't need your gun for protection, I figured it couldn't hurt to have it."

"Your dismissed. Not just to the kitchen but out of my house. Thanks for stopping by." She nudged by him in the hallway, realizing she was still in her underwear. She headed toward her bedroom again as he started for the stairs. "Hold on! I want to see something." She moved toward the top of the stairs, knelt down and examined the first few closely. Not seeing what she expected, she stood up and continued to her room.

As Lindsay closed the door, Grayson said, "Coffee's ready. See you downstairs."

Lindsay stopped and listened to Grayson. She shook her head. She had to get him to leave. She needed to check the house out more thoroughly and couldn't do it with him underfoot. She pulled on sweatpants after checking herself out in the mirror and went downstairs to the kitchen, where breakfast smells hit her.

"Ah ah ah, off to the couch you go. Breakfast is almost done." He took her by the shoulders and tried to move her out of the kitchen. "Don't make me carry you again."

"I thought you didn't cook? Why are you cooking breakfast?"

"Because you need to eat. And rest. I think

you took a pretty good fall this morning. The fact that you puked tells me you may have a concussion."

Lindsay didn't argue. She walked to the couch as fast as she could, in fear that she was going to be sick again.

A few minutes later, Grayson walked in carrying a tray. "Coffee and omelets, my queasy queen."

"How do I know you aren't trying to poison me?" Lindsay tried to look concerned, but the look came across pitiful.

"If I wanted to kill you, there are better ways. Breaking into your house at the crack of dawn is not one of them, nor is poisoning you."

"Really, tell me more." She picked up the cup of coffee and slowly took a sip. It actually made her feel better and she realized she was hungry. "I guess if you were going to kill me, you would make it worth photoing?"

"Is that a word? Photoing. Let me ask you something, Kendall, why would I want to kill you? Why would anyone want to kill you? Isn't that something that you do in your books as a writer? Maybe I should be careful. Are you setting me up?"

Lindsay couldn't help but laugh. If he only knew how ironic this was. She was no more a writer than she thought he was a photographer. She hadn't seen him with a camera once. She also wondered why he didn't ask what she had been looking for on the stairs.

38

Lindsay did not want to get off the couch to answer the door, but who ever it was, was not going away. She dragged herself through the dining room and into the kitchen to the back door. She couldn't hide now, or not answer; Lance saw her immediately.

Lindsay opened the door and stood silently.

"Well, good evening Kendall. Oh, that's right, I'm to call you Miss James. I'm sorry to bother you, but have you seen Mrs. Wigley today, or this evening?"

"No, sorry. Has she escaped again?" Lindsay shuddered at the thought of having to deal with Mrs. Wigley's shenanigans tonight.

"It appears so. She isn't home and the car is still in the garage. Her grandson is due back tomorrow to check on her but called tonight." He stood there looking bored.

"Since when are game wardens babysitters?"

"I spend a lot of time around here since it is a pretty big lake, in case you hadn't noticed. The local cops call me when they need help."

"That appears to be a lot. You are the only officer that has knocked on my door since I've been here. Where are the others?" She wondered to herself why she was asking him questions. She wanted him gone so she could go back to the couch.

"Looking for Mrs. Wigley, but I was closest so here I am. You do know there is usually only one cop on duty for the most part this time of year, right? So, I help out when I can."

"How sweet of you." Lindsay batted her eyes at him. "Hey, by the way, can you get me statistics for this area, like crime rate, number of break-ins, car accidents, hunting accidents?"

"I can, but you can search on-line for all that information. Why in the world do you need that? Most of the activity around here is caused by Mrs. Wigley." Lance chuckled at his own comment. "It's not high crime. Did something happen?"

"No, I'm thinking of putting it in my next book and I just thought you could give me more accurate and updated records than the internet. If you can't, it's fine."

"I think I can handle it, but I also think you could find a zillion better places to write about than here. Are you okay? Your wrist doesn't look good and you have a bump on your forehead." He looked at her more closely.

"I'm fine. I took a little fall on the stairs this morning." She grinned sheepishly. "I can be a hazard to myself in the morning without coffee." Now why did she say that? She needed to stop talking.

"You don't really look fine. Did you get that checked out?"

"Oh look, it's past my dinner time. I really need to run and eat." She gave him a beaming smile now.

"If I didn't know better, I would say you are avoiding me. What is it exactly you don't like about me, Kendall?"

"It would be easier to ask me what I like about you. I would suggest we do that over coffee, but I can tell you faster than you can order coffee. Good luck with Mrs. Wigley." She closed the door and went back to the couch.

An hour later, she was awakened by banging on the door. She wasn't going to get up and answer it this time, regardless of who it was. This place was supposed to be peaceful and quiet. It was anything but.

Lindsay was grateful the knocking stopped. Then she heard footsteps on the deck outside the huge living room windows. All she could do was groan to herself.

"Kendall, open up! I need to make sure you didn't die." Grayson was tapping on the window on one of the sliders to the deck.

"I didn't die. Look, here's a thumbs up." Lindsay gave him the thumbs up as she said this but didn't get up. Just yelling that to him zapped her energy.

"C'mon Kendall, open up." Lindsay wondered how stubborn Grayson was. She thought about waiting him out, then thought better of it. She would get up, show him she was good, then go to bed.

As she opened the door, she couldn't help but take in the sight of him. "Why do you need to make sure I didn't die?" She tried for the serious look again and failed. It took to much energy.

"Because it wouldn't look good for me if my neighbor died and there was something I could have done. And how would I explain what I was doing here with this casserole?" He held it up now with both hands.

"Who made that?" Lindsay took a big whiff once the smell hit her. This time, the smell didn't make her nauseous, and in fact, made her mouth water. She realized she hadn't eaten since he made breakfast at dawn. She moved back to allow him in.

"I did. It's my specialty."

"It doesn't smell like cereal, so there's that." She followed him into the kitchen.

"Omelets are my real specialty but you already had those this morning. I just came by to check on you and bring you food. I'm sure by now, and tomorrow, you are going to be quiet sore. How are you feeling?"

"I am a little sore. I'm sure tomorrow will be worse. Let me get some plates."

"Just one for you."

"You aren't staying? Did you eat?" She hoped he didn't see the look of disappointment on her face.

He did. "Do you want me to stay to eat or because you don't want to be alone after this morning?" He looked genuinely concerned. So did Sam last time she saw him. Saw him for what he was, too. She wondered where that thought came from.

"No, I uh, I'm fine. Really. But if you haven't eaten, it wouldn't make sense for you not to now." Lindsay was getting herself in deeper. She didn't like where this conversation was going.

"I did eat, but I can stay if you are more comfortable."

Grayson stood in her kitchen with one leg in front of the other and his fist on her counter. There was something comfortable about his stance. "No, really, I'm good. Thank you though. I appreciate that, and this food. What am I eating?"

"Comfort food. My grandmother made this for me when I was a kid and not feeling well. It's chicken parm casserole. It has a white sauce instead of marinara. Easier on your stomach. Go back to the couch and I'll get you set up."

As she went back the couch, she had a feeling of dread. Grayson was completely at home in her kitchen. She wasn't even that comfortable in her kitchen. He was gorgeous, muscular, sweet, smart, could cook and shoot. He was obviously too good to be true. And overwhelming her senses. She was here to make sense of her life, not complicate it. She still needed to figure out what she was going to do with Sam, if anything.

"I left my number on this for you, in case you need anything. Can I get you anything before I leave?" He had set a plate in front of her and a fresh water, along with a note pad.

"No. Thank you. I'll eat and go to bed. I appreciate your help, but really, I'm good. Thanks for dinner." She hoped he didn't see the sadness she was feeling. If he did, she could blow it off as sore from the fall. Grayson had a way of seeing through her when most people didn't. "Good night, Grayson."

"Good night, Kendall. I'll show myself out."

39

The next morning, Lindsay was looking through the garage when she heard a car pull into the driveway. She groaned when she saw Lance's car. She didn't want to do this with him today. She pretended to be lost in what she was doing. She had woken up feeling a little dizzy and nauseated, thinking she may have gotten a concussion during the fall down the stairs. But there was no way she would mention that to anyone.

"Hey, Kendall. How are you?" He smiled that smile Lindsay was sure made women melt.

"I'm good. And you?" She barely acknowledged him, except for the glance to see those straight, white teeth behind his full lips and that smile.

"I don't mean to disturb you, but wanted to check on you. And bring you this." Lance handed her a coffee.

"Why would you need to do that?" Now she looked at him.

"Because I know how much you enjoy your coffee. And it's white chocolate mocha."

"I'm not talking about the coffee. But how did you know it's my favorite?"

"I figured you had heard. There were a few break-ins recently. We haven't heard from you so we figured you were fine but wanted to make sure."

"Break-ins? Really? Like Mrs. Wigley getting

loose? She's harmless." Lindsay continued to look at the shelves on the garage wall like they were of upmost importance.

"No, not Mrs. Wigley. A few houses were broken into. We haven't caught anyone yet. It's probably just some of the camp kids getting bored out there, but we can't be sure. You are all good here?"

"Yup, hadn't heard anything. Good thing we all have you to protect us, right?" Now she turned toward him and started walking past him.

Lance turned and watched her walk to the garage door that was open where he had come in. "You aren't walking right. You look stiff. Is that from your fall yesterday?"

"Probably. I'll be fine in a few hours. You probably should be out figuring who has broken into these houses instead of standing here worrying about me." She leaned against the outside garage wall.

"Actually, that's not my job, remember. I deal with animals mostly."

"Then why are you here?" She gave him her most alluring smile. Then crossed her arms to diminish the effect.

"Honestly, to check on you and see if you are willing to go to dinner with me?" Now he gave her his most alluring smile.

"Woah, how did we go from coffee to dinner?"

"You won't agree to coffee so I figured I would try to feed you. I promise I don't bite, much."

"No, I'm perfectly capable of feeding myself, but thank you."

"You'll give in eventually. In the meantime, stay safe." He started to walk past her but she stopped him.

"Why do you always have to have the last word and end every conversation with something egotistical or glib?" What she was really wondering was how he knew white chocolate mochas were her favorite and where did the "stay safe" come from. Jack popped into Lindsay's mind.

"You're wrong. I don't end every conversation that way. The night I changed your tire, I didn't." Now he was smirking.

"The night you changed my tire, you didn't say one word!"

"Still counts. Want to go to dinner and finish discussing it?"

"Bye, Lance. And thanks for the coffee."

He started to saunter off, thinking he may be wearing her down, but then turned back to her. "If you see anything out of the ordinary, please call me." He started to turn again but stopped when Lindsay responded to him.

"Wait, is there anything ordinary here?" She almost said something about the raccoon but thought better of it. He was a game warden and had ease and access with animals. Was Lance trying to make her feel weak so she would call on him?

40

"C'mon Sam, you have to go back to work. You can't keep doing what you are doing without eventually going crazy. It's obvious Lindsay doesn't want to be found. She is a tough cookie and can handle herself. We have a ton of people working on finding her. Either they will find her or she will turn up on her own, when she's ready."

"Please don't. I don't want to do this with you again. If you want to discuss Lindsay's case, I will. Other than that, I don't want to hear it." Derek knew Sam well enough to know when his brain cells where on overload. "You have another thought. Let's hear it." Derek didn't know what do to about Sam. He refused to talk about anything other than Lindsay. The only time they got input from him and it wasn't about Lindsay, was one day in Robert's office when they were discussing another case. Sam had a great plan. He just happened to be sitting there waiting on a report from the field about Lindsay.

"Remember the day Deacon talked to her in Atlanta at the airport?"

"Of course. What about it?"

"Remember when we got back to Philadelphia and shortly after Jack disappeared. What if he went and found her and is now holding her somewhere? Don't we need to keep an open mind about Jack since we aren't sure if we can trust him?"

"I wish I could say I doubt Jack has anything to do with Lindsay staying away so long, but I can't. That is exactly why he is being followed. We're already on it." Derek knew the second he said it, he shouldn't have.

"Why the hell didn't anyone tell me?" Sam looked exasperated.

"Because you are a hot head where Lindsay is concerned. Look, Sam, I really need you on this case that came in. Why don't you work it with me while you wait for Lindsay? You've exhausted every angle regarding her."

"No, I haven't. I'm going out west where the boys are. Lindsay will go see them, eventually. Or she's already nearby."

"No, she won't. She knows someone will be expecting her to do that. We shouldn't have told you we found the boys. You also can't let them see you. You are dead, remember? Did Lindsay tell them you are alive, risen from the dead? Listen, Sam, she obviously does not want to be found, give her some space."

"Do what? You've got to be kidding me! What if she is in trouble? If she is, and we stop looking for her, then it's on us."

"News flash, my friend, her disappearance is already on us. You, Robert and Jack. Robert played dead for years! You played dead for how long? Now it's her turn to play dead. Jack was…is her handler and he was willing to kill her, as far as she knows. The three people in her life that she should have been able to trust, lied. Horrifically. I get it. Just give her space to sort through it." Derek couldn't take much more of Sam's pity party.

"Whose idea was it for me to play dead? Now

I have to live with Lindsay thinking I betrayed her and lied to her! I can't bear the thought of Lindsay never trusting me again. All because of Robert's life choices and lies. He's poisonous to everyone around him. So is Jack. There are things that we should know, or do you already?" Sam wiped both his hands down his face like he was trying to wipe away dirt. One minute Sam was furious and the next he was like a beaten dog.

"You didn't have to fall in love with her. That's on you and you of all people should have known better. I should have taken you off this case the moment you made your feelings clear. That's on me. You don't know all the facts. You can't judge Robert and his decisions based on your feelings. Sam, it's clouding your judgement and I'm tired of the pity party and blame game. You need to get your head back on straight." Derek was getting furious.

"Get out!" Sam's veins were popping in his neck. He couldn't remember ever being mad at Derek before. Maybe Derek was right, he was losing his mind.

41

"Jack, do you really believe that I don't know you have people trying to find Lindsay before we do?" Robert was itching for a fight and this was a great opportunity to have it out.

"Just because I met with my guys, doesn't mean they are looking for Lindsay. Some are looking for Charlie. We do have a business to run here in case you forgot. One that we have gone to extremes to make successful. There are plenty of people looking for her but we also have cases that still need to be taken care of. We don't know how long before we find her or she turns up." Jack gave Robert a hard stare.

Robert knew what Jack said was true. "I hate that I can't trust you where Lindsay is concerned. I'm not sure that I ever will. Would you have really shot her?"

"How many times are you going to ask me? You know damn well I wouldn't have!"

"That's the problem, I don't!"

"Then let me make this clear. Listen carefully. I'm tired of beating this dead horse. Lindsay has been like a little sister to me. I have protected her as long as I can remember. I've also protected you most of my life. I have done things that I shouldn't have had to do, for you. For Lindsay. Maybe instead of questioning me, you should question yourself. Look in the mirror, Robert. All these problems started with you. You made decisions that the rest of us have had to pay for, in one way or another. I've gone along with you because you saved my life. I'm not the bad guy here. My loyalty has always been to you. I tried to protect you even against yourself and your daughter. Now you have the audacity to question my loyalty. I've played clean up for you more times than I can count. Sure, I have a lot to lose if Lindsay does anything to harm this company, but you ultimately have everything to lose. We are where we are because of you, not me!"

Robert didn't say anything for a few minutes. He put his finger on his lips. The quiet in the room after Jack's outburst was more deafening than the tirade.

Finally, after several minutes, Robert spoke again, in a quiet voice. "What were you going to do?"

"The only thing I could think to do. I was going to introduce her to the boss. I was in the process of getting an old acquaintance to play you. I figured she would only have to meet him one time, then we could move on. It probably wouldn't have satisfied Lindsay. She knew there was a big reason she was never meeting you. Maybe we should have let her believe I was the boss when we pulled her in from the beginning. We underestimated her and never realized she would get obsessed about it. The more we hid it, the more she wanted to know. The idea came to me the day before she and I met that morning. I had contacted him and was to meet him later that day. I couldn't take Lindsay to him that morning but if I could have bought some time until I filled him in… that was my plan. It was a long shot, but we were out of time. I knew she was getting close. We underestimated her, Robert. We all did."

Robert shook his head slowly. "This proves we were too close to the situation. It's our number one rule and we broke it. Now we pay for it."

"What is your number one fear?"

"Lindsay right now. I doubt Lindsay wants to destroy this organization. She knows we do good work. Even if she wants to destroy me, she can do it without harming the organization. Besides, she has friends here. She won't hurt them."

Jack interrupted, what appeared to be, Robert talking to himself, out loud. "Robert, I doubt Lindsay is thinking she has any friends here. The last time she saw us all together was the night Joe caught her in the woods in the back of the neighborhood. She felt betrayed then, if I know how I would have taken it if I were in her shoes. I wouldn't count on that."

"What I think we can count on is that Lindsay is a good person. Have you ever known her to get revenge on anyone?"

Jack thought about that for a minute. "The only ones she would have had reason to get revenge on was husband number one and two. Mostly, two. He put the boys through hell. Lindsay maintained decency and the boys' best interest through that whole mess. Honestly, Robert. She hasn't had any reason to...until now. I'm not sure how she is handling this. As well as I know her, I can't say what she will do. She isn't emotional or vengeful. But I also don't know how eager to forgive she is. As Kendall, she's always been even keel in her professional life. As Lindsay, she seems to be the same. She walked away from her mother and brother. She walked away from two bad marriages. I don't know if she is going to be able to walk away from this. And Sam complicates it."

Robert sank down into the closest chair. "That is what concerns me. Not that she'll destroy the organization, but that she'll walk away. We can't lose her. We need her."

"Is that professional or personal?"

"Both. She did mention that I've been able to be a part of her life, even if from afar, but that she's never been part of mine. I don't know that she can forgive me for what I've done. I haven't had a chance to explain anything to her. We can't seem to get past the first few minutes of any conversation. There is so much that she needs to hear from me. I just hope I get the chance to explain. It's probably selfish of me because it doesn't matter what I say, she's not going to understand how I deserted her and left her with those monsters. How I was never there for her. I was there, but she's not going to see it that way."

Jack was always candid with Robert and now was no exception. "No, she's not. As far as she's concerned, she would have done fine without this organization or us. And she'd be right. Have you told anyone she knows the truth?"

"No. I won't until I talk to Lindsay about it. If I ever get the chance."

Jack could see the toll this was taking on Robert. He didn't want to add to it but he had to get it out in the open. "Robert, there are some other things you need to know. About Charlie, who's still MIA."

42

By late morning, Lindsay was sick. Very sick. She couldn't get up without reeling. She had started vomiting again, but much more intensely. Laying down, the vertigo was overwhelming. It wasn't from the fall. She recognized poison when she saw it. The abdominal pain and sweating were from poisoning.

She had made her way upstairs to her bedroom. There was no way she was dying like this. Although she felt like she might. She had slept on and off the rest of the day, only waking up for brief periods before dozing back off.

Late that evening, she made her way downstairs. She needed water. As she slowly crept downstairs, she thought she remembered seeing Lance sitting in the chair in her room. She must have been dreaming, or delusional.

As she reached in the cupboard for a glass, something caught her eye outside. It was a flash so she wasn't sure if she had seen something or was imagining things. It was something the size of a man, but she was too sick to care. The doors were all locked. She had made sure of that before she had headed upstairs earlier. She got her water and headed back up the stairs. Halfway up, she heard someone knocking. She ignored it and continued back to her room and climbed into bed.

It seemed like the knocking went on forever. Lindsay hadn't fallen back to sleep right away.

The abdominal pain was intense again and she had lain there holding her stomach for a while. Finally falling asleep again, she slept soundly for a few hours.

She was awoken by the sound of gunfire. She tried to sit up in bed but was too weak. She laid there listening. A few more shots were fired, but they weren't close to her. Someone was probably shooting coyotes. She fell back asleep.

The next time she woke up, Lance was sitting in the chair in her room. This time, she talked to see if she was delusional or if he was really there. "Hey."

"Hey! You're awake. I was getting worried."

"Why are you here? How did you get in?"

He just looked at her and didn't respond.

Later, Lindsay awoke again. This time, able to move a little better. She had her back to the chair where Lance was earlier. She turned as quickly as she could. The chair was empty.

She tried sitting up in bed. She was able to do that much. After a few minutes of sitting without being overly dizzy, she eased her legs over the side of the bed. She needed to get up and see if Lance was in her house. Her head was starting to clear. She also had to go the bathroom.

Once she was able to stand, she held on to the bed for a few minutes. The dizziness wasn't completely gone but it was much better. She slowly took a few steps and stopped again. Then kept moving until she finally made it to the bathroom.

She was able to take her time and make her way downstairs. The kitchen door was locked. Nothing appeared out of place. She sat down at the kitchen table for a few minutes before she was able to move to the garage door, then the living room door. All the doors were still locked and everything appeared to be as it was when she had gone to bed.

Lindsay was questioning whether Lance had been in her room. She continued with her own questions. Had it been the fever? She wasn't sure. She didn't like this at all. She sat down in the chair closest to the big windows in the living room, pondering the last few days events leading up to her getting sick.

She wasn't sure of much but she was sure she was poisoned. She wasn't sure if it had been intentional or not. The only things she had eaten are the things Grayson had made. The breakfast was from her kitchen. The dinner was from his. She needed to research him more thoroughly. Then she remembered the coffee Lance had given her that morning. Too bad she couldn't contact Casey. Or could she? If she did it quickly enough, she could. No, she couldn't. He was obviously working for Robert Langston. If they didn't find her, they may find Grayson, which means they would find her. She let out a string of curse words. She hated feeling so paralyzed. She was on her own.

43

Two days later, Lindsay was sitting on her deck overlooking the lake. The sun had only been up about an hour and she was enjoying her coffee while watching the rays on the lake. The thoughts of the last couple of months playing out in her mind. She didn't have much more information about any of the men or companies as she had hoped. She hadn't made a decision about Sam.

Lindsay knew she loved him. Whether or not she could trust him was the nagging question. He had made decisions for her, just like Robert and Jack. How could she justify Sam's behavior but not theirs? Was the level of dishonesty excusable? Or less offensive? It shouldn't be. The major difference was Sam was trying to protect her where Robert and Jack were protecting themselves. She surmised that Robert and Jack excused their behavior by thinking they were protecting her from finding out Robert was her father. What they were protecting was that her father had faked his own death, then controlled Lindsay's life through the organization. An organization that walked a fine line between right and wrong.

Robert had obviously built a multimillion-dollar organization over the years. Lindsay didn't know if he was respected or feared. She suspected both, depending on which side of the fine line one was on. Lindsay didn't know much about the organization when it came right down to it. She knew they had contacts in the FBI, CIA and other government organizations. She knew they did assignments for them. She also knew they had contacts in the criminal world and did jobs for them as well. She didn't think the work the organization did on the criminal side of things was evil against good. It was evil against evil. She had figured that much out.

Now that she thought about it, most of the people she had come in contact with were good. Some knew of her photographic memory and they were all the good guys. No criminals that Lindsay knew of, were aware of her memory.

For the thousandth time, Lindsay asked herself what makes a man fake his death, leave his family and start an organization like Robert's.

She wondered how she started thinking about Sam and always ended up thinking about her father and the organization. The fact was, they were all tied together. They were all neatly webbed together. A web of lies. Everything in her life centered around her father. And the lies. She knew better than to wonder how many more lies there were to uncover, but she did.

Lindsay's thoughts were interrupted by someone on the lake screaming. It only took her a second to see someone struggling to stay on top of the water. Without giving it any thought, Lindsay took off at a dead run into the lake. She didn't have to swim far to reach the last spot she saw the person before they went under. Diving under the water, she saw a body starting to float.

She swam underwater to the body that had its back to her. As she reached for it, it swung around and grabbed her. She was startled but instantly recognized Grayson. Lindsay was furious. He was a diver. What was he doing? She got away from him and surfaced. He was right behind her.

As she gulped for air, he appeared on the surface with a big grin, until he realized Lindsay was furious. He didn't think he had seen that look before. She didn't say anything but started swimming back to shore.

Grayson caught up to her quickly and caught her around the waist. "Don't be mad. It's just a little water."

Lindsay couldn't believe he was playing around. "What's wrong with you? Why would you do that to someone?"

"C'mon Kendall. You need to lighten up. You are too uptight. A little water never hurt anyone. Let's have some fun."

"Why didn't you just ask me to go for a swim? That would have been much easier."

"And what would you have said?" Grayson gave her a look like he already knew.

"No. At least not in my clothes. I have bathing suits appropriate for swimming." Lindsay started swimming toward shore and was determined to make it this time.

"Ok, I'm sorry Kendall. Let me make it up to you with breakfast."

Lindsay didn't answer. Now walking up her yard toward the deck, with Grayson still following her, she turned and glared at him. "What is up with you wanting to feed me all the time?"

"I'm hungry and you need to eat and we are together. Two single people at the same place at the same time. Breakfast time."

"The last time you fed me, I was deathly ill."

"Is that why you haven't answered your door or been outside? Why didn't you tell me?"

"You didn't know?"

"Know? How could I know! As I said, you didn't answer your door." He gave her an incredulous look. "Did that fall down the stairs make you lose a few braincells? I also ate the same things you did."

"You didn't eat the casserole that you cooked for me. I'm going inside to dry off and change clothes."

"I actually did. I made two batches. I told you poisoning is not how I would kill you. Come on over to my place after and I'll get breakfast started."

Lindsay didn't respond but walked into the house. She didn't look at Grayson because she didn't like him reading her expressions.

Despite all that had just happened, she decided she was going for breakfast. She wanted to get into his house and to talk to him a little more. If she couldn't pull his electronic information, she would do the next best thing.

44

Lindsay jumped in the shower. As she dressed, she finalized her next move. Ready to get this over with, she went down the back stairs to the kitchen. As she opened the door, Lance was standing there, with his hand raised and about to knock.

"Hi, Miss James." Lindsay wished he didn't have such a captivating smile.

"Officer Becker. What brings you by this early?"

"I happened to be in the neighborhood. Brought you some coffee. Just checking in on you." He held out another latte.

"Do you make house calls to everyone or am I special?" She took the coffee and set it on the counter.

"Oh, you are special but I needed to stop by and check on Mrs. Wigley. I figured since I was next door, I would brighten your day. Going out?"

"How's Mrs. Wigley?"

"She's fine. Her grandson is coming in later today but she had a rough night last night." He shifted from one foot to the other.

"Did she wonder off again?" Lindsay was thankful she hadn't seen the crazy old lady lately.

"No, she just didn't sleep well."

"Interesting. It's so sweet of you to check on her. She really needs to be in a home."

"We agree, but she doesn't. She has good

days. It's the nights that tend to be bad for her."

"Well, I hope she stays safe. I really need to go. Thanks again for the coffee. By the way, where do you get it?"

"At the café in town. You should meet me there for coffee one morning." Lance gave her a serious look. There was no amusement in his face.

"Bye Lance."

Now she was stuck. Lindsay didn't want Lance knowing she was going next door. She wasn't sure why, but he didn't need to know. As they walked outside together, Lindsay said she forgot something and turned to go back inside.

She watched from the upstairs bedroom as he backed out of the driveway and headed toward the main road at the end of the lane. As she started out of the spare room, she noticed a piece of paper on the dresser that she hadn't put there. She walked over and picked it up. It was blank. She didn't remember putting it there so where did it come from? She glanced around the room but everything was as it was supposed to be.

Lindsay wanted to check out the rest of the house, but decided to wait until she got back from next door. She was already later than she wanted to be getting to Grayson's. She had the rest of the day to look around the house. Now she wanted to look around his house.

Grayson answered her knock quickly. He was wearing a tight-fitting t-shirt and shorts. His tan was one she would kill to have. Her body was as fit as his and her mind went to places that made her blush.

Grayson noticed but let it go. "I wasn't sure you were coming."

"I got held up by Officer Becker."

"Officer Becker? What did you do this time?" He flashed his straight, white teeth.

"I didn't do anything this time, or last time, or the time before that."

"Does he stop by often?" Now he was scowling.

"Often enough, I guess. Usually because Mrs. Wigley is acting crazy or is missing, or whatever crazy old ladies do."

"Are you her keeper, or is he? I thought her grandson took care of her." Grayson looked puzzled.

"He does, but he's usually only at the lake on the weekends. They do courtesy checks on her, I guess. And no, I'm not her keeper. Only met her a few times."

"Isn't Lance Becker a game warden? Why does he check up on her?"

"He is, but I guess it's usually pretty quiet here at the lake so he has time and he helps out the Sheriff."

"You know quiet a bit about that situation, huh? I try to keep to myself. It's much more peaceful that way." Grayson was now busy making breakfast as they chatted.

"Really, because you tend not to keep to yourself as much as you end up in my yard." She gave him a silly grin to soften that statement. Lindsay realized he was asking all the questions. She came here to question him. Breakfast was a bonus and since she didn't drink the coffee Lance brought over, she would know if Grayson was poisoning her. Not that she wanted to go through that again, but it was worth the risk.

"You need more caffeine, Miss Sassy." He handed her a cup of coffee. She hoped it wasn't laced. What could he want with her anyway? Surely, he didn't know her real identity.

"Indeed. Between your drowning and Lance, I'm not sure there is enough. Why did you do that this morning?"

"What, pretend I was drowning to have you rescue me? I told you, I knew I could get you into the water. I doubted you would stay, but it was worth a try. And you happen to be sitting there so….". Lindsay softened at his amused smile.

"You seem to be a pretty good swimmer from the way you swam back to shore." One of the few things Lindsay had found on him was that he was a diver. There wasn't much information on that and she wanted more.

"You got me. I am a professional diver. So yes, a pretty good swimmer. I swim every morning, usually around dawn. It's one of the reasons I'm here. I love the lake. No sharks, no alligators, no rip currents. But my love is still the ocean. Do you swim?"

"Interesting. I can swim. You said one of the reasons you are here?" Lindsay didn't think this was too personal since he made the comment that it was one of the reasons. He opened that door.

"Yeah. I messed up my knee pretty good and need to give it time to heal. I didn't want to be in a pool so the lake was the next best thing."

Lindsay didn't think he sounded sincere. Maybe her overly sensitive mind was kicking in. Being super suspicious of people may be her new thing. "I'm sorry to hear that. How did you get started diving?"

"My dad. He was a diver. We had a summer home in Puget Sound. He started us off cold water diving. The rocky walls and reefs are some of the most spectacular. It's a great place for beginners and experts alike. Dad never got bored and I guess since he started me so young, I didn't have any fear but also was enthralled by the colorful anemones and marine life that can be seen only underwater." Grayson seemed lost in thoughts while he said this and almost burned the toast.

"That's beautiful. Are you and your dad still close?"

"Yeah, we are. We get together at least twice a year and dive. We take turns picking the dive spots. We've basically been all over the world diving."

"You're lucky to have that kind of father. Where is your favorite dive spot?" Lindsay felt a pang of hurt over the fact that his dad spent time with him and taught him things. And, even now, still made time for him. Isn't that what dads did? The pang of hurt was for herself, not him.

"It will always be Puget Sound because that is where I learned and fell in love with diving. But my second favorite spot is Belize. It's my dad's favorite, too. The Cook Islands off the coast of Australia are another close favorite."

Lindsay could see the passion in his eyes. "It must be great to do work that you love and with people you love." That hint of hurt was back, again.

"It is. But how about you? You love writing, right?"

"I do, but it's a solitary life. So, you mentioned that your father took 'us.' Do you have siblings?"

"Yeah, I have two sisters. They dive also but not often. They are both married and have children so it's not as easy for them."

"That's nice. So, no wife or children for you? I'm sorry. I don't mean to be so personal."

"It's fine. No, never been married. Almost married my high school sweetheart. She was a flight attendant. She had called me on a Friday and said she wouldn't be home until Saturday due to a flight delay. I stopped by my best friend's apartment that night since I was on my own. You can imagine my surprise when I walked in on him and her. It didn't end well. At least for me. Now, they are married with four children."

"I'm so sorry. I can't imagine what you went through." Lindsay did, genuinely, feel sorry for him.

"It's water under the bridge. I got over it. It's not easy to meet women in the ocean. Not a lot of people hanging out there. The work keeps me busy and I love what I do so I can't complain. How 'bout you?"

They were just sitting down to eat breakfast. Grayson put a plate in front of her then set his own plate down. Lindsay jumped up and asked, "Do you mind if I sit on this side?" She didn't wait for an answer and quickly sat down in front of his plate.

Grayson actually laughed. "No, you can sit where ever you are most comfortable. I promise, I am not poisoning you. Here, we can share the breakfast. We'll eat from both plates. Would that make you feel better?"

"I just watched you make this so unless you are extremely suave, I think I'm safe." They sat down and began to eat.

"You mentioned that you were also a photographer. Tell me about that." Lindsay was here to find out about him. At least to see what he would say. She knew most people didn't tell the truth. So far, a deep-sea diver wouldn't have any reason to want her dead. If that is what he was.

Grayson realized she changed the subject. Now he wasn't sure if that seating arrangement was a distraction or she really was worried about someone poisoning her. "One summer, my sister was in a car accident and couldn't dive with us. I had the idea to get an underwater camera and bring the scenery back to her. My parents realized quickly I had an eye for photography and bought me more expensive equipment. It progressed from there. While I was in college, my sister, unbeknownst to me, submitted some photos to a magazine. That blew up and I did a few contract jobs for a major photography outlet. Left college debt free. It all worked out well. I get to combine the two things I love most."

"That's great! I would love to see some of your work. Who do you work for now?"

"I do freelance work. That's enough about me. Tell me how you became a writer." He reached over the table and stuck his fork into a hash brown on her plate and popped it in his mouth.

Lindsay hated this part and hadn't given it enough thought. She didn't want to lie to him, but that's all she had done since she met him. "I was always a storyteller and very detail oriented. When I would start to tell a story, people would say things like, is this going to take long, or how many side stories will there be to get through this one? I used to get angry then just shut down. I started writing what I couldn't say."

"That's actually sad. I'm sorry. But it looks like you turned it to good. Why do you ghostwrite? I mean, why not do your own stories?"

"I don't want recognition." Lindsay watched as he reached across the table again and stuck his fork in a piece of her egg.

"But you could write under a pen name?"

"I could, but there would still be appearances to make and people to deal with. I'm not interested in that. I just want to write and not be bothered with the rest of it. It works for me. I get paid well and enjoy it."

"I can see that about you. How come this is your first time here at Lake Dare?" He gave her a straight forward look as if to say he knew whatever she was about to say was going to be a lie.

"I just never took the time and was always traveling. There's a huge world out there to see. I'm lucky that I get to travel when doing research. I love that part. The experiences are invaluable and there's always something new to explore."

Grayson didn't say anything for a moment and Lindsay wondered what he was thinking. She didn't need to wait long.

"What about family? With that much travel, it must be difficult. Are you close with your parents?"

There it was. She wanted to shut this down quickly. There was no way she was going to tell him her mother was a monster and her father faked his own death, controlled her life from afar and was resurrected as her boss. "They died in an accident when I was in college."

"Kendall, I'm so sorry." Grayson looked hurt for her and it made her feel badly. Although Lindsay didn't think he was necessarily who he said he was, she believed most of what he told her. There was just more to his story. She couldn't shake the feeling. She was straight up, blatantly lying to him.

"Thanks." It was all she could mumble.

"So, tell me, do you like boating?" Grayson could see Lindsay was uncomfortable on the topic of family. He could read her fairly easily.

"I love boating! It's one of my favorite things. If I were staying here long term, I would get one." Lindsay couldn't help but light up at the thought, remembering her time on the water in Annapolis.

"You're in luck then. I have one coming to-morrow. I will have to keep it at the yacht club on the other side of the lake though. My dock needs some work first. I should have waited but I was pretty excited to get it."

"You are more than welcome to dock it at mine. It's not being used, as you know, and it would be closer and more convenient for you." Lindsay wondered where that came from. The last thing she wanted, or needed, was for Grayson to have free access to the front of her house. She was clearly losing her mind.

"Really, you wouldn't mind? I promise I'll be discreet and not bother you. I mean, if it wouldn't bother you, that would be great." He seemed to be holding his breath for her to confirm.

"Sure, it's no problem." Lindsay seemed to lose her excitement quickly but gave him a reassuring smile.

Lindsay could clearly confirm she had lost her mind. She thought to herself, "It better not be a damn problem." She either just assigned herself a part time bodyguard or gave an assailant easier access to her.

45

Lindsay walked quickly back to her house from Grayson's. Breakfast was delicious. She hoped it would stay down and not make her ill. He had eaten from her plate. She found that endearing. He appeared very thoughtful. They had done the dishes together while talking about their different boating experiences.

Grayson had taken a call while Lindsay was drying the dishes. He excused himself then went into the garage. She looked around his house as much as she possibly could without being suspicious had he walked back in. He was on that call for about ten minutes, coming back and apologizing profusely. He didn't give any indication of who had called and hadn't made any excuses for taking so long.

Lindsay was now anxious to get back to her house and check things out. She was remembering that slip of paper in the spare bedroom. As she dug for her keys to unlock the door, she realized she had left them at Grayson's house.

She walked back to his house through the front yard, avoiding the lane and the woods. Coming up the front yard, she noticed him on the second level through one of the floor to ceiling windows. He was on the phone and appearing angry at who ever he was talking to. She walked slower to be able to watch him as long as she could. He was raising his arm and making a slicing movement as he paced. He appeared very angry.

Hoping to avoid an uncomfortable situation, Lindsay decided to see if, by chance, the door was unlocked. She wanted to grab her keys and leave and without disturbing him. She tried the handle and the door opened. She gently opened it enough to walk through and spotted her keys on the table. She could hear Grayson on the phone but couldn't make out his words. She walked over quickly and silently picked up her keys and started back to the door when Grayson's voice rose above a normal conversational volume. Now she could hear every word clearly.

"I told you I'm working on it. I gave you everything I have up to this point. I can only move so quickly without causing suspicion. You of all people know that this takes time."

Then it was quiet again. Lindsay tiptoed closer to the stairs. Now in a quieter tone, she heard Grayson talking again. "I understand. I have to handle this gently. Nothing is causing alarm right now and if I move any faster, it could jeopardize this whole situation."

There was another pause, then Grayson started speaking again, now at a normal level. "I'll let you know when I have anything more."

Lindsay hurriedly made her way back to the door and flew out as if someone were following her. She rounded the corner of the garage and jogged across the yard back through the trees to her house.

She rushed into her kitchen and locked the door behind her. She strolled through to the living room and stared out over the lake. She loved looking at the lake. She did her best thinking here.

Lindsay ran Grayson's one-sided conversation through her mind again. He could have been talking to someone about a job but she doubted it had anything to do with deep sea diving or photography. She still hadn't seen him with a camera and according to him, he took pictures under water. He wasn't working at the moment, while recuperating and he wasn't deep sea diving in the lake. The lake wasn't that deep even though it was huge. It still didn't mean any of his conversation had to do with her. As far as she knew, he didn't know her real identity. Maybe she was being super suspicious again. Someone was breaking into her house, though, and someone did poison her. As much as she vowed to herself to stay away from him, he kept creeping into her life.

Even if she could run him through the Deep Web, it may set off flags if the wrong people got ahold of an inquiry and there was more to him than she knew. If he was working for Robert, why would he want to spook her while watching out for her? She wasn't making sense of this. Unless, he was one of Robert's enemies that she was warned about. Then again, how would he have found her if Robert and Sam hadn't?

Lindsay hated dead ends. She would figure this out, but for now, she wanted to check out more of her house. She headed upstairs to the guest bedroom where she found that blank piece of paper this morning. She was sure she had put it back on the dresser after finding it. It was gone.

Thinking if may have fallen off, Lindsay checked around the dresser. It had vanished. She looked around the rest of the guest room. It was sparsely decorated, as it was never used, so it didn't take her long. Lindsay went as far as checking for surveillance equipment everywhere in the room. She didn't find anything.

Lindsay moved into the other room, where Ava had stored her things. Ava had used the master bedroom when she lived here but had moved things to this room when she married. Everything appeared fine, except Ava's clothes were missing.

She checked both of the bathrooms attached to each room and their closets. Everything was as it was supposed to be, except Ava's clothes. Lindsay found them in the guest bedroom closet. Lindsay knew they were moved. She had checked the house out thoroughly when she first arrived.

She checked all the pockets of Ava's clothes. They were all empty. She checked the seams for any flaws. Lindsay didn't know whether to be happy she didn't find anything, or disappointed. At least if she had found something, it would have been a start. She was coming up empty again.

Lindsay moved into her own bedroom. The first thing she checked was the safe. One of two in the house. This one was in the master closet because that was the first place anyone looked. It was a decoy for anyone looking for a safe. Should they find this one, they may not look for another. The safe was intact.

Next, she went into the master bath. Everything appeared fine. She opened the closet in the bathroom where she kept towels. On the top of the towels, she found another piece of paper. She scanned her memory back to when she took a shower this morning. That paper was not there then. Someone had moved it from the guest room

194

dresser to here while she was at Grayson's. Someone had been in her house again.

Lindsay moved out to the garage. She kept the doors closed. She removed the door off the electrical panel box, then slid the entire panel out. Making sure all the wires were clearly out of the way, she hit the button hidden behind the sheetrock to slide the safe over to where the electrical panel had been. Her IDs, guns and meds, as she liked to call them, were all intact. She loved this safe. The tracks were well hidden and anyone opening the cover to the panel would never suspect anything.

She was going to have to get cameras but they weren't fool proof since they could be hacked, blocked, painted over, covered, or any number of things. She had another idea. But it would have to wait until she was out of town again. She also needed to get into Grayson's house.

46

Lindsay spent the rest of the day thinking about Robert, Jack, Sam, Joe, Derek and the others, along with the various companies they owned. Trying to put all the pieces together that she could. She reviewed what little she had on them. It was disappointing. Looking at the information from her professional perspective, it was all too neat and tidy. Obviously, well planned and limited. She was beating her head against the wall. She contemplated going to Philadelphia and giving her father the opportunity to be honest with her. He had been willing to talk to her, but she couldn't stay in the same room with him long enough to get past the first five minutes.

She wasn't getting much accomplished here. Lindsay wasn't able to relax and this wasn't peaceful. She needed to consider going back, but she still didn't have any answers for Sam.

Just as she walked into the kitchen to make herself something to eat, she glanced out the window and saw Lance's car pull in. She thought about hiding out in her own house, but that was silly. She had a better idea.

She opened the door before Lance could knock. "Officer Becker. You may want to find a job that keeps you busier than having time to check on me. What crazy thing has happened now in this peaceful lake town?"

"Nothing new really. Just wanted to check on you, Kendall."

"Then come on in and check." She moved away from the door to let him in. She started to pull things out of the cupboards to make chili. "Have a seat. I'm starving so I hope you don't mind if I make dinner while you do your checking."

"I don't mind and glad I'm not keeping you from anything." He sat down at the table where he could easily watch her work. He wondered why she didn't correct him when he called her Kendall and not Miss James.

"Have you eaten? I'm making chili and there will be more than enough for you." She smiled at him and continued to work. She was glad she could keep busy.

"I haven't eaten but wouldn't want to put you out. I could always take you out to dinner and save you the trouble." Lance watched her as she worked.

"It's no trouble and I was going to make it anyway. Please stay."

"Who are you and what did you do with Kendall?" Lance wasn't sure who this sweet lady was or what brought out the nice side of her.

"I'm not sure what you mean. Are you working? I noticed no uniform, but you are driving the game warden SUV."

"No, but I was on my way over to the dock. We have a new boat coming in late tonight and I need to check it out."

"So, what brings you by here if all is well in Lake Dare?"

"As I said, I just wanted to check on you. And I was going to check on Mrs. Wigley since I had some time to kill."

"Okay, I can see why you check on Mrs. Wigley, but in case you hadn't noticed, I'm not old or crazy, so why keep checking on me? Is there something I should know?" Lindsay stopped stirring the hamburger and looked at him.

"That's exactly why I check on you." He let out a chuckle. "You aren't old and crazy. Well, you might be a little crazy. That's yet to be determined."

She could see he was teasing. "What makes you think I'm crazy?"

"Besides the fact that you pulled a bullet out of your neighbor, didn't tell me about it, and you carry a gun. You rarely leave your house, except when you do, it's for days at a time. Nothing. That's completely normal for a young, beautiful, single lady."

"That's the life of a writer. Except I rarely pull a bullet out of people. That only happens every few years." She winked at him and continued cooking.

"How did you know how to do that?" Lance gave her a steady glare now, but she wasn't looking at him to see it.

"I'm a writer. I know all kinds of useless things. I guess you found out through the doctor after Grayson's wound got infected?"

"Yes, all doc visits like that get reported, even in this small town. How well do you know Grayson Tyler?"

"Not well at all. I believe he's a photographer. Just here recuperating from an injury. How well do you know him?" Lindsay spoke very matter of fact but friendly.

"Only what you just told me. I stopped by there after I heard about the shooting but never spoke to him. I guess he was out of town when I went by and never caught back up with him. Haven't had any issues so no reason to worry about it. Have you had any issues with him?"

"Nope. Seems nice enough. Keeps to himself. Why is it that you are here all the time and I know more about my neighbors than you do?"

"That's usually how it goes, isn't it?" He looked at Lindsay questionably.

"I really don't know. I'm not usually home this much. Writing and researching, as you probably know, keeps me traveling pretty much most of the time."

"I heard that's why this is your first time spending any time here. Your Aunt had been living here for years before she married and moved. Do you still see her with your traveling and her in Europe?"

"See, you know more about me than you do Grayson. Why is that?" She stopped cooking again and looked at him questioningly.

"You caught me. You are much more attractive than Grayson Tyler."

"How do you know if you haven't ever seen him?"

"That's fair." Lance liked her sense of humor. "I couldn't help but notice you the first time I came here to rescue you from Mrs. Wigley." She looked at him and he gave her a wink. He noticed her slight stiffness come on quickly. "It was only natural that I find out if you lived alone." Lindsay gave him a look. "That didn't sound right, did it? It was part of the police report information needed."

"Ahhhh, now that sounds better. I was thinking you might be a stalker."

"Do you worry about stalkers? Had any experience with them?"

"No, well, only in one book I wrote. It was about a serial killer who became infatuated with one of the women he was going to kill. She fought him off during his initial attack. After almost killing him and breaking a few bones and several ribs, she got away. He had never had that happen and became infatuated with her. Then stalked her."

"Do tell me more. Sounds exciting."
"I may worry about you after all. She was an undercover agent for a secret organization and trained to kill."

"You're killing me. Who won in the end?"

"Guess you'll have to read the book." She laughed as she continued cooking. "Almost done."

"What else have you written?"

Lindsay proceeded to tell him about a few other books until she was ready to serve the chili.

"How many have become best sellers?"

"All of them. Surprised you would ask that. Do you read?" Lindsay gave him a shocked look, pretending to be offended.

"Yes, on occasion. Who is your favorite author?"

"Telling you that may give too much away." She smiled an all-knowing smile. "Very clever, Lance. Tell me how you came to be a game warden."

Lindsay was surprised at how easily she could lie to Lance. She didn't feel the least bit bad about it. And he was law enforcement. Maybe she figured he should know a liar when he hears one or he just spends too much time with animals instead of people. Maybe he was just a challenge.

"My uncle took me camping as a boy. I fell in love with nature. As I got older and had to start thinking about a college degree, I couldn't imagine being in a cubicle eight hours a day. That would be torture for me. What better job could I possibly have then this?"

"Where did you go to college?"

"University of Maryland. It was the best for criminal justice and my uncle went there. I figured since he was paying for it, I should follow in his footsteps."

"That's cool. Is your uncle a game warden? Are you still close?"

"No, he's not a game warden but he's in law enforcement. We are still very close. He raised me after my parents died." Lindsay was great at reading people. She had a hard time with Lance most of the time, but she could see the sorrow in his stunning eyes when he said this.

"I'm sorry to hear that. It's good that you have an uncle that could do that."

"How about you? Family?" Lance's sorrow was gone, but not completely.

"No, just Aunt Ava. I wish I could see her more than I do but circumstances make that difficult." Lindsay could fake the sorrow on this subject. "Did you grow up around here?"

"No, actually, Dallas, Texas."

"Are there places to camp in Dallas? Or Texas?"

"Some. It's not the same as the East Coast. My uncle loved the East Coast so we came here more often than not."

Lance was lying. Lindsay wasn't sure what was truth and what were lies. But he was definitely lying. She could see it when she looked in his eyes. He was also a professional. He was either lying about his current job or he had military experience along the way. "Were you ever in the military?"

"That's an interesting question. Why do you ask? Do I look like a military guy?"

"Just curious. I've always had a special place in my heart for our military guys and gals." Lance was looking at her curiously so she continued. "A series of books I wrote had vets who were active duty at the time in them. I researched a lot of what they do. Then interviewed them after they retired."

"Put that way, yes, I'm prior military." He couldn't hold his laugh in and Lindsay couldn't tell if he was joking or not. She didn't get the answer she wanted.

"You were the class clown, huh?"

"No, honestly, I was the shy guy. Stop smirking! I was!"

Lindsay hated the fact that she liked Lance like this. "I would bet money if I pulled your yearbooks up, that would not be what I would find."

"Indeed, you would. Probably why I spent so much time in the woods. Animals loved me more than the girls."

"I find that impossible to believe." Lindsay couldn't help but laugh at the thought of Lance as a gangly, acne clad kid. "I would have to see a picture to believe that."

"Maybe I'll get you one, then again, maybe I won't. I'm having a hard-enough time to get you to go out with me as I am now."

"About that. I have to be honest. I'm just not in the market for anything. I'm extremely busy on this book and they keep moving the deadline on me. I originally thought I had some down time to enjoy the lake, which is why I'm here. I may not make the deadline as it is."

"Ahh, were you doing research for your book a few weeks ago when you went out of town?"

"How did you know I went out of town? I never told you that. You are stalking me!" Lindsay tried to feign shock.

"I just noticed you hadn't been around. At least I assumed you were gone. If you weren't, you were ignoring me then. I came by several times to chat with you about Grayson and the shooting. I questioned you once then you disappeared. It's my job to notice these things."

"Were there any break-ins during that time?" Lindsay watched his face closely.

"I don't recall off the top of my head. Why, did you have a problem? Kendall, if there's something going on, I need to know."

"You are an animal guy, not a criminal guy. Why would you need to know?"

"Law enforcement is law enforcement. I told you, I help out the local Sheriff when needed. What is going on?"

"Not a thing. Remember, I asked you for statistics for this area."

"Is there more to the shooting with Grayson than you admitted to me before? I can question him again. Do you think he's up to something?"

This was not how this conversation was supposed to go. "No, no, no. It's nothing. I thought I left a TV in the garage, but now can't find it." Lindsay almost blanched at the weakness of that stupid statement. She should have thought faster on her feet.

"They were stealing TVs. Is that the only thing missing?"

"Yeah, I probably just put it somewhere else. It was a really small one. There isn't anything else missing, so I doubt they were here. There are a few paintings upstairs and some speakers. They would have taken more valuable things had they come in here." Lindsay needed to change this conversation quickly.

"So how are the campers at the campground on the other side of town? Staying pretty quiet?" Lindsay was having a hard time trying to look interested. She could not care less.

"Yes, for the most part. Occasionally, there is a fight between the drunks or kids doing stupid things. Nothing alarming."

"Still only need one cop on duty this time of year?" Now she was looking more interested.

"Yes, there is never really more than one on duty unless we get a wave of problems. Even with the break-ins, we've just got local citizens watching out. Small town. Everyone knows everyone. Just the way I like it."

"I'm such a city girl." That was a slip up and Lindsay realized it the moment she said it. She had internally cringed at the thought of living in a small town permanently or in the country. She was sure she would die first.

"I already pegged you for that. You made a few faces when we were talking about camping and animals. Where did you grow up?"

"All over the place really. Aunt Ava being an artist, liked to move around a bit. We never stayed in one place long. I think that is why she stayed here for so many years. Now, she's traveling a lot but still in the same home in Europe they bought when they got married. Hey, by the way, how would a raccoon get in here?" Lindsay watched Lance's face closely.

"A what? A raccoon. In here, the house?"

"Yes, for my book."

"Unless you have a doggy door or an open window or door, I don't see how they could. What are you writing?" He looked amused, not guilty. But Lindsay thought she already had figured him out, he was a professional. He had access to raccoons.

And he was a liar. Just like the rest.

47

Lindsay waited patiently, leaning on the building across the street from the FBI office in Philadelphia. She knew Agent Scott Preston was there today. She would wait as long as she had to for him to come out. She had called his office saying she had a tip and requesting he meet her at the café two blocks away from his office. Of course, she hadn't given him her real name.

Lindsay could see the café from where she was. She had gotten here early to watch if any agents went before him. So far, none had. They would either cross in front of her or walk a block or two up, then cross the street. The café was on the side of the street as she was. She didn't mind waiting. It gave her a chance to watch people.

She loved human nature. She found herself putting stories to the people who walked past her. Lindsay realized that they all had happy endings in her own imagination and they were all trustworthy. Maybe she was trying to convince herself that, generally, people were still good. And honest. Not everyone was out to deceive and lie. She wanted to believe that. She needed to believe that.

An hour after Lindsay arrived, Scott walked casually out of the FBI building and strolled to the first corner. He stopped to wait for the walk signal to change. He was a rule follower and a good guy, although he had infuriated Lindsay once before regarding Cowboy and Jack.

Lindsay watched as Scott crossed the street, keeping his eyes moving. He didn't recognize Lindsay. As he walked by, and was now slightly beyond her, Lindsay said, "Good day, Agent Preston". He turned around so quickly, had Lindsay not been watching him, she would have thought he was coming from the other direction. Without a hint of surprise he asked, "Can I help you?"

"Maybe. It depends on if I can trust you." Lindsay removed the overly large, blacked out sunglasses she was wearing. It took Scott a minute to recognize her beyond the pink wig and blueish black lipstick. "Kendall Thomas? What are you doing here dressed like that?"

"Hi Scott. You once told me you were on my side and here for me. Although you betrayed me and reported back to Jack, I wanted to try again. I need a favor. Can I trust you not to tell anyone you've seen me, or spoken to me?"

"Kendall, I apologized for that. We were looking out for you since we didn't know Cowboy's intentions. I apologized."

"You didn't answer my question. I'm a grown woman, perfectly able to take care of myself. Now, I will ask one more time, can I trust you not to report back to Jack this time?" Lindsay eyed him closely. She knew his lying face. She had seen it once and it was ingrained in her memory.

"First, let me ask you a question. Are you in trouble?"

"No."

"Yes, you can trust me. What do you need?"

"I need you to get me information on a man named Jerry McDermont."

"Okay, but I have to ask why you can't get it? You have access to almost all the information I do. Kendall, what's going on?"

"I have some things I'm dealing with and can't involve the organization. Nothing criminal. I don't want any information that I retrieve to pass through their system. I would also appreciate it if you didn't tell anyone about this meeting."

"Kendall, let me help you." Scott put his hand on her arm. "Please?"

"You are helping me by getting me information on this man. That's all I need right now. Once you get the information, I will need you to call this number and relay it to me. How long do you need?" She handed him a slip of paper with a cell number on it.

"A few hours. I have a meeting I'm on my way to."

"No, you don't. That was me you were meeting at the café. Thank you." Lindsay nodded and walked off, disappearing around the corner of the building she had been leaning on. Once she was in her rental car, she called a number and waited for an answer.

Drama Llama answered after the first ring. "I'm here at the address you gave me. No problems getting in. Surveillance ready. Now we wait?"

"Yes, good job. Did you get the cameras set at the back door in case they go in that way?"

"Yes."

"Good. Did you get another guy in case this takes longer than we expect?"

"Yes. Ye of so little faith. I'm good. Followed your instructions to a tee. Relax."

"Let me work on that. How's the girlfriend?"

"I don't know. She's not around much. I'm not sure how I feel about her. She was great in the beginning but something's changed. Haven't figured out exactly what yet. But I will."

"I'm sorry. I was hopeful for you. Maybe she'll come around."

"I wouldn't take you for hopeful. What's up with that?"

"I would like to believe that most people are genuinely good. It's a thing lately."

"Are you okay? You know you can…."
"Yeah, yeah, yeah. I'm fine and I know I can talk to you. Listen, gotta' go. I'll be in touch soon. Thanks for doing this."

Lindsay didn't wait for Drama Llama to say anything more. She thought by now he would have realized when he starts with the whole "you can talk to me" thing, she shuts him down. Lindsay wasn't accustomed to talking to anyone about personal things. Even Robin and Courtney were limited. They didn't know much about her at all in the grand scheme of things. The only one she had ever completely opened up to was Sam. And look where that got her. Damn it. She wanted to believe. She just didn't know if she could.

Lindsay drove around Philadelphia for an hour before convincing herself she would drive by the neighborhood where the guys all lived. She wasn't sure what she was hoping to see, but she couldn't stop the gut feeling that was telling her to go. She had checked Sam and Derek's location on their trucks earlier and they were in Baltimore. First, she stopped at the truck stop and traded the pink wig character for that of a jogger. She kind of liked this pink wig and matching punk rocker outfit. Too bad Scott had seen it.

Parking a mile outside the neighborhood, she started on her run. This meant going through the woods again that Joe had caught her in. She hated the woods but they did provide good cover, for the most part. She was hopeful that Robert and Jack were at the office in the city or on an assignment.

Lindsay jogged toward Langston Drive, this time staying in the woods that ran alongside Joe's house at the end of the street. This way she could look down the street since she never saw anything from the back of their houses. She slowed as she neared the spot she wanted.

Lindsay laid on the ground and took out her binoculars. She was far enough away that she might not need them but wanted to be prepared.

There were a few cars parked in some of the driveways near the start of the street and only one visible at Robert's house. Lindsay didn't recognize the Audi A4. She loved the blue color it was and suspected it was custom. She hadn't seen any like that.

After about fifteen minutes of waiting, Robert and an elegantly dressed lady stepped out the front door of Robert's house. Lindsay wasn't close enough to hear them but she was close enough to see that Robert was furious. She lifted her binoculars and was in time to read his lips. "Get Charlie here immediately. No more excuses!" The woman got in her car, backed out and squealed her tires all the way down the street.

Lindsay searched her memory but was sure she had never seen this woman before, nor had she heard the name Charlie. She thought back to all the people she had worked with.

Robert was still standing in his driveway, facing her. He had pulled out his cell phone and was now holding it with one hand and had the other hand in his pants pocket. He looked frustrated. Lindsay was still looking through the binoculars. Reading his lips again, Robert said, "Follow her and don't loose her. We have a tracker on her car but once she gets out, I want to know every single detail." He hung up. He stood there a moment looking up at the sky. Knowing Robert, there was a helicopter up there following this lady. Or a satellite reading her every move. Lindsay was letting her overactive imagination run wild again. He was probably just stretching his neck muscles. Of course, had she known him better, or at all, she would be able to answer which of these thoughts it was.

Robert went back inside. As Lindsay was getting up, she saw Derek's truck had just turned up the street toward her. She fell back to the ground quickly, holding her breath to see where they ended up and hoped it wasn't in front of her.

Derek pulled into Robert's driveway. Someone was with him but had his head turned away from her, looking at Derek. They sat there for several minutes. Lindsay couldn't get a clear visual of Derek's lips to read them.

Finally, Sam got out of the passenger side and stood there. He pulled a cigarette out and lit it. Lindsay didn't remember Sam ever smoking. Huh, she wondered what else she didn't know about him.

Derek got out of the truck and headed inside while Sam smoked his cigarette. Lindsay pulled the binoculars back out and zeroed in on Sam. He looked like hell.

48

Lindsay stayed lying in her position for a moment after Sam went into Robert's house. Lindsay couldn't shake feeling sorry for Sam. He didn't deserve this. Neither did she. It was an internal battle and Lindsay didn't know if either would come out the other side.

She had to move or she might never be able to get up. She considered waiting for Derek and Sam to come back out. But she thought better of it and didn't want to miss Agent Preston's call, which might be coming in soon.

Lindsay started slowly back to her car. Once she was a safe distance from the houses, she jogged the rest of the way. She thought she heard someone on her way back, but couldn't see anyone so she kept going. Before she walked to her car, she looked around and, not seeing anyone suspicious, jumped in and drove off.

As she approached the traffic light leading into Robert's neighborhood, she saw Derek's truck, along with a few Mercedes speeding out of the neighborhood. They were turning the same direction she was going. She wondered where they were all off to in such a hurry. She recognized Joe and a few others. Something was going on. She considered following them, then thought better of it. They were professionals and she didn't want to take the risk of tailing them and being recognized.

Since Lindsay knew where Sam was, she decided she would visit him, or at least his house. He was busy with whatever he was doing in Philadelphia. Just as she turned onto the highway to head south toward Baltimore, the phone rang. It was the phone that she had given Scott the number of.

"Yes?" She answered monotone.

"I have the information you requested. Do you want me to send it somewhere?"

"No, you can tell me now."

Scott gave her the information he got on Jerry McDermont. He gave her everything she already knew, except two things. Scott didn't tell her Jerry was in the witness protection program. She already knew that because she was the one that brokered the deal between him and the CIA. He wouldn't tell her that, which she expected. The other thing he didn't tell her was that Jerry was now contracting work from both the FBI and the CIA.

"Where does he work?" Lindsay waited.

Scott hesitated. "Classified."

"Thanks. I'll be in touch." Lindsay disconnected. She heard Scott start to say something but had disconnected. She was sure it was a question she didn't want to answer. That call proved he would give her information to a certain point. She had FBI security clearance and he had given her what she wanted to that extent. Now she would wait for step two in Scott proving himself.

As Lindsay drove to Baltimore, she thought about Sam. He had so many opportunities to tell her that he was working for the organization. He didn't have to tell her exactly what he did, but he could have warned her. Did he think she was incapable? Instead, he chose to lie, repeatedly. It may have been to protect her, but that didn't make it okay. He wasn't protecting his own skin, so it was about her. What gave these men in her life reason to think they had to protect her? She had been protecting herself, taking care of herself and the boys and doing a fine job. Until they butted in. Maybe she was a challenge to them. Maybe they wanted to see if there was anything they could do better than she could. She heard that men sometimes considered strong women a challenge. This thought led back to the ex-husbands and the competition she was in, even if unbeknown to her. The only thing she could do differently was play the victim. And that she would never do. She despised her mother, who did just that. So much so, that's what she became.

Thinking of her mother, she wondered if she knew Robert was still alive and thriving. Lindsay wouldn't think about that now. She had too many other decisions to make.

The phone Drama Llama was supposed to call vibrated and buzzed.

Lindsay picked it up, excited for news. "Go."

"They're here. Eight of 'em. Two at the front door, two on each side, and two in the back."

"Any on the street?"

"I'm not sure. There's a bit of traffic here and lots of parked cars. Busy place for a residential street."

"Did anyone answer the door?"

"Not yet. They've been here about two minutes. The two guys at the door look professional. They're in suits. The others are in combat gear looking outfits."

"Describe the two guys at the door."

Drama Llama described Agent Scott Preston.

Lindsay suspected the other was Jerry's Witness Protection Program handler. Lindsay wanted to ask about a white truck with a blonde driver but if Derek was there, so was Sam. Drama Llama would recognize Sam. She didn't push it.

"Still no answer?"

"No. They look like they are debating on going in."

"Okay, hangout and call me back when they leave."

"Will do." Drama Llama disconnected. He wondered what was really going on and how Lindsay knew they would show up. They were definitely FBI or CIA and SWAT. He knew she was into some crazy things but he couldn't figure out what side she was on. It didn't matter. She was his friend. Some day maybe she would trust him with more.

Agent Scott Preston failed step two. Lindsay was disappointed. It seemed he was more loyal to Robert's organization than to her. She couldn't wait until the next time she saw him, to hear his excuse. Maybe she would call him and hear it now.

Lindsay pulled off the highway and parked at the first place she could. She pulled out her computer and checked the tracker for Derek's truck. He wasn't at the location that Drama Llama was watching. He was at Robert's office in the city.

Lindsay decided to call the boys since she had a bit more of a drive and she was on the last phone she used to call them. They answered on the first ring and were excited to hear from her. They assured her they were having a great time. One, or two less things she had to worry about.

She made it to Sam's house in record time. He lived in an apartment in a gated community but she had no problem getting in the gate. She followed the car in front of her in. She often wondered what the point was of gated communities. Must just be to give the residence a false sense of security and jack the price of the apartment. All gates did was keep the honest out. Lindsay was honest but today, she probably fell into a lesser category.

She easily made her way into Sam's apartment. She was an expert in picking locks. Thank goodness he hadn't put the deadbolt on. Now that she thought about it, it would have been easier if Sam had given her a key, and now that she knew what she knew, it made sense why he hadn't.

Lindsay walked through Sam's apartment, making sure she was alone. She loved that he was neat and tidy, but in this case, it made this a little harder. If she didn't leave everything the same way, he would know someone had been here.

She wasn't sure what she expected to find. She looked in all the obvious places but came up empty. She ran her hands under, in and around everything. Still nothing. The only thing with an ounce of hope would be his computer. She was sure it was locked up tightly, but it was worth a try.

Pulling out her cell phone, she opened the program that would crack his password. She connected it to his computer's USB and started it up. She watched as digits, alpha and numeric, flashed faster than she could read them. Finally, a password popped up.

"KT you are in trouble" was the password. KT is Kendall Thomas, her organization name. Lindsay unplugged the cell phone from Sam's computer and connected an external hard drive. She copied the entire contents of his computer to her hard drive.

While she waited, she checked the tracker on

Derek's truck. He was still in Phili. She called Scott.

"Stop disappearing on me!" Scott was obviously angry.

"Nice job on paying Jerry McDermont a visit. Find anything?" Lindsay asked in her most sarcastic tone.

"I had to after you inquired, but that's all I did."

"With SWAT? Is that a new standard procedure I'm not familiar with?"

"Okay, while I was researching him for you, something else came up. Don't ask. It was just a precautionary visit." Scott let out a sigh.

"How do you know my inquiry wasn't related to what you found?"

"Trust me, it's not."

"Did you tell Jack I contacted you?"

"No, but I think you need to contact them. Jack contacted me a few weeks ago. It's what I was trying to tell you earlier. They think you are in danger."

"What else did he tell you about me?"

"Nothing. Said he couldn't get into details. Listen, I know you can take care of yourself and I don't know what's going on, but at least let me help you. I feel like I owe you that much."

"You do. I'll be in touch." Lindsay hung up, shaking her head. She could add another person to her growing list of people that she didn't trust. Agent Preston.

49

Robert was sitting behind his desk. He put his hands up and rubbed his temples. Jack said what they were all thinking. "Robert, you may need to consider bringing the FBI in."

"I don't understand why we haven't?" Sam was tired of the delays, excuses and lies. He was starting to understand Lindsay more and more when dealing with Robert Langston.

"It's not that simple!" Robert slammed his hands down on his desk. "Instead of telling me what to do why don't you guys just find her? It can't be that hard. Our percentages of finding people are damn near perfect! She isn't a ghost."

"She was well trained by us. We all will agree that Kendall is one of the best agents we have, not even considering her photographic memory which puts her in her own league. We trained her. She excelled and is now better than most of us. I just had no idea she was paying that much attention." Jack was out of options. "Robert, I've given this considerable thought. We can tell the FBI we think she may have been abducted. I've worked out all the details and outlined them in this." Jack put a sheet of paper down on Robert's desk.

Robert looked at Jack with fire in his eyes. He picked up the sheet of paper outlining the story they would tell the FBI. He read over it and considered it for a second. "And how are you going to explain it to them when they find her and she's alive and well and lying on a beach? Don't forget, Deacon already had contact with her so he knows she wasn't abducted."

"Robert, that's not where she is and we all know it, with all due respect. She could have been abducted since the Atlanta incident." Derek was concerned more so now than he had been in the beginning of Kendall's disappearance. The information, although scarce, that they had gathered, indicated she had left on her own.

"Joe, how much does Deacon really know about what we do? Does he only know the good stuff, or all of it?" Derek asked as he raked his fingers through his hair. It needed a cut.

"He doesn't know much, but he does know we do exceptional work and have helped the agency out considerably, especially Kendall. He may be worth talking with, Robert. If he can't help, he will tell you."

"Fine, get an appointment with him here as soon as possible. The only ones sitting in on this meeting will be the five of us and I don't have to tell you, it's confidential. I don't want anyone else in on it until I make a decision to bring them in. Understood?"

They all nodded in agreement but Jack didn't like Robert listening to Joe more than him. "When I said we should involve the FBI, I was thinking of Scott Preston. He may be more beneficial in this area and he's worked with Lindsay, as Kendall of course."

"Deacon has more pull than Scott. Call Deacon." Robert didn't like overriding Jack but he wanted the best man for the job and in this case, it would be Deacon. Robert also trusted Joe more than he did Jack, at least where Lindsay was concerned.

Jack was mad. Derek and Joe were glad they were pulling in the FBI, which would give them more boots on the ground and a bigger reach. Although the organization was huge, no one had found her yet. Adding in the FBI would only benefit them and expand their resources now.

Sam hadn't shared with them that Lindsay had been in his apartment. He silently thanked his elderly neighbor, who happens to be extremely nosey. She had taken a picture of Lindsay and had shown it to him, asking if she were his new girlfriend. He couldn't come up with one reason to share this information. If it was only to give them peace of mind, he wasn't willing. He wasn't sure Jack knowing she was looking for something was in her best interest. He hadn't decided if he was going to tell Derek. They never kept secrets. This might be the first. Hopefully, it would be the last.

50

Lindsay awoke in her bed at Lake Dare with a raging headache. She had driven back from Sam's apartment, only stopping to use the ladies' room and grab a quick bite. She had left before dawn the day before and got back to the lake at two in the morning.

Getting in at that time of morning, she had glanced around the house but hadn't thoroughly checked it out. She was more careful than usual about the stairs. She didn't want another fall. They were clear.

Lindsay made her way to the bathroom for medicine. She wasn't sure if the knocking she was hearing was from her head or if someone was at the door. She didn't have it in her to answer if it was. She looked out the bathroom window, but didn't see a car. She made her way back to bed.

She crawled in and tried to go back to sleep, but the knocking would not go away. She got up and put on sweatpants, but didn't change her tank top. Lindsay made her way down the stairs. Once she reached the last step, she tried to peek around the corner to see who was at the door. It was Grayson.

Lindsay walked over, opened the door and looked at him. Grayson noticed right away her eyes looked swollen and glazed. She didn't look good. "Are you okay?"

"No. What can I do for you?"

"You weren't here yesterday when the boat was delivered and I wanted to make sure you're still okay with it being on your dock. What's wrong? You weren't poisoned again, were you?"

"No, I have a killer headache but I'm alive. Thanks for stopping by." It hurt just to speak and the sunshine coming in wasn't helping. Lindsay tried to close the door but Grayson put his hand up to hold it open.

"When was the last time you ate? Let me make you something. Leave the door unlocked and I'll be right back." He bolted off before Lindsay could argue. She headed for the couch. She didn't want Grayson in her bedroom.

Sometime later, Lindsay woke to the smell of omelets. Grayson liked his omelets. She started to get up when she realized her neck was cold. As she sat up, she looked down to where her neck had been on the couch pillow. Grayson had put an ice-pack behind her neck while she was sleeping. Lindsay found it disconcerting that he had been able to do that without waking her.

"Look who's vertical. How're you feeling?" Grayson was speaking just above a whisper. She appreciated his thoughtfulness.

Lindsay looked at him for a moment. "I'm not sure yet. Thank you for that." She pointed at the ice pack, but didn't move her head.

"Well, hurry up and feel better because it won't be any fun poisoning you if you are sick." He winked at her and flashed those perfectly white teeth. "Can you stay sitting up for a minute?" Before she could answer, he had started back to the kitchen.

"I'll try." Lindsay wasn't sure of anything right now.

Grayson was back with two plates and held them out. "Pick one. They're the same but I know how you are." He was still almost whispering.

Lindsay pointed to the one in his right hand. He set it down in front of her then set his down on the opposite side of the coffee table. He picked up a napkin, unrolled it and set a knife and fork on it then laid it down in front of her. He moved quietly to other side of the table and sat on the floor.

"Thank you. You can sit up here."

"I'm good. This way you won't have to turn your neck to see me or talk to me. Well, you probably don't want to talk anyway. Want to listen?"

Lindsay could only nod and that was painful.

Grayson noticed the flinch. "You really are hurting. I'm sorry you have a migraine."

"How do you know it's a migraine?"

"My sister gets them. I had a few, but nothing like she does. She has medication, but they can still put her out for a few days."

Lindsay and Grayson ate in silence. Lindsay could only take a few bites before she would have to stop for a minute, then continue. She had eaten about a quarter of the omelet. She thought that was a lot considering the omelet covered the entire plate. She fell over on the couch. "Keep eating. I'm going to lay here for a minute."

Grayson jumped up and came around to her neck. Feeling the ice pack, he took it and walked out. He was back a minute later with it completely cold. "How did you do that?"

"It's a different one. Ssshhhhh rest." He sat down on the floor beside Lindsay and gently took her hand. He started massaging it. Lindsay could feel the throbbing in her head start to ease up.

Lindsay must have fallen asleep again because when she opened her eyes, the house was dark. At first, she thought it was nighttime and she couldn't imagine she had slept that long. She sat up and realized someone had closed the window blinds. The amount of light coming in was minimal through the blinds. Now that she was up, there was just enough light to see someone sitting in the chair across from her.

She sat looking at him, waiting for her eyes to adjust. Normally, they adjusted faster than the average persons, but the headache wasn't helping anything right now.

At least she recognized the voice. "You're awake. I was starting to worry. I was considering hooking you up to a brain wave machine or something. How's the head?" Grayson was speaking in a very low voice.

"What are you doing? Have you stayed here all day?"

"Guilty. I had some reading to do and I was out on the dock a few times, so it was nothing. I may have taken a nap myself."

"Watching me sleep is creepy. Napping in that chair is stupid. You didn't have to stay. I'm a big girl and this isn't my first rodeo. What possessed you to stay?" Lindsay was a little dumbfounded.

"It wasn't putting me out and if you woke up and needed anything, someone would be here. You are making a bigger deal out of it then need be, Kendall. I didn't mean to make you uncomfortable. Besides, I wanted to make sure no one came in and poisoned you, again." He was trying to lighten the uncomfortableness with teasing. He was studying her now with a look that said he wasn't sure which way this was going to go.

"Well, put that way, thank you. But really, you didn't have to." Lindsay still wasn't comfortable with it. To soften the last sentence, she added, "I do appreciate it."

"Good, glad that is over, phew. Now, are you hungry? Since you slept peacefully all day, I'm going to poison you with my superior cooking skills. Feel like eating at the table or would you prefer to stay there?"

"Really, you cooked again? I'm going to weigh five hundred pounds if you keep this up. And the table is fine."

"Right this way." Grayson held his arm out for Lindsay to take it and, once she did, he led her to the table. He had already set two places. Lindsay thought he was getting entirely too comfortable in her house. It was a nice gesture so maybe she should let it go.

Before she sat down, she excused herself. Lindsay headed up the stairs and Grayson headed for the kitchen. Lindsay entered her bathroom and checked the piece of paper that she had left on top of the towels. It was still there. She checked her overnight bag for her laptop. It was as she had left it. She pulled it out and opened it. She turned it on and once it was ready, she checked the log in history. It had been logged into three hours earlier. She had been sleeping for the last four hours. Had Grayson put something in her breakfast to make her sleep so that he could check it? Who else would have been in here to do that, she wondered? It was a stretch. She was starting to think maybe her house was haunted.

Lindsay went down the back stairs as Grayson came back in to the kitchen. She eyed him suspiciously and he noticed. "Everything okay?"

"Yes, fine." Lindsay would get through dinner and test him. She would also get him out of here as soon as she could. She had another plan.

51

Lindsay was relieved when Grayson left. She checked all the doors and windows, then headed back to her bedroom and her laptop. She pulled it out of the bag slowly and deliberately, trying not to add any additional finger prints and not smudge any new ones.

She gathered the extra bag from her car, the mirror off the wall and the laptop. She had everything set up on the dining room table and was ready to get started.

Lindsay pulled the contents of the bag out and set each item on the table. She had Titanium Dioxide, brushes, Mikrosil, tape and a flashlight for oblique lighting. She went into the kitchen and got the glass Grayson had used for water at dinner. He wanted to rinse everything off before he put it in the dishwasher. At least he was great at cleaning up after a meal, but Lindsay wondered if it was for a bigger reason that he was a neat freak, which he was. She wondered if there was a specific reason for this.

She opened the cupboard where she had put the coffee cup Becker had delivered to her to retrieve it. It was gone. She looked through the other cupboards, but it wasn't there. She knew she had put it in there. Someone had obviously found it and disposed of it. She stood still, going back through her memory thinking of anything else he had touched that she could positively pull his fingerprint. She would have to get a new one from him.

Lindsay dusted the glass used by Grayson. Once she acquired his fingerprint, she made a mold of it for future reference.

She dusted the laptop. There were tons of prints but most of them would be hers. She examined it closely for any matching Grayson's fingerprint mold. She didn't find any but that didn't rule him out. There were just too many to be sure. He could have also used gloves.

Lindsay was frustrated at having to wait on getting Becker's prints and not being able to positively match Grayson's on her laptop. She spent the rest of the day cleaning every surface possible, thoroughly enough to wipe all existing fingerprints. She cleaned the outside door knobs as well. Several hours later, she was satisfied she would be able to pull any new ones, once touched.

Lindsay went around the house setting all the doors a specific number of inches open and making a mental note. She taped all the closet doors, like she had last time she went to Denver.

Satisfied everything was how she wanted it, she pulled out the external hard drive with the copy of Sam's computer she had gotten from his apartment. Driving back to the lake yesterday, Lindsay had thought about his password, KT you are in trouble, and concluded it was from when she had first met him. That thought process had taken her down memory lane on the drive back. Lindsay still wasn't sure how she felt about Sam's involvement in her life. She just wasn't sure if she could get over his betrayal. He didn't see it as betrayal, which was part of the problem. He saw it as protection.

Lindsay scanned the folders. There didn't appear to be anything of interest to her. She opened a few folders and read the files. Still nothing of interest. She knew on her own computer that she intentionally "mislabeled" folders and files. She had all day tomorrow to read through them, but now she needed to get to bed. She had early morning plans.

52

Lindsay was awake at the crack of dawn, showered and on her deck drinking coffee before the day truly started. She had plans to get Lance's fingerprints and check out Grayson's house if he left.

She watched the beautiful sunrise over Lake Dare, taking in the orange and yellow hues. She focused on the colors and just breathing in the clean air. It was serene and carefree here, for the moment. Lindsay had expected it to be this way all the time, but it hadn't been. With Mrs. Wigley and her creepy grandson, Lance and Grayson, coyotes, raccoons and other strange happenings, it was anything but peaceful and quiet.

Her mind drifted to Sam. She instantly blocked any further thought of him out. She had gone as far as she could with finding information out about any of them. She had made up her mind to take the next couple of weeks and do nothing. Simply exist. After today. She had plans for today. As she was enjoying the rest of the sunrise, she drifted to a better place. She thought of what she would be doing right now, if life wasn't so complicated.

Staring off into the sunrise, Lindsay forced her mind to run wild. Her thoughts were of traveling around the world, hitting all the best beaches and drinking coffee from other countries with her boys. Lindsay wasn't sure how long she let her imagination go, until she realized Grayson was standing on his boat, watching her. Once she realized he was there, she blushed. Thankfully, he was too far away to see it. She waved to him and he waved back.

He hollered something but she was unable to hear him. She slowly got up, not wanting to end this tranquil moment yet, but also not wanting to be rude. She walked down the front yard toward the dock.

"Good morning, Kendall. You're up early." Grayson was entirely too perky for this time of day.

"Good morning, Grayson. Trying to enjoy the start of the day while it's still tranquil and beautiful."

"I'm sorry. I hope I didn't ruin the moment."

"Not really. If you didn't, someone else would have. It never lasts around here, does it?" Lindsay followed this up with a resigned sigh.

"I think it's really quite lovely this time of day." Grayson said this with a British accent. Lindsay couldn't help but smile. Now speaking in his usual tone, "I didn't realize you find it not so lovely, here."

"I guess you don't get the traffic I do."

"I don't. I also didn't realize you get so much traffic. Ohhhhh, you are referring to me?" He looked at her with an appalled expression and stopped pulling the rope he had been focused on. "I'm sorry if I have been an intrusion."

"No, I am not referring to you. Well, mostly." Lindsay grinned, realizing she didn't think of him as an intrusion. "I was more referring to Mrs. Wigley, Officer Becker, coyotes and raccoons."

"Ahhh. I didn't realize they stopped by so often. Have you seen any more animals?"

"Yes, you didn't hear them last night?"

"Not at all. I did hear Mrs. Wigley about midnight though. I heard someone yelling and walked outside. She was yelling at her grandson as they walked down the lane toward her house."

"Glad I missed that. At least she hasn't tried to get in my house again. I didn't realize her grandson was here. I thought he only showed up on weekends?"

"I have no idea. I rarely ever see either of them. Want some peace and quiet today? Come out on the lake with me."

"I can't. I really have a lot to do today." Lindsay felt a tug. She really wanted to go. It had been too long since she had been boating.

"I can see it in your face. You want to come out. C'mon. We can make it a short trip if you want." "I don't want you to cut your day short because of me. I guess it can wait until tomorrow. Let me get a few things. How long before you leave?"

"Whenever you're ready. I'm glad you're going." Grayson didn't hide his enthusiasm.

Lindsay couldn't help the excitement she was feeling since she decided to go. She was long overdue for something she enjoyed. "Give me ten minutes?"

"Perfect. Meet you back here then." Grayson threw the rope he had been pulling up back into the water.

As Lindsay made her way up to the house, she realized she must be the crazy one. She suspected Grayson had been breaking into her house and going through things. And she had gone so far as to make a mold of his fingerprint. She thought he may have poisoned her and now here she was, going boating with him.

He had also cooked several times since and she hadn't gotten sick. He had taken care of her yesterday when she had a migraine. She was conflicted over him. At least everything she had been able to dig up when researching him had matched most of what he had told her. She hadn't found anything incriminating. The only incriminating thing that bothered her was the conversation she had overheard when she had gone back to his house to get her keys. He was usually at her house, except that morning. They had eaten breakfast at his house while, apparently, someone had been in hers. He had also disappeared for ten minutes while on the phone, so she didn't rule him out.

While these thoughts trickled through her over active imagination, Lindsay put her bathing suit on under her shorts and tank top. She gathered a few things from the bathroom and, while there, she checked the piece of paper again in the closet. It was still there. She had already put the external hard drive in a secure place, along with her laptop. She glanced at the doors of the other rooms. All was well upstairs.

She made her way to the kitchen. She filled two travel mugs with the rest of the coffee, grabbed two waters, checked the doors, did her thing with the drawers where they weren't completely closed and headed out. She grabbed a beach towel from the downstairs closet on her way to the living room door.

She hoped whoever was getting into her house would do it today. It would exclude Grayson because she would be with him. She had to check herself with that thought as she made her way to the boat. She realized she was hoping he was who he said. She wasn't sure when she started to really like him. She tried to remain cautious around him and thought several times to avoid him, but he seemed to find his way back in easily. These thoughts almost made her change her mind about going with him today, but now she was standing in front of him and the boat and wasn't going to miss out. It was only one day.

53

Robert crossed the room extending, his hand before he reached Deacon. He shook Deacon's hand and thanked him for agreeing to meet on short notice. He introduced Deacon to Jack, then Derek and Sam. Deacon shook each of their hands then sat in the only seat left. Joe also thanked Deacon for coming in on short notice and told him how much he appreciated it.

"I'm not sure I can help yet, until I know what this is about, but I'm listening." He acknowledged Robert.

"We have a situation. You met Kendall Thomas in Philadelphia and again in Atlanta. Thank you for agreeing to go to the airport and try to talk to her."

"I'm sorry that didn't work out as planned. I didn't realize she didn't want to be 'found'." The look on Deacon's face let them all know he wasn't impressed.

"I apologize for that. We had limited information and weren't sure what to expect. We do have new information since then. You are correct, Kendall didn't want any discussions at that time. Now, we believe she may feel differently. We believe that she is being held against her will." Robert stopped speaking to let that sink in and gauge Deacon's reaction.

"I'm listening." Deacon appeared to sit

straighter in his chair.

"We believe that she has been taken. She was to return home three days ago. She didn't, nor have we been able to contact her. She was to contact Sam once she was home. Sam hasn't heard from her. He went by her house. It's been ransacked and her safe has been broken into." Robert picked up several photos from his desk and handed them to Deacon. "We have fingerprinted and checked the local street cams. There is no sign of anyone suspicious, or Kendall."

"Why the secrecy?"

"For someone to take Kendall, they would have only one reason. We don't want an all-points bulletin and we also don't want Kendall's name out publicly. She has been able to go deep undercover and easily move around. We don't want to jeopardize future assignments. However, as large as my network is, yours is another layer in locating her. We called you because we can't afford any mistakes in how this is handled."

"I see. And you are sure she's not hiding on her own for some reason? She did not want to be found the last time I saw her. Everyone in this room knows of her talent?" It was a question, not missed by any of them in the room.

"Yes, everyone here has knowledge of her photographic memory." Jack appeared bored.

"And you believe someone has found out about that and is using her for such purpose?"

"Yes. That is what we believe." Robert seemed to be holding his breath.

"Let me make sure I understand. What you expect is to put something out to the entire field, without her name, real or otherwise, not specify what she may be being held for and hope someone just happens to see her?" Deacon waited patiently for Robert to confirm.

"Basically. We know it's a long shot. The problem is, if we were to put her name, there are many agents that know her as Kendall Thomas and we don't want to cause alarm until we have more information. We also don't want to cause panic among her FBI friends. We don't want a massive hunt for her."

"You know this is BS. Either she is in danger or she isn't. You don't know. She wouldn't talk to you before and she's not responding now. What happened that she wouldn't talk to you before three days ago?"

"We aren't at liberty to discuss that at this time." Robert looked uncomfortable.

Deacon didn't like any of this. "Let's try another angle. Is there anyone in the FBI or CIA she would reach out to; that she trusts?"

They each looked at each other. "I'm afraid, if there is, we don't know." Robert looked uncomfortable again.

"There was one, but she tested his loyalty and he failed." Jack was now uncomfortable. "She wouldn't go to him again."

"I see. There is obviously some secret here that you want to remain that way. That secret can't be shared with me. I can't help you. If I don't know what I'm working with, I'm not going to be an asset either. If Kendall doesn't want to be found, I'm not going to find her. Unless you can give me more to work with, we're done." Deacon stood, nodded at Robert, looked at Joe and said, "Joe." He turned to leave.

Joe followed him out of the office. "Look Deacon, I'm sorry. I thought they might give you more to work with."

Deacon stopped in the outer office. "I'm sorry too, Joe, especially if Kendall is in danger. She is respected and admired in our world by those that know her. If anything comes up that I can assist with, please call me."

Joe shook Deacon's hand and nodded. Joe watched Deacon walk out the door. He stood still for a few moments, thinking.

"I thought we agreed to give him a little more than that." Sam was disappointed and not trying to hide it.

"I can only give him so much. If I give him too much, it could hurt the organization should he dig." Robert hadn't moved from his position since Joe and Deacon walked out.

"Hurt the organization? I guess I shouldn't have expected any more from you. All you've done is hurt everyone around you to protect this organization, including your own daughter! And dragged the rest of us down with you!" Sam stormed out before anyone could react to his outburst.

"Derek, get him under control or I will." Robert didn't need Sam being a lose cannon. "He's no longer privy to this investigation. Keep him out of the loop." Robert said this to Derek's back as he was already on his way out of the office.

As Derek left the office to catch up with Sam, he thought to himself, "What investigation? Kendall has become a ghost."

With only Robert, Joe and Jack now left in Robert's office, Robert looked at Jack. "Don't say it. There's no indication that Agent Scott Preston could do any more than Agent Wyatt."

"Deacon can do something; he just chooses not to." Jack shook his head.

"Lose the almighty attitude, Jack. You haven't delivered Charlie, either."

54

Lindsay and Grayson had a great time on the boat yesterday. She was glad she had gone. They had kept the conversation to current events, although he did seem to try to steer it back to Lance a few times. She blew it off.

Lindsay wasn't sure if she had been happy or disappointed that her house was just as she had left it yesterday morning. No one had been there.

Lindsay researched Lance, looking for some background on him but also trying to figure out where he lived. She was coming up empty on that.

Today was the day she would make progress with Lance and Grayson, at least on some under-cover work. She hated not having access to all the regular information she was used to and she hated not having resources and people she could trust. Technically, she had access to all the information; it was just that she didn't want anyone tracking her should she access it. And Casey would track her. Lindsay was sure, the minute she logged in to their system, they would know.

Lindsay went to the kitchen to grab coffee and head out to the deck for the last bit of sunrise. She figured Lance typically worked nights and finished early morning. At least, he usually stopped by in the early hours of the morning regarding Mrs. Wigley and other times early enough to bring her coffee. She hoped she was right. She planned to head into town and follow him from the police station. If that didn't work, she would hang out at the game warden's office on the other side of the lake and follow him from there. She hated following people and waiting on them, but what other choice did she have right now?

It had crossed her mind that Mrs. Wigley's grandson was the one breaking into her house, but she would rule out Lance and Grayson first because she was suspicious of both of them. Then again, who wasn't she suspicious of anymore.

She hated this. She hated the lies. She hated the deception. She hated not having anyone she could trust. She hated fighting. She hated dead ends. She hated no answers, no truth. She hated this life. All the work she had been doing had gotten her no further ahead. No answers. She was determined to work hard today, then end it. She would relax and enjoy a few more weeks here at the lake house then head back to reality and find new angles. If someone were trying to drive her crazy, so be it. She figured she was halfway there. If someone was trying to kill her at this lake house, they had opportunity already.

If they were trying to figure out what she was doing, she wished them luck. They could torture her and she wouldn't tell them because she had no idea herself.

Just as she started out of the kitchen with coffee in hand, there was a knock at the door. Lindsay thought of ignoring it but then thought better of it. Coffee still in hand, she opened the door. "Good morning, Lance. What can I do for you today?" Lindsay welcomed him with a smile. "Business or pleasure?"

"Both. I can mix them, right?" He had a twinkle in his eye. Lindsay thought it was a little early for that. "I brought you coffee." He held it out for her.

"I already have one but come on in and you can drink it while you tell me what's going on." She raised her cup to him and moved back to allow him entrance.

"Is the deck okay? I want to see what's left of the sunrise." She didn't wait for an answer but led the way.

"It's a beautiful morning." He followed her to the deck.

"Aren't you getting off work soon. I assume you are still working with having business to discuss."

"Yeah, both. You're my last stop before I head home." They both were taking their seats. Lindsay positioned herself so that she was facing Grayson's house and he was facing Mrs. Wigley's house.

"Where is home for you?" Could that have been more easily handed to her on a silver platter, she wondered.

"I live in the back of the game warden's office. It's a perk of the job. It's not much, but I don't need much. And it's convenient. It puts you and Mrs. Wigley half way between me and town so, you see, it's not inconvenient to stop by and check on you and her. Easy to bring you coffee from town on my way home." He raised up the coffee he brought for her.

Lindsay watched that cup of coffee carefully, wondering if Lance was going to drink it or just hold onto it. Time would tell.

"Ah, I see. So, what is the business you want

to discuss?"

"Can you tell me if you were home all night last night?"

"Yes, I was home from about sunset yesterday to now. I haven't left since last evening. Why, what's wrong? Mrs. Wigley again?"

"Uhhhh, no. You are sure you haven't left this house at all?"

"Yes, I'm positive. What is going on?" Lindsay was curious now and didn't try to hide it.

"There was a robbery last night at one of the jewelry stores in town."

"What does that have to do with me?" Lindsay gave him a genuinely confused look. He saw it but continued.

"Well, we have you driving your car through town at about the same time. Driving away from the jewelry store."

"That's impossible. What do you have, a picture, a video?" Lindsay already knew there were no street cameras and most businesses didn't have cameras outside, or if they did, they were only showing the immediate area around their doors.

"We have an eye witness who saw you."

"Ha! That's impossible because I didn't leave. Have you thought maybe your eye witness is the robber?"

"No, the eye witness is trustworthy."

"Oh, well, that explains everything!" Lindsay looked at him like he was the dumbest person on earth.

"How so?"

"If he, or she, is trustworthy and I'm not, you have a case. Where did you tell me you got your degree?"

Lance looked at her for a moment, like he was trying to remember what he had told her. He ignored the question and asked her if she was prone to sleepwalking.

"Okay, look. I know this little town is weird, with strange people, such as Mrs. Wigley, however, even you know this sounds absurd. Did your witness get the license plate off my car?"

"Yes."

"I mean, from when he, or she, supposedly saw me last night, not off the internet 'findpeople. com'."

"Yes. They described you also."

"Well, that's convenient. Did you put a dose of stupid in your coffee this morning or are you just bored and yanking my chain? Surely, you could come up with something better than this as an excuse to stop by."

"I'm afraid I'm not joking, Kendall. The Sheriff will probably stop by at some point and question you further, once the fingerprints come back."

"Good luck with that. I've never stepped foot in the jewelry store." Lindsay wanted to keep him longer because, as ridiculous as this story was, he hadn't drunk from the cup of coffee he was still holding.

"I just wanted to give you a heads up."

"Complete waste of my time and yours. So, what are you doing with the rest of your day? Surely, not investigating this further." Lindsay now smirked at him. They both knew it was absurd.

"I'm going fishing. I find it relaxing. Want to go?"

"Yes, I can see how after a busy night at the office, you would need some relaxation." She smirked again. "I don't think it's in your best interest to be seen with a suspect in a robbery. Are you going to drink that coffee or just hold it?" She took a big sip from her own cup.

"It's cold now. I despise cold coffee."

"I can warm it up for you." Lindsay started to stand and put her hand out to reach for the coffee.

"No, that's just as bad. You can dump it for me, though."

"Sure thing. I'll walk you out. I need to get moving."

Lindsay walked him to the door. When he hesitated, she asked, "Am I safe to leave town, Officer Becker?"

Lindsay could tell Lance was thinking it over. He finally answered, "I'm sure it will be cleared up soon. Are you planning a trip?"

"Maybe. I have some research to do. If I do, I'll only be gone a few days. I'll be back, especially, because I have nothing to worry about."

Lance nodded and left. Lindsay closed the door and leaned on it for a minute. She wondered why chaos followed her. She was a just a girl trying to live her best life.

55

Lindsay had showered and dressed after Lance left, taking her time to give him time to get home and go out fishing. As she turned to lock the door behind her, she heard a loud whistle. She looked in the direction of the whistle and spotted Grayson coming toward her, across the side yard.

"Good morning, Kendall. You're off early."

"And you're perky this morning, Grayson. Whatcha' up to?"

"I'm always like this. I was just coming to invite you out on the boat with me today. But looks like you have plans."

"I do have plans. Yesterday's plans I put off, remember? I'm sorry. I would love to go out again though. Maybe next time?" Grayson went from perky to disappointed to hopeful and Lindsay noticed as she spoke.

"Sure. I would like that. I won't keep you. Have a great day."

"Thanks, Grayson. Have a good time on the lake today. Long trip or local?"

"I thought about going to the other end of the lake today and doing a little more sightseeing."

"Enjoy! And be safe." Lindsay was disappointed but was determined to figure something out today, no matter how small.

Grayson winked and started to leave, but stopped. "Hey, by the way, was that Officer Becker

I saw here first thing this morning?"

"Indeed." Lindsay didn't elaborate, but waited.

"You weren't kidding about him stopping by a lot, huh? I didn't realize he did it so early. Business or pleasure?"

Lindsay found his curiosity interesting. "Both." She would see how curious he was.

"Ahhh. Personal business?" Now Grayson grinned, trying to pretend he wasn't that interested. "If he is giving you a hard time, you can tell me. I'll take care of it."

"Really? What are you going to do? Duke it out with the game warden?" Lindsay couldn't help but laugh at the mental picture of them fighting in the yard, like middle schoolers.

"I'm more mature than that. I can talk to him if you like."

"Do I look like I'm two? I can handle him. It's good to see chivalry isn't dead." Lindsay's face gave away her thought, which shocked her. Isn't that what Robert and Sam were doing? Good grief! What a thought. "Hey, have fun. Gotta' go." With that, she turned around and sprinted to her car.

She jumped in and sat there for a moment, stunned at her own thought. Were Robert's and Sam's actions chivalrous? No, they weren't. Their behavior was that of deceitful liars, lunacy, maybe even mentally unstable. Now she wondered if she really thought that of Sam. Did he really fall into the same categories as Robert? No, he couldn't. Could he?

Lindsay compartmentalized these thoughts. She had things to do. She glanced over to where she had been talking to Grayson. He was still standing there, watching her. He had a concerned look on his face. Lindsay gave him a smile, a quick wave and backed out of the driveway.

Five minutes later, Lindsay pulled back into her driveway. She thought since Lance was going fishing, she would have a little time to do something else first.

Lindsay grabbed her house key and headed inside through the kitchen door. She walked carefully into the dining room and then into the living room, staying low. She could see Grayson on his boat. He started the motor and took off toward the middle of the lake. She effortlessly and efficiently made her out to her car then jogged through the trees to Grayson's house.

She picked the lock and slid inside. She walked through his house, taking everything in to her memory. She found the stairs and headed up, glancing over her shoulder through the windows facing the lake and caught sight of Grayson's boat far out on the lake. She continued to the top of the stairs and found two bedrooms. She scanned through them not finding anything of interest. She did note how clean he kept his home.

Entering the master bedroom, she searched through everything being careful to keep things as he had them. Finishing her search, she was dismayed at not finding anything out of the ordinary. She stood in the middle of the room, taking it all in. Her eyes were drawn to the tiled fireplace. She wasn't sure what instinct kicked in but she began pushing on each tile. One popped open, startling her.

She pulled it out further, and looked in. She was surprised to find pictures. She removed them from the hidden drawer and looked through each one. They were all of Lance. They appeared to be taken over various days based on his clothes and his surroundings. She wondered out loud, "Why would Grayson have photos of Lance?" She put the pictures back and closed the drawer. She got a towel out of the bathroom and wiped her prints off of the tiles. Sure, her prints were everywhere but she had been very careful where she touched other things.

Being satisfied she had checked everywhere upstairs; she made her way back to his kitchen. Lindsay went through every cupboard and his pantry. She was looking for something one could use for poisoning. She was again dismayed at not finding something, some kind of proof. She headed out to his garage.

Although it was extremely organized, it would take her all day and a ladder to look through the totes and tool storage benches, then the shelving units. She looked through what was easily accessible, realizing nothing would likely be out in the open. If she were to find anything out of the ordinary, it would most likely be hidden or up high. She would need to wait for that opportunity. Today wasn't it.

She left the same way she came in, making sure to lock the door behind her. As she jogged back to her car, she realized she hadn't seen a camera anywhere in Grayson's house, nor anything that would indicate he was a photographer or diver. That was something, wasn't it. Maybe, but it wasn't enough for Lindsay.

56

As she drove to the other side of the lake to the game warden's Office and Lance's place of residence, she wasn't sure what she was looking for. Once inside, she hoped whatever it was, would present itself. Maybe there wasn't anything to be found, but she doubted it.

Lindsay pulled onto a dirt road that looked like it didn't go anywhere. She was about a mile from her destination. She would jog the rest of the way, avoiding having her car seen on any cameras at the office, or Lance's home.

Before she got out, she put her hair in a messy bun, put a hat on and tucked her gun in her waistband at her back. She grabbed the two tools she would need to break in through a locked door. She also grabbed the internet scrambler. She began the jog, calculating she would make it there in less than seven minutes at a good pace. Lindsay hoped this road wasn't well traveled at this time of the morning.

She covered the distance in less than seven minutes with only one truck passing her in the opposite direction. As she approached the office, she moved off to the trees lining the long driveway. She wanted to check the outside for cameras, without being seen herself. She had Googled the area and checked it in satellite view so she was well aware of the surroundings.

The long driveway led to a two-story building sitting directly on the lake with one separate garage off to the far left. Lindsay knew there was a short area in the front leading to the dock where two game warden boats were located. On the satellite, there were no other boats but that didn't mean Lance didn't have a boat of his own and Lindsay hadn't thought to ask that morning. She wouldn't be able to tell from how many boats were docked if Lance had left or was still here.

She slowly made her way to the back of the building, then to the far-right side. The woods hid her well enough that she made it far enough in the front side to see two boats. They were both game warden boats so that was no help in determining if Lance were there. She did notice that there were no cameras outside, nor any indication of an alarm system. Thank goodness for small town trustworthiness.

Seeing no vehicles around, Lindsay went back to the driveway and walked to the left side of the property, then through the trees to the area behind the garage. It was a metal garage with four windows along the back. Lindsay, still seeing no indication of outside cameras, made her way to the closest window. Peeking in she could see a white, four door truck she had never seen before, the SUV Lance usually drove, along with several kayaks, two jet skis and other equipment one might expect to find at a game warden's location.

She continued along the back of the garage until she could see the side of the office. Everything appeared quiet and still no cameras in sight. Thinking it would be better to be safe than sorry, she pulled out the scrambler that would interrupt the wireless connection going into the office. She would at least disrupt that long enough to get in and out.

Now she moved to walk along the side of the office to the nearest window. She slowly looked in from the side and, not seeing anything, moved to the next window, closest to the front of the building. Still seeing no movement, she walked across to the front door. It was locked and had a sign that said, "Be back at 2 pm." More benefits of being in a small town.

Lindsay continued walking across the front of the building to the other side, where there was another door. She tried this door only to find it locked as well. Looking in, all she could see was a set of stairs. She picked the locked and let herself in. Closing the door behind her, she stood still, listening. Not hearing anything, she sprinted quietly up the stairs, the whole time looking up. Near the top of the stairs, she stopped again, listening. Still not hearing anything, she made her way up the last few stairs and was surprised to find herself in a large room, apparently a very large living room with part of the back wall a kitchen area. The front of the room, facing the lake, had large windows with a great view. Lindsay started in the kitchen, looking for food poisoning products although she knew how ridiculous it would be to find that in someone's kitchen. Whatever was used to poison her, was a small amount, just to make her sick but not kill her. It could have been anything.

Lindsay made her way to the back wall to the left of the kitchen area where a door was partially opened. She carefully peeked in the room. Obviously, it was Lance's bedroom. Seeing it was empty, she breezed through the dresser drawers, then onto the nightstand drawers. Nothing unusual. She opened the closet door and peered in. Everything seemed typical. There was another door in the back of the room, which Lindsay suspected led to the bathroom, putting it behind the kitchen wall. Opening the door, she was surprised to find a set of steps going downstairs, which meant the office could be accessed inside. There was another door beyond the stairs. It was a bedroom, but being used as an office. Lindsay glanced out the window to the back of the house/office. Everything was as she found it.

Lindsay glanced around the room then moved over to the desk. A laptop was sitting closed on the desk. Lindsay scanned all the desk drawers, then opened the closet. Not finding anything of interest, she made her way back to the laptop. When she opened it, she heard a faint noise. She listened intently for a full minute. Off in the distance, she heard a boat. She couldn't tell if it was coming or just going by. While she waited for the laptop to fire up, she went into the kitchen and found a glass in the sink. On her way out, she would take it with her.

Going back into the office, she checked the laptop. It was ready. She couldn't believe that Lance didn't have it password protected and wished she had her portable hard drive to copy everything. She visually scanned the folders and files for anything of interest.

The boat outside was getting closer but before she could go check it, she heard the door open at the bottom of the stairs where she had come in. She immediately jumped up and squeezed herself into the closet. It had slat doors and she hoped

Lance, or whoever it was, wasn't going to be here long. She wasn't sure she could stand like this for long.

Lindsay held her breath as someone came in the room. She heard them fumbling around like they were looking for something. With the slats pointing down, she couldn't see too far across the room, but only about two feet in front of the closet door.

Then a cell phone rang. Lindsay wasn't sure if whoever was in the room answered it or made a call back out because there was only one ring then a full minute of silence. Next, she heard a very nasty sounding female, "Where the hell are you?" Then silence again. Then another nasty reply. "Ridiculous. I'm at the salon now but leaving. Meet me at the usual place in fifteen minutes. Don't be late."

Lindsay hoped Lance's place wasn't the usual place this nasty lady was referring to. It could be a long wait in the closet. She only had to wait another few minutes when she heard the lady leave the office, then a moment later, the door downstairs open and close. The boat that she had heard earlier was very close now. She peaked out the window of the office to see a Mercedes leaving the driveway. It was a very quiet car as Lindsay hadn't heard it coming, nor leaving. Sadly, she couldn't see who was driving it. She headed into the kitchen, grabbed the glass out of the sink and checked the front windows, over-looking the lake. The boat was almost there and Lance was driving it. She had to hurry out.

She made her way down the same stairs the other lady had used and crept around to the back of the house. She would have to go straight out the back so Lance wouldn't see her from the dock. Once she was far enough down the driveway, she could move into the trees lining the driveway, hopefully, without being seen.

Only one car had passed her on her jog back. It was a Mercedes, the same one that had left Lance's while she was there. It was traveling the same direction as she was, but only slowed once it had passed her. It came to a crawl before she almost caught up to it, then zipped off, speeding out of sight. She didn't get a look at the driver this time either. The windows were blacked out. She did memorize the license plate, although it was a rental.

57

Lindsay made it back to her car. She wondered who the lady was, what she was doing there and who she had called and lied to. What did it have to do with Lance, was the bigger question? She couldn't help but wonder again if she were being overly suspicious.

If the lady had been speaking to Lance, he would be driving by soon to meet her. Instead of hurrying back to go through Grayson's house, Lindsay wanted to wait and see if Lance was meeting this woman. With her time frame, if Lance were meeting her, he would be along soon. He had returned from fishing rather quickly, if that is what he was actually doing.

Lindsay turned her car around so that it was facing the road, but pulled it farther away from sight. She didn't have to wait long before Lance drove by. He was in the white truck she had seen in the garage.

She let Lance get around the first bend in the road before she pulled out. Lindsay was able to catch up to him, but stayed a safe distance away. He passed the road to her house and continued toward town. He drove through town and took a right on the road that led to the campground. If he was meeting the lady from his office, he was going to be late. Part of Lindsay didn't want him to be meeting her.

Lindsay followed Lance to a bar about a mile before the road led into the campground. Once he pulled in, she continued to drive past, not looking at his truck, but staring straight down the road. She turned around once he would have enough time to get inside. Driving back by, she checked out the parking lot. The bar sat alone, along the road to the campground. There were woods on each side of the bar. The parking lot had enough spaces to park about ten cars. Lindsay scanned the cars for the Mercedes but didn't see one. There was no way she could have missed it with only eight other cars and trucks there.

Lindsay didn't know if she should be mad at herself for thinking the worst of Lance or be relieved he didn't meet the woman. She decided she didn't care. She didn't need to know. Did she?

Lost in thought, Lindsay hadn't realized she had driven to her lake house. She sat in her car in the driveway, exhausted from chasing her tail. She felt like she was going round and round with everything in her life. She had come here to sort things out and only ended up creating more chaos and wondered, again, if she were being overly imaginative. Then she had a second thought, she knew the facts, although she did not know the why in reference to her father and Sam. Did it really matter and would knowing change the future? Was the truth that important?

Lindsay wasn't sure how long she had been sitting there but it had to have been quite a while. She was jolted back to reality when she heard a woman scream. From Grayson's house. She pulled her gun from under the seat and bolted through the trees, not bothering to close her car door. She made her way to the door leading into the kitchen. Peering though the window, Lindsay didn't see anyone. She heard another shrill scream. She pushed the door and it opened. She slipped into the kitchen then made her way through the dining room and into the living room. Still no one. Lindsay crept up the stairs.

Just as she stepped on the top one, she heard a shrill scream, but with words. "Get out of my house you fool! What are you? A Peeping Tom. Get out!!"

The voice was that of Mrs. Wigley. Lindsay wasn't sure who, if anyone, she was talking to and why the long pause between the first scream and this. Lindsay stepped into the doorway of Grayson's bedroom just as someone was running toward her from the master bath. She pointed her gun and said, "Stop!" just as the man realized she was there. He was dressed in black and had a matching mask. It was too late. He plowed into her.

Lindsay flew backward on impact through the doorway landing at the top of the stairs, with the guy on top of her. She was still clutching her gun. He was fast and pinned her arm down. She grabbed him by the neck and swung her legs straight up, flinging him down the stairs. With the grip on her arm, he dragged her down with him.

At some point during the fall, they had become disconnected. Lindsay landed on top of the guy at the bottom of the stairs. Mrs. Wigley was now standing at the top of the stairs wrapped in a towel and screaming.

The guy jumped up as he pushed Lindsay off of him. He was poised for a fight, but didn't get one. Lindsay wasn't moving. He reached down and felt a pulse in her neck. She was alive. She may have internal injuries or brain injuries but he didn't care. He wasn't here for her. His target wasn't the crazy lady at the top of the stairs either. He left the same way he came in.

Mrs. Wigley rushed down the stairs to Lindsay's side. She felt for a pulse and shook Lindsay. She went and got a cold cloth for her. Once she put it on her head, Lindsay began to move. Mrs. Wigley insisted she lay still.

As Grayson entered the kitchen, he was frustrated that the boat had something wrong with it and he had to end his day early. All he wanted to do was jump in the shower and head back over to Lindsay's dock and figure out what was wrong. He had only taken two steps in when he heard a female voice coming from the living room. He made his way in and was bewildered at an old lady leaning over a body he couldn't fully see.

"Excuse me? Who are you?" Grayson spoke to her back and spoke softly in an effort not to startle her.

"I'm the owner here. Come quickly and help me with Kendall."

Grayson had already moved around to get a better angle on what was going on and when he realized Kendall was laying on his floor. He rushed to her side. "What is going on, Kendall?"

Lindsay heard his voice and understood it clearly but his face was blurry. She was having a hard time moving. She tried to sit up.

"Woah there. You might want to stay still a minute. Mrs. Wigley, can you tell me what happened?"

"Well, I was taking my bath when some fool dressed like it was Halloween or something crept in and was peeping on me while I was bathing. Kendall must have heard me scream and came to my rescue. First thing I know, I hear loud booms, like them falling down the stairs. Which, as you can see, is exactly what happened. Damn fool ran off when he saw Kendall not moving. Now, we need to get her to the hospital after that fall knocking the snot out of her."

"Mrs. Wigley, while I check Kendall out, can you go get dressed, please?" He had already started for her when Mrs. Wigley grabbed his arm.

"You can't move her. What if she has an internal injury or brain damage or her back is broken? I'll call the ambulance people. They'll know what to do."

Lindsay found her voice, "No, no ambulance. Just let me lay here for a minute."

"Mrs. Wigley, go get dressed. Kendall, does anything hurt? Can you move all your limbs?" Grayson's concern was valid but Lindsay was mad.

"Go find that guy instead of sitting here!" She started to get up again, but laid back down instead. "Go!"

"He's long gone. Just answer me."

"Yes, I think I can move all my parts. It's my head when I move it. Was I out cold?"

"I think so. Do you remember what happened?"

"I just came home when I heard a shrill scream. I came over to check it out and once I entered the bedroom at the top of the stairs, a guy with a mask on charged me. And Mrs. Wigley told you the rest." Lindsay had her eyes shut but opened them to look at Grayson just as she finished. He didn't look impressed.

"We need to take you to the hospital."

"No. You need to tell me why someone would break into your house. What was he looking for?"

"Are you police or does this make a good story for one of your books?"

"It might tell me who you really are."

"Huh, interesting. I hadn't thought of that." He winked at her. "Probably just someone burglarizing the neighborhood. You haven't been inside your house since you returned from where ever?"

"No. Who burglarizes houses in the middle of the day?" Lindsay was having a hard time focusing but wasn't going to admit it.

"The guy that charged you. Ok, let's get you moved over to the couch and off the floor." Grayson had been watching her move her limbs around to make sure everything worked. "At least nothing appears broken."

"Except my ego."

"That can't be fixed but it can be ignored." He chuckled as he lifted her up. "Damn Kendall, you weight more than you look."

The color drained from Lindsay's face. "Put me down. Quick!" She tried to wiggle free of his hold.

"No way." Grayson had barely gotten it out when Lindsay puked all over him, and herself.

Grayson carried Lindsay to the bathroom upstairs, off one of the guest bedrooms. He held her while he filled the tub with water. Once there was enough water, he set her down on the toilet. "Get undressed and in the bath. Once you are in the tub, let me know. I'll run next door and get you some fresh clothes."

"No, do you have a t-shirt I could borrow. The rest of my clothes are fine. I just need a shirt. If you could leave it on the bed, that would be great." Lindsay was mortified but felt too badly to argue. She didn't want Grayson or any other man going through her drawers and certainly not picking out clothes for her.

"Yes. I'll get it and check on Mrs. Wigley. Just let me know when you are in the tub safely. Can you stand up on your own?"

"I'll be fine." Lindsay knew she would be fine but she may never get over the mortification. She had never puked so much as she had since coming to Lake Dare. And in front of Grayson, every single time. She wondered if he was the cause of all them.

58

Lindsay soaked in the tub and thought she needed to do this more often. She enjoyed it for quite a while until the water got cold. She slipped out of the tub, dried off and got dressed. Wrapping the towel around her, she went in to the bedroom where she found Grayson's shirt.

She dressed and sat on the bed for a minute. Her head was a little fuzzy. She got up slowly and made her way to the door. Just as she reached it, Grayson knocked.

Lindsay opened the door. "Hey, thank you. Where is Mrs. Wigley?"

Grayson's eyes grazed over her face then her body. "She's downstairs, having coffee. I'll walk you home and then take her. I thought of having you stay here, in this room, but I think your house is safer for you, considering what happened today." Lindsay didn't miss his hair being wet, figuring he had jumped in the shower. She found it disarming.

Lindsay thought of questioning him but decided to wait. He walked her home, with his hand on her back the entire way. Once there, Grayson made sure her house was empty and no one had been there. When he was comfortable everything was as it should be and Lindsay was settled on her couch, he told her he would be back once he got Mrs. Wigley home and settled in. "You don't have to come back and check on me. I'm fine."

"It wasn't a question." Then he walked out.

Lindsay thought about the height of the masked man. She couldn't be sure because he was in motion and bent slightly when she had seen him. She could confirm he was in excellent shape. It was surprising he hadn't knocked the wind out of her when he slammed into her. She was sure she was going to be sore from the fall down the stairs and rolling with him hadn't helped.

Lindsay wondered why he didn't use her gun to shoot her and Mrs. Wigley. She never saw a gun on him, but she couldn't be sure. Either he was there just to rob the place or he was there for Grayson, not her and Mrs. Wigley. But why would he be looking for Grayson and in the middle of the day, dressed like that? Then again, why did Grayson have hidden photos of Lance in the fireplace? She was sure there was more to all this than she was piecing together. Maybe she should just ask Grayson why he had those photos. Maybe she should mind her own business.

Grayson came back within minutes. "Mrs. Wigley's settled in. How's your head?"

"Much better. Thank you. I'm fine. It isn't the first time I've been knocked out since being here. Seems to be a habit."

"Are you hungry?"

Lindsay noticed he didn't comment on her remark, but changed the subject. "No."

"Actually, I have to run into town and can grab something there. Want Mexican? That little restaurant in town is delicious. I won't be gone long and if I could get out of it, I would."

"That sounds good. I do have to ask though,

who was that guy at your house, honestly? I know there is more to you than you've told me."

"I honestly have no idea. I'm pretty simple, Kendall. I don't have anything to hide from you. I could ask you the same thing. What are you hiding?"

"What makes you think I have something to hide?"

"You shoot and move like you've had formal training. It's not just a hobby for you. Who tries to stop a burglar or masked man? Show me the novel you are working on."

"I can't show you that. The contract has a Non-Disclosure clause and I could be sued. I haven't seen you with a camera or any pictures that you've taken."

"Okay, truce. I have to run. Are you comfortable here or would you like to go upstairs? You have your gun, right?" Grayson knew she did. She pulled it out of his waistband when he first lifted her off the floor at his house. She was quick and efficient. She had put it in her waistband when he set her down on the toilet. He had also seen it when he was walking her home after her bath.

"Yes, I have it. I'm good here." Lindsay proceeded to pull her gun out, then reach into her sock and pull out the bullets. She reloaded her gun. She hadn't taken her eyes off his. He watched her, amused.

"So, you unloaded it before I walked you home. Was that in case I wanted to use it on you? I could have done that when you were out cold or still weak afterwards. Or, for that matter, a million other times. Trust issues, Kendall?"

"Bye, Grayson." Trust issues. That was a solid

yes. She wondered if he was going to meet the lady that was at Lance's. If so, he was very late.

59

"You're late. Don't ever keep me waiting." She could glare with the best of them.

He could glare back, just as intense. "Calm down, Princess. I'm here. Don't keep you waiting? Don't demand I jump when you get a whim."

"You have forgotten you work for me, haven't you?"

"Why do you insist on thinking I work for you?"

"As long as I'm pulling the strings, you do. Now, what new information do you have for me? You haven't been scaring her much."

"She doesn't scare easily. I'm not sure why you expected she would. I'm telling you, there is nothing at the lake house other than she appears to be a writer, just writing a story. She hasn't had contact with anyone, except on her trip to Philadelphia. She met with Agent Preston for two minutes, and it didn't look like a friendly meeting. She doesn't trust anyone so it's going to be impossible to get close enough to her for her to confide in anyone."

"She hasn't had contact with Robert, Jack, or Sam?"

"No. What is it you think she is up to that has you so worried?"

"Do I look worried?"

He knew it was rhetorical, but took the opportunity to let her know what he thought of her.

"You seem worried but look desperate. Blackmailing someone is desperation. Look, it's all irrelevant to me. I could not care less, but I think your wasting your time. She appears to be on a hiatus if you want my professional opinion."

"I don't. I know she is up to something. Maybe it's time I had a face to face with her. If you can't find anything, or figure out what she is up to, then I will."

"What are you going to do? Bump into her and pretend to become friends? She would see right through you."

She looked at him like she was just seeing him for the first time. He could see the wheels spin. "Speaking of friends, she has two very close friends…."

"You wouldn't. You're taking this too far."

"Robin and Courtney would cause her to come running."

"If you want to have a face to face, you know where to find her."

"Only because she doesn't know me. Hell, I doubt she even knows I exist. According to Jack, she doesn't. But I don't trust him."

"You apparently don't trust anyone, otherwise, you wouldn't have to blackmail me."

"Stop being so dramatic. I have another plan that is failsafe. I'll let you know when the time is right. Good bye. Oh, by the way, you can still continue with our plan. I'm not releasing you yet." And just like that, she waved her hand as if to dismiss him.

"We aren't done yet. Who have you sent to my home?"

"No one. Why? What's happened?"

"Don't look so innocent. You don't have an innocent bone in your body."

60

Lindsay was dozing off when the knock at the door woke her. She wanted to ignore it, like she always did, but assumed it was Grayson returning with dinner.

"Hold on, I'm coming." She was moving much better than this afternoon and her head wasn't as clouded. She didn't hide her surprise when it was Lance. "What do I owe this honor? Ready to take me in, in handcuffs? Can I at least go feed my cat first?"

"You're safe. That won't be necessary. You don't have a cat and your fingerprints didn't come up a match."

"Really? And just where did you get my fingerprints from and when did I give you permission?" Lindsay didn't comment on the fact that he knew she didn't have a cat.

"You are smarter than you let on. We hit a match on the fingerprints from our system. We suspect he is from the group that has been burglarizing homes around here as well."

"Gee, let me get my shocked look." Now Lindsay gave him a flirty smile followed by her pretend shock look. "Did you really think I did it?"

"I've learned in this business, trust no one. Now that you are cleared, can we have dinner?"

"I bet you get lots of women with that smile

and those eyes. Sorry, it takes more than sexiness for me. If it was only that, you might have stood a chance. Look, I need to get back to writing, so thank you for stopping by and giving me the good news." Naturally, the last part was full of sarcasm. "Bye, Lance."

She had wanted to ask him if he had stopped by to check on Mrs. Wigley, but didn't want to give him a reason to if he hadn't. Lindsay wasn't sure what Mrs. Wigley would tell him, unless Grayson had asked her not to say anything.

Five minutes later, Grayson was back, with food. "Oh, you just missed Lance. I thought about inviting him to dinner with us but wasn't sure you bought enough." She studied him closely.

"Why would you do that? I thought you found him to be a pain in the ass for the most part." Now he watched her closely.

"Just to see your reaction. What is it about him you don't like?"

"Who said I didn't like him?"

"Do you?" Lindsay was watching him though pretending to be focused on getting out plates and silverware for dinner.

Grayson knew she was watching him closely and got tired of the game. "I don't really know him to judge. Are you going somewhere with this conversation?"

"Nope. Conversation closed." Now Lindsay was more curious. There was definitely something Grayson was not telling her. Like who he really is and why he would be taking pictures of Lance.

They ate dinner in the dining room and kept the conversation light. They told boating stories they each had. Eventually, they agreed to go boating the next day.

As Lindsay was reaching to put a plate away, she let out a painful cry and dropped the plate that shattered on the tile floor. Grayson pulled her into his arms just as she leaned forward holding her head with both hands. He led her to the couch and sat beside her. "What happened?"

"It was a sharp pain in my head. It's okay now. It's gone."

"Okay, taking you to the hospital." He started to get up.

"No, please. I've had those shooting pains before with headaches and migraines. They only last a minute and go away."

"Have you had these checked out by a specialist?" Grayson looked genuinely concerned. He still got up and gently led her to the living room. She didn't fight him for once.

"Yes. They are unexplainable. Goes along with the migraines."

"But you don't have a migraine now, right?" Grayson looked directly into Lindsay's eyes and could see they weren't right.

"Grayson, it's fine. No, I don't have a migraine. I probably just need some rest."

"Then rest you will get. I'm staying here tonight. I'll sleep on the couch so no fuss necessary."

Lindsay could tell there was no wiggle room. He wouldn't negotiate. "Is this because you are worried about me, afraid I'll sue you, or because you know who broke in today and you are worried they will be back?" As soon as Lindsay said the first option, she regreted it.

"The last two are ridiculous. Look, people have been breaking into houses lately and you aren't up to par to take care of yourself. There isn't anything for them at my house so no reason to worry about that. I do have to run next door though. I'll only be gone a few minutes. You have your gun, right? Not that you could probably hit your target right now."

Lindsay pulled her gun from under the cushion and aimed at the picture on the other side of the room. "Want to bet?"

"Sit still. I'll be back in a few minutes." He walked out shaking his head.

Lindsay laid the gun down and rested her head on the back of the couch. Naturally her mind started to whirl with questions, but she was exhausted. She blew it off as the events of the day and the fall down the stairs.

She didn't realize how exhausted she was until she was vaguely aware of being carried up the stairs. As she started to stir, she heard the comforting words, "Sssshhhh, I got you." She mistook the voice to be Sam's.

Grayson tucked her in bed and, as he was pulling the covers up, she grabbed his hand and pulled him down saying, "Stay with me tonight."

61

Lindsay opened her eyes but didn't move. She was aware it was still dark. She was aware she was sleeping on her side, which she rarely did. She was aware there was an arm around her and she was wearing a t-shirt and underwear. She moved the arm away from her as slowly as possible then, with the same speed, slipped out of the bed. It was too dark to see his face, but there was only one person that arm could belong to. Grayson Tyler.

She made her way to the bathroom and shut the door, without turning on any lights. She leaned her back against the door and tried to figure out what had happened to land Grayson in her bed. Her head seemed clear. She concentrated on her memory. She usually had what could be described as scenes playing in her head, like slow motion of past events.

Now she was only getting two second flashes of images. Muscular arms. Six pack abs. Falling down the stairs. The gun in the back waistband of the masked man, which she hadn't noticed herself. Grayson's face with passion all over it. Smoky eyes. Sweat. No, she did not. She couldn't have slept with him. She couldn't have had sex with him. The flashes were from before. Someone else. It couldn't be. Her mind had to be playing tricks on her.

She was sore as she moved toward the shower

and turned the water on as hot as she could stand it. She was sure that was from the fall that had knocked her out. She couldn't get her memory to show her anything other than flashes. She wasn't sure what was happening, but it did scare her a little. She may have to go back to her regular doctor, which meant leaving the lake house. She stayed under the hot water until it turned cold.

She dried off and wrapped the robe tightly around her before walking into her bedroom. She let out the breath she hadn't realized she was holding. The room was empty. The bed looked like it had barely survived a battle. The sheets and comforter were piled in and around each other. Did she really sleep with Grayson? Yes, she had. Did they have sex? But he wasn't here. Maybe she just had a dream. Yes, that was it.

She dressed conservatively and made her way to the kitchen where amazing smells greeted her. She stopped in the doorway and just watched. Grayson was making breakfast and singing. Singing! He was dressed in jeans and a tight-fitting t-shirt. Without stopping or looking at her, he held a cup of coffee out. Lindsay took it and didn't bother with thanking him, but did wonder how he knew she was there. He was beyond intuitive.

Grayson finally stopped and turned around with two plates of omelets and hash browns. "Good morning."

"That's yet to be determined."

"Aww, not a morning person. I forgot."

"Ahhhh, an irritating morning person who functions before coffee. It's irritating."

"I guess that's why that thought started with 'irritating morning person', because we are irritating?"

Lindsay just looked at him. It was too early to have a conversation. She wasn't sure how she was going to ask him if they had sex, let alone try that without any caffeine in her system.

"Would you like to grab the coffee and follow me to the deck for breakfast and the sunrise?"

Lindsay nodded and followed. Once they were seated and Grayson had taken his first bite, Lindsay couldn't stand the silence. "So, nothing interesting happened last night, huh?" She instantly blushed. Why did she have to say that, of all things?

Grayson saw the blush, but didn't acknowledge it. Instead, he raised his eyebrow, smirked and said, "Depends what you call interesting?"

All Lindsay could do was look down at her plate. She didn't dare open her mouth for fear of saying something stupid again.

"I guess last night gave you a hearty appetite?" Grayson wasn't smirking now. He was serious.

"I didn't realize how hungry I was." Lindsay looked down at her plate and realized she had eaten the entire omelet along with the hash browns. She had never finished the whole thing before. She wondered if it was her appetite or just that she didn't know what to say, so she had kept eating.

"I'll get us more coffee." Before Grayson could say anything, Lindsay was up, grabbed both cups and headed for the door.

As she stepped back out onto the deck, she heard Grayson's cell phone ring. She realized she had never heard it ring before. But it brought back the memory of the time she overheard him talking to someone about things taking time and he was working on "it".

He looked at the phone, punched a few keys and put it in his pocket. Standing up quickly, he asked Lindsay if she was okay.

"Yes, I'm fine."

"I have to go. I have to take care of something. I'll be back shortly. Sorry to eat and run."

"Go take care of what you have to. I'm fine." Lindsay watched Grayson sprint across the yard and disappear into the short strip of woods separating their houses.

She couldn't help but think that may be the last she sees of him. She had a feeling of dread. How could she have slept with him? She was a fool.

Lindsay gathered the dishes and took them inside. She took her time putting them away. She had to figure out how to talk to Grayson about what had happened. She felt like a fool and worse yet, she felt like she betrayed Sam. How would she ever face him again. Then reality set in. She didn't owe Sam anything. He had lied to her. She hadn't seen or talked to him in two months. For all she knew, he had moved on. Then she felt badly again. She shouldn't have stayed away from Sam this long. He was probably hunting for her all this time. She decided it was time to go back and face reality. This hiatus just left her more confused and added more players to this crazy, deceitful life.

She would leave right after she talked to Grayson today. Feeling better about her decision, Lindsay collected the trash and opened the kitchen door to go out when she almost stepped on something. She had to stop and think of the date. It was the date of her father's death. Or fake death. The dead flowers were delivered every few years. This meant someone knew she was here. She had never figured out who delivered these dead roses. She was finally convinced she wasn't crazy and the things that had happened were planned by someone. The question is who? Without her connections, she would be less likely to figure it out. She needed to go back.

Lindsay would need to tell Robert about the lake house to use his resources. She wasn't sure she could trust Jack yet. She had no idea where things stood with him and Robert, or herself. Maybe she could bring Sam and Derek here to plant listening devices and cameras. She was determined to figure this out and if it meant going back to reality, she would.

She put the dead roses in the trash can on the side of the garage and looked around to see if anything else were different, but everything was as it should be. Now, time to put her life as it should be. She headed upstairs to pack.

62

Lindsay had just finished packing the last of her things and was ready to take it all downstairs when someone started banging on her door. She held still. She didn't want to talk to anyone, except Grayson, and she would stop by his house on her way out. She just wanted to close up things here and get on the road.

Now along with the banging, she heard Grayson yelling her name. She stood still, unprepared to talk to him just yet. Then decided to let him in to get this over with. Before she could make it down the stairs, he was in. She continued down toward the living room.

He stepped into the living room and looked up at her. As she started to speak, he put his finger up to his lips, in a gesture for her not to say anything. He nodded his head in the direction of the deck. She came down the stairs and followed him out. He put his finger to his lips again and took her hand. She started to speak but he stopped her by the look he gave her and the shake of his head. He led her to the boat. Once onboard, he told her to give him a few minutes. He needed to check for something.

Lindsay watched as he went over the boat looking for what she suspected was listening devices or cameras. Placing them on a boat would be difficult, or at least difficult not to find on this size boat.

Once Grayson was sure there were no devices, he told her he wanted to go toward the middle of the lake for safety. She didn't say anything but nodded in agreement.

Once they were half way between each shore line, Grayson cut the motor. He didn't waste any more time, "Kendall, I'm not who I told you. Well, I am, but I didn't tell you everything. I am a contract diver, but my real job is at an agency." He paused for a moment. He could see Lindsay's face change but wasn't sure what the look was.

Lindsay had been holding her breath from his first sentence. She was right, there was more to him. If he said he was hired by Robert Langston, Jack Cooper, Sam Stone or one of the others from her organization she was going to shoot him right then. She had been sitting with one hand behind her back the whole ride, not knowing what to expect with his behavior. Now she pulled her gun from her waistband, aimed it at him and stood in one motion. She was fast and Grayson hadn't expected it.

"Whoa, Kendall! I'm not going to hurt or threaten you. I'm not sure who you are, but I think you might be in danger." He held both of his hands up.

"Turn around." Grayson did as she requested. "Where is your gun?"

"It's the same place you had yours, apparently."

Lindsay pulled his gun from his waistband. Setting it well out of his reach behind her and keeping her gun on him, she patted him down. She pulled his knife from its strap on his right calf and another gun from his left calf. She also took his cell phone from his pocket.

"You are well prepared for something. The suspense is killing me. Who do you work for?" Her sarcasm flowed easily.

"I work for myself, as I told you. Right now, I'm under contract by the FBI. I'm investigating an FBI agent. I would prefer to talk to you face to face, if you don't mind."

"Turn around slowly. I would prefer that also, to gauge your lying face." Lindsay was furious.

"Apparently, you aren't who you say you are either. That makes us both liars, Kendall. Who are you?"

"What makes you think I'm not who I said I was?"

"You're professionally trained. You wouldn't have that kind of training unless you are law enforcement or criminal. You're not a criminal. That leaves one option."

"Back to your story, Superman. The suspense is killing me. What do I have to do with any of this?"

"I think you're a target. I know someone has been in your house. Not once or twice, but a few times. I know someone is trying to make you crazy. I think you were poisoned."

"How do I know it's not you?"

"Wait. You think it was me doing this?"

"I haven't figured it out yet, but I'm getting there. Since you know so much, who is behind this?"

"I'm going to need you to tell me who you really are, Kendall."

"Tell me what you know about me."

"I only know what you've told me. Your name is Kendall James, a ghost writer and you are here writing your next novel. But we both know that's not true. I should be hearing back any minute on who you really are. You aren't on my radar, Kendall. But I do think you are involved in some way with who I'm investigating. I think he's here for you."

"Who?"

"It would be easier for me to tell you if I knew who you really are."

"Why didn't you wait until you got confirmation on who I am before bringing me out here to have this little chat that is going nowhere quickly?"

"Because I believe you're in danger."

Lindsay laughed. "You do know this sounds ridiculous. You don't know who I am, but you know someone has been in my house, driving me crazy and poisoning me, but you won't tell me who. It could be you."

"How well do you know Lance Becker, really?"

"Only that he's a game warden. He wants more from me than friendship and he randomly checks on me since he is usually around the area checking on Mrs. Wigley. You already know this."

"I'm investigating the man you know as Lance Becker."

"What? Are you saying he isn't Lance Becker or that he isn't a game warden?"

"He's FBI. He's on leave. Extended time off. He has a stellar record, until recently. Things have been 'off' but before an official investigation could be opened, he took leave and disappeared.

I tracked him here." Grayson's phone rang. They both looked at it.

"Don't touch that. You aren't making any sense. If he's FBI, how do you figure I'm in danger? You're trying to tell me that I'm in danger from an FBI agent? Then who are you to try and protect me from an FBI agent?" Grayson's phone rang again.

"That's probably important." Grayson looked at his phone expectantly.

"Who is it?" Lindsay was watching him closer.

"My boss."

"Ha. I guess that could be the call telling you who I am. You are on a need-to-know basis, and that you don't need to know. I do, however, need to know why I am in danger from an FBI agent." Now Grayson's phone chirped. Lindsay cocked her head at him, but didn't say anything.

"If I knew who you were, I could piece that together. I was hopeful that you may be a little more forthcoming in who you are, which would answer a lot of questions. And I thought you trusted me by now."

Lindsay turned to stone. Grayson softened.

"Ahhhh, now I get it." Lindsay was boiling under the cool exterior.

Grayson didn't understand what Lindsay meant by that and before he could ask, Lindsay's phone rang. Only four people had this number. Keeping her gun pointed at Grayson, she pulled her cell phone out. Holding it up so that she was still looking at Grayson beyond the cell screen, she saw Drama Llama's number. She put her cell back down. That call would have to wait, although she didn't doubt it was important.

Lindsay picked Grayson's cell phone up. His screen was locked. "Give me the code."

"I can't do that. Now if you want to tell me who you are, we can work from there."

A boat in the distance caught Lindsay's eye. "We have company. Talk fast. Who is Lance Becker, really?" Lindsay also lowered her gun but kept it pointed at Grayson. She was too far away for him to make a move before she could fire.

"He's an FBI agent. I already told you. Do you know Charlize Torrington?"

"No, I never heard that name. Who is she?"

Before Grayson could answer, she heard her name being hollered from the approaching boat over a defining speaker.

"Kendall! Kendall!" Lindsay looked over to see her "Aunt Ava" waving and hollering her name, from the game warden's boat, being driven by Lance Becker.

Lindsay looked at Grayson, then back to the boat. "That's my aunt with Lance. Does he know your real identity or intentions?"

"No."

"Walk toward me and stand slightly in front of me, facing them." Grayson did as she instructed. Lindsay never took her gun off of him and once he was in front of her, she put her gun in his back. "Pick your cell phone up and give it to me."

Grayson did as instructed. She flung his phone toward the cabin of the boat, just as the boat with Ava pulled alongside Grayson's boat.

"Aunt Ava! What are you doing here? I wasn't expecting you."

"I called you from the airport and left you a voicemail. You didn't get it?" Lindsay hadn't seen

Ava in a few years but she knew instantly there was definitely something wrong. Lindsay hadn't received a call and the look on Ava's face was obviously trying to tell her something.

"Lance, thank you for bringing Aunt Ava out. Is everything okay?" Lindsay faked her smile for their sake.

"Yes, everything is great. I stopped by to check on you and met your aunt. I figured you would be happy to see her and she mentioned how much she loved boating, so here we are." Lance was moving onto Grayson's boat as he rambled, which he wasn't one to do. Ava wasn't making a move, but instead was very much frozen in place.

The hairs stood up on Lindsay's neck. This was all very wrong. Just as Lindsay was about to ask Lance how he knew where she was, a lady appeared on the other boat. Lindsay noticed the gun in her hand immediately. It was pointed at Ava's head as the lady moved to stand directly behind her.

"Well, well, well. It's nice to meet you, Kendall Thomas. Or do you prefer to be called Lindsay, or Miss Phillips?" The lady gave her a beaming smile. Lindsay could see the evil in her eyes.

Lindsay looked at her, then at Lance, then back to the woman with her gun pointed at Ava's head. "Call me whatever suits you. Do I know you?" Lindsay recognized the striking green eyes. She was the lady Lindsay had seen in Charlotte at the downtown location during lunch and then again at the hotel.

"No, honey, you do not. But you should. Lance, tie them up, Mr. Sexy first."

"You said you only wanted to talk. Don't do something stupid, Charlie." Lance gave her a threatening look.

Grayson didn't miss the connection between Charlize and Charlie and he had taken pictures of her and Lance together. He had sent them off to his boss and already gotten word back on her identity. Lindsay didn't make the connection between the two names, nor did she appear to know her.

"Shut up and do as I say. It will be more enjoyable talking when I don't have to watch their hands reaching for things they shouldn't."

As Lance moved toward Grayson, Lindsay put both her hands behind her back. Lance tied Grayson up then turned toward her. No one had spoken a word as this was done. Everyone was busy watching everyone else, waiting for their moment. It never came.

As Lance approached her, Lindsay turned her head toward her shoulder and whispered, "You are FBI. What does she want?"

With his back to Charlie, Lance whispered back, "Just to talk. She's crazy, but not a killer. Just play along with her. I won't make yours tight."

"Leave my gun."

"That's enough! Lance don't get any ideas." The lady was calm, cool and collected. Quite sure of herself. She and Lindsay stared each other down.

"Lance, throw her gun in the water, along with her cell phone. Where is Mr. Sexy's cell phone?"

Grayson looked at her then at Lance. "It's at the house. I have a radio on board so I don't bring it."

As Lance turned back around to face Charlie, she shot him. He went down, blood quickly soaking his shirt from the bullet to his chest. Ava screamed and covered her face with her hands.

Charlie pushed Ava forward onto Grayson's boat. "Get down in the cabin and don't let out a peep or you're next."

Charlie waited for Ava to go below then moved onto Grayson's boat as well. Gun now pointed at Lindsay.

Grayson was the first to speak. "What do you want?"

Charlie looked at him and studied him for a moment. "Listen, big guy, you're next if you dare flinch a muscle. This doesn't have anything to do with you, so I'll need you to join Auntie Ava. Be a good boy and do as instructed and you'll leave here alive."

Lindsay and Grayson exchanged a look. Grayson stood up and moved backward toward the stairs. Once there, he moved backward down the stairs and into the cabin.

"Well, isn't this fun. I've waited a long time for this. Now I'll need you to answer some questions. Lie and you die. It's pretty simple. I'm sure you have lots of questions, and if you don't die first, I'll answer yours after. Now, my first question, do you know who I am?"

Lindsay looked at her, studying her face. This wasn't going to end well for one of them. "No. But I did see you in Charlotte during lunch and followed you through the store. Then you were at my hotel."

"You and that photographic memory of yours. Tell me about your family." Charlie wasn't hiding her contempt and apparent hatred.

"I suspect you know as much as I do. What do you want?" Lindsay hated games and this woman was playing one.

"Just answer the questions as asked, then it will be your turn."

"I have a mother and brother, who I have no relationship with. I have Aunt Ava, that you've met."

"No father?"

"He died when I was very young." Lindsay didn't like where this was going.

"Have you enjoyed the dead roses every few years?"

"Who are you? Answer me and stop toying with me! You are too young to the be the woman who supposedly died in the car with my father. Are you her daughter?"

"Oh no, honey. Nothing like that. Tell me, what are your intentions where the organization is concerned and don't play stupid."

Charlie had been pacing slowly as she inter-rogated Lindsay. She was now close to Lance and looking down at him.

Lindsay took her time "I'll return to work when my vacation is over."

As Lindsay finished answering, Charlie turned around to face her. Just as she opened her mouth, Lance kicked his leg up enough to knock Charlie off balance, taking her by surprise.

Lindsay got her golden opportunity. She yanked hard on her hands as she stood up and went for Charlie. Lindsay rammed herself into Charlie, taking them both down.

While Charlie had been interrogating Lindsay on deck, Grayson had Ava get his cell phone that had landed under the cabinet. He had told her the code to unlock the phone. He had three messages from his boss, Deacon Wyatt. The first message read, *"Kendall James = secret ops agent Kendall Thomas aka Lindsay Phillips reported missing."* The next message was, *"On our way."* Then one more message, *"Death hit on you. Get out of there. Unknown internal or external."* Grayson had Ava text Deacon back, *"On water. Lance down. Charlie & Kendall on boat. Both armed."*

After reading the messages and having Ava respond, he had her work on freeing his hands. Just as she got his hands free, he heard scuffling above on deck. As he made his way on deck, he saw Charlie shove Lindsay backward. As Lindsay fell backwards, she fired Charlie's 9mm at her. The impact blew Charlie back and off the boat. Lindsay landed on the opposite side of the boat, knocking her head on the railing. She slumped forward and didn't move.

Grayson rushed to Lindsay's side. She was out cold and bleeding mildly from her head. Checking her over quickly and finding no bullet holes, he hollered to Ava. As she ran up the stairs onto the deck, Grayson instructed her to grab a towel and hold it on Lindsay's head where she was bleeding. Holding Lindsay and waiting for Ava, Grayson heard helicopters. He looked up to see three coming toward the boat. He also saw several boats headed toward them. He glanced at Lance whose eyes were closed. He wasn't sure if he was dead or alive, but no time to check. He instructed Ava to keep pressure on Lindsay's head until help arrived. Then he jumped overboard.

63

Ava couldn't stop pacing. She replayed the day in her head over and over. The doctor tried to talk her into getting checked out but she wouldn't leave Lindsay's bedside. She hated seeing Lindsay hooked up to all the machines. All of them making strange noises. She never did like hospitals. This hospital in Atlanta, where Lindsay was flown, was huge.

There were two FBI agents standing outside of Lindsay's hospital room. She wasn't sure why they were there. They had arrived while Lindsay was having tests done, which took way longer than Ava was comfortable with. She had called Drama Llama; the only contact Ava knew to call concerning Lindsay. He had caught a flight and should be there any minute.

Ava looked up to see a tall, dark, handsome older man talking to the FBI agents. He appeared to be arguing with them and wanting to see Lindsay. The FBI agents weren't letting him in and Ava could see how furious the man was getting. He wasn't the first one who had tried. Ava wished she had spoken to Lindsay more often and kept in closer contact over the years.

Drama Llama finally arrived and was escorted to a private room, where FBI agents searched him and confirmed his identity. After that, he was led to Lindsay's room, where Ava immediately hugged him, relieved to have someone there with her.

"I'm so glad you came. Thank you. I don't know who all these people are or why the FBI is guarding this room. I was told they are searching the lake house as well and I can't go back there until they are done. I'm not leaving Lindsay's side anyway. Do you know who these people are? I'm sorry for rambling."

"How is she? Is she.... going to be okay?" Drama Llama's voice cracked mid-sentence and he was having a hard time looking at Lindsay lying in the hospital bed.

"I'm sorry. I should have told you that first. They said it's too soon to tell much. The test showed that she's hit her head a few other times lately, but I'm not sure why or what happened. I don't do well with medical stuff. It all makes me queasy and I don't understand it."

"Ava, I'm not sure who else is in Lindsay's life. I know she has two boys and an ex-husband. I wish I were more help."

Ava was wringing her hands and couldn't seem to stop. "You know her family doesn't know about me. If the boys see me, they will know I'm not her real aunt. I don't want to lose her."

"I don't have any answers for you. I'll do everything I can to vouch for you, but it depends on who shows up."

They sat in silence, one on each side of the bed. Neither knowing what to say and not liking the unknown with Lindsay.

Finally, Drama Llama had to ask. "Which name was Lindsay using while here and what was she doing?"

Ava didn't know how much Lindsay had shared with him and didn't want to overshare and have Lindsay upset with her later. But Drama Llama knew all of her names since he made the fake IDs and histories for each one. She remained quiet for a moment.

"We need to have our stories straight in case we get questioned." He looked at Ava with more of a pleading look than anything. "She called me while she was 'out of town' and had me help her with something in Philadelphia. I don't have details but I know the FBI was involved. I'm not sure which side Lindsay was on. I don't want to say anything to jeopardize her in any way. I'm the only one who knows who you are. Help me out, Ava."

"They will know about her alias, Kendall James, because of the lake house. It's in both of our names."

"As far as you know, I'm only her friend and the only mutual friend we have. We met when you were in Baltimore doing artwork and that's how you know Lindsay. You and I met through her years ago. Nothing about fake IDs or aliases."

"I understand. I'm not sure how I will explain both of us being on the deed to the lake house or why we have the same name." Ava was worried.

"Tell them you know her as Kendall James, and that she hates Kendall so goes by Lindsay sometimes."

"The whole town thinks we are related. If people start snooping around, they may find more than I am comfortable with."

"It's okay, just tell them the minimum. Play stupid."

"Well, where this gal is concerned, aren't we?

I don't think either of us knows much about the real Lindsay Phillips."

64

"Get Deacon Wyatt in here now!" Sam shouted at the two agents in front of him.

"Mr. Stone. You will need to stop yelling. Agent Wyatt will be with you shortly."

"I need to see Lindsay, now." Sam ran his fingers through his hair for the fifteenth time.

"Sam, if you don't stop doing that, you are going to lose your hair. Calm down my friend. I know this is tough." Derek hated to see Sam go through this. Now that they had finally found Lindsay, it was getting impossible to keep Sam out of her hospital room. The doctors wouldn't speak to him and he needed Deacon to confirm who he was.

Robert came through the door with the same impossible look Sam was currently perfecting. "No word yet?"

Derek spoke up. "No, not yet. Where's Deacon?"

"From what I understand, he's on his way. There was a mess at the scene. I'm not getting much information either. Joe is working on getting what he can. Jack is in touch with Agent Preston. I can't stand this waiting."

"If it weren't for you...."

"Sam, not now. It's not going to help anything right now." Derek put his arm on Sam's shoulder.

"Sir, you and Mr. Stone have been approved

to speak with the doctors. If they approve, you can visit Lindsay. She's not awake though. I just want to warn you. Follow me, please."

"Thank you, agent." Robert and Sam followed the agent out into the wide corridor and onto the elevator. They finally arrived in the area of Lindsay's room. They could see the two FBI agents, but not into her room. A doctor came out to speak with them.

"I'm Dr. Davis. Lindsay's neurosurgeon. She has suffered a TBI, traumatic brain injury. We believe it is mild but won't be able to tell until some of the swelling goes down. Most of the swelling appears to be external at this time. She is sleeping comfortably. We will keep her in this state until we feel it's safe to gradually reduce the medication and awaken her. We do not believe that she is in serious condition but we won't know any more for a few more days. Do you have any questions?

"Are you saying she's in a medically induced coma? Is that the same thing?" Sam didn't want to hear the answer but had to know.

"It's a step under a medically induced coma. She is breathing on her own at this point. It's more of a deep sedation than an unconscious state. Keeping her sedated will help her to relax and get plenty of rest, which is the most important thing for her recovery. All of her organs, including her brain, are functioning."

"I understand. Will she make a full recovery?" Again, Sam was hesitant on the answer but had to know.

"We expect her to make a full recovery, unless there are any changes. Only time will tell at this point."

Robert was deep in thought. "When you say she is expected to make a full recovery….she has a photographic memory. Will she loose that?"

"That's what you are worried about right now?" Sam's fists balled at his sides and he could feel his blood pressure rising.

"I'm only trying to gauge her recovery expectation."

Sam couldn't look at Robert and didn't wait for the doctor to respond but, instead asked if they could see her.

"I will allow you to see her but remember, she is still fragile and shouldn't be upset. We don't believe she can hear you, but it's hard to say in these cases for sure. We encourage positive communication at this time while in her room. Thank you, gentlemen." The doctor nodded to the two FBI agents outside of Lindsay's room.

As Sam and Robert approached Lindsay's room, Deacon intercepted them. "Sorry, I was held up. I see you are going in now. I will need to speak to both of you after your visit so please let the agents at the door know to find me when you are done." He shook both of their hands and nodded to the two agents. One of the agents went in to Lindsay's room and escorted a man and a woman out. Deacon greeted them as they walked by Sam and Robert. Sam recognized the man but couldn't place him.

Sam and Robert didn't say anything to each other as they each went on separate sides of Lindsay's bed. Neither could stand seeing her lay in that bed. Motionless and lifeless. Robert's eyes teared up several times while looking at Lindsay and he would walk over to the window and stare out while he got himself under control. Sam let the tears flow. He was sure his heart was breaking in two. His heart rate sped up and he could feel his body getting hot. He became overwhelmed with emotion a few times and put his head down on Lindsay's bed. Robert didn't miss the way Sam's body would shake when he did this. They were both concerned with all the machines. There seemed to be a lot of monitors for her "mild condition".

They had been in Lindsay's room for about an hour when Derek came in and asked Robert if he would come with him. "I understand you want to be here when she wakes up, but the doctor has assured us, it won't be for at least the first few days. Deacon wants you now."

Sam had been holding Lindsay's hand and slowly let it go. As he turned toward Derek, Derek noticed the haunted look in his eyes. Derek would have to have a long talk with him. He already knew he was beating himself up for what Lindsay was going through, had gone through, of which they really had no idea yet.

As Robert and Derek walked out of Lindsay's room, they both acknowledged the FBI agents guarding her door. Neither were sure why that was necessary, but they were both glad for them.

Derek led Robert to the top floor of the hospital where it appeared there were lots of doctors' offices and conference rooms. They walked through double wooden doors where Deacon and a few other agents were in deep conversation. Seeing Robert, Deacon excused the other agents. Once they were all out, Deacon asked Robert to sit. Derek nodded to them and closed the door behind him as he left the room.

"Who were the man and older lady leaving Lindsay's room as Sam and I went in?" Robert was direct and expected an answer.

"That was David and Ava. They are being questioned as we speak."

"Do David and Ava have last names?" Again, Robert was direct and expected an answer.

"They do. I have some other information that I have to share with you."

65

"Robert, I'm sorry to have to be the one to tell you this. Let me start with saying that there were other people on the boat. Ava, who you passed and asked about, was there. An FBI agent, who was on leave and is under investigation was also there. He was shot and is in surgery. His prognosis isn't good. There was one other person there. Charlize Torrington." Deacon waited for his reaction.

Deacon wasn't surprised that Robert had no reaction. It was his life's work. After only a moment, Robert asked the inevitable, "Where is she now?"

Robert and Deacon studied each other. "I'm sorry, Robert. She didn't make it. She was shot and fell overboard. I'll give you a few minutes if you need it." Deacon stood up.

Robert didn't react, only shook his head in agreement to having a few moments. Deacon walked out.

Derek was waiting in the hallway. Joe walked up at the same time and joined them.

Joe studied Deacon's face for only a moment. "Did you tell him about Charlie?"

"Yes, I told him I would give him a few minutes. How is he going to take this?" Deacon studied Joe's face.

"I'm not sure. Once ballistics come back..."

Joe bit into his bottom lip.

"Someone want to fill me in on who Charlie is?" Derek was lost.

Both Deacon and Joe looked at each other. "Someone Robert knew very well." Joe didn't look at Derek, but instead looked past Deacon as he answered Derek.

"Like a girlfriend, an employee, an enemy? What?" Derek was still in the dark. He knew there was someone at the scene who died but that was it.

They were both silent for a moment. Joe needed to change the subject quickly, "Derek, can you call Jack? I left him a voicemail earlier. Find out where he is and how much longer before he gets here."

"Yeah, sure. Then I'm going to check on Sam." He walked off. Apparently, Charlie was another mystery. So much secrecy in this world. Robert's world. Derek again understood why Lindsay disappeared. Although, he wasn't sure now that Lindsay was exercising free will at the end. If he and Sam found out she was being held against her will, there would be hell to pay for someone. As he made his way back to Lindsay's room, he tried a few different scenarios in his head.

"Guys." He nodded at the FBI agents as he went into Lindsay's room. Sam had his head down on the bed next to his hand that was holding hers.

"Any change?" Derek asked in just above a whisper in case Sam was sleeping.

Sam raised his head. "No. Have you gotten any more information?"

"Very little. You know that there was a boating accident on Lake Dare. There were a few other people on the boat, one of which was the older lady you saw leaving here as you came in. The only thing I know about her is that her name is Ava James. No real affiliation yet. She's still being questioned. I'm sure we'll know more once that is done. There were two other people on the boat. An FBI agent and a lady named Charlize that goes by Charlie. That's all I have. Jack should be here in about an hour. Joe is back from the scene. It's all pretty hush-hush and I'm sure they are trying to put the pieces together."

"Do we know the FBI agent? Who's Charlie? A friend of hers?"

"Sam, I don't have those answers yet. Except that Charlie is known by Robert and he had a close affiliation with her, although I don't know exactly what."

"Has anyone notified Lindsay's sons yet? I doubt Lindsay would want her mother and brother contacted yet."

"Yes, Deacon had the FBI contact her ex-husband to let him know. The boys are still at the ranch."

"If I was willing to leave Lindsay right now, I would go see them."

"My guess is they don't know any more than you do. Let's not forget, you are dead to them." Derek gave Sam a sympathetic look.

"Do you know where the man that was here earlier is? I want to see him."

"I believe he's being questioned. Want me to see if I can find him?" Derek would do anything to get out of the room. He hated seeing Sam hurt and hated seeing Lindsay lying in the bed, lifeless.

"Sure."

66

Derek headed to the top floor of the hospital in search of the man Sam wanted to talk to. Luck was on his side. He found him sitting outside one of the conference rooms just off the elevator. The lady wasn't with him.

Taking a seat next to him, Derek stuck his hand out and introduced himself. "Hey, I'm Derek, a friend of Lindsay's. And you are David?"

Drama Llama looked at him and reluctantly shook his hand and introduced himself, "I'm Dave, also a friend of Lindsay's. I saw you with the man who I think was Sam Stone earlier?"

"Yeah, actually, I was looking for you. He wants to talk with you." Derek gauged Dave's face.

"I thought he died? I don't understand."

"Yeah, that's kind of a long story. He can tell you about it. Want to take a walk?"

"Do I need to tell someone where I'm going? I mean, the agent told me to wait here. And I want to be here when Ava comes out." Dave wasn't sure what to do, but he was sure he wanted to know more. He just wanted to talk to Lindsay to find out how much to say. Sadly, that wasn't going to happen.

"Nah, I gotcha. I'll take the blame."

Dave looked at Derek suspiciously. "Are you an FBI agent?"

"Nope, not really. Just think of me as a friend of Lindsay's."

They took the elevator down to Lindsay's room, not knowing what to say to each other.

Dave walked into Lindsay's room to come face to face with Lindsay's supposedly dead boyfriend for the second time. He didn't know whether to sit, stand or punch him. It just occurred to him that he hadn't ever really had a conversation with Sam. What was he supposed to say now? He wasn't even sure if he liked the guy. Sam had disappeared on Lindsay several times during their relationship, without any explanation. He was supposed to have died, yet, here he is. Standing in front of him, alive and well. It was too much for Dave. He could only imagine how Lindsay would take it. He nodded toward Lindsay and blurted out, "Does she know you aren't dead?"

"Yes. I saw her a few months ago. She's known for a while. Thanks for being here. I assume you are better friends than I ever knew, or do you work with her?"

"We're friends." He wasn't ready to tell Sam much more than that and wasn't going to tell Sam or the FBI he was her source for fake identities. That would be up to Lindsay, if….

"Do you mind if I ask how you made it to Atlanta so quickly? Or were you with Lindsay all along?"

"No, I wasn't with her. I didn't know where she was until Ava called me to let me know she needed me. Ava needed me."

"Who is Ava? I mean, to Lindsay? I've never met her or heard of her." Sam was watching Dave closely.

"She's on old friend of Lindsay's. It was her lake house that Lindsay was staying at. Do you know who Charlie was?"

"Charlie? Never heard of him." Sam looked at Derek.

"Charlie was a female. She was on the boat and was shot. She died at the scene. That's all I know about her. Not sure what she was doing or who she was." Derek shrugged. He wasn't going to say much in front of Dave. Maybe Jack would shed more light on who Charlie was.

"Care to tell me why you aren't dead? Are you FBI?"

"It's classified." Sam looked at Dave and felt badly for keeping him out of the loop. There was no other way to handle his questions, since no one really knew much about Dave. It was obvious he cared for Lindsay, but Sam wasn't sure how much he already knew about Lindsay. Sam suspected it wasn't much. Unless, Dave was working for her. Apparently, he didn't know Lindsay as well as he thought he did.

67

The next morning, Robert was in Lindsay's room when Jack came in, looking tired and beat up. He had no idea what he was walking into. Jack had tried to get information out of Agent Preston, but everyone was tightlipped, including the FBI. Jack didn't like not knowing what to expect. Especially this, because it involved Lindsay and Charlie. It was going to be a mess, and he was probably going to get the blame for Charlie's death. He had spent half the night being interrogated by the FBI and this was the first chance he had to see Robert.

"Robert, I'm sorry. I don't know what to say."

"Jack, nice of you to join us." Robert hesitated, "I'm sorry. That was uncalled for."

"Robert, I tried to find Charlie. I didn't think she would go after Lindsay. And I didn't see it coming to this."

"What did you tell the FBI?"

"I told them what we had always agreed to. It's ironclad, Robert. I know we haven't agreed on some things lately, but it's not only your lie. It's mine, too."

"You don't have as much to lose as I do." Robert felt himself tense up and his pulse quicken. He hated having this conversation.

"I am an accomplice. I don't have the number of humans to lose as you do. But this is my life now. And I owe you."

"Did you tell them Lindsay is my daughter?"

"Of course not! But they did ask why you are so close to her." Jack clenched his fist. He took a few deep breaths to calm himself. Had Robert really just asked him that?

"What did you tell them?" Robert studied Jack's face.

"We've rehearsed this so many times, I believe our lies. I hate to ask right now, but what are you going to tell Lindsay about Charlie?"

"You sound sure that I will have to tell her anything. I hope she wakes up from this with no repercussions."

"Lindsay's tough. She'll make it through, but you didn't answer my question, Robert."

"I don't know."

"I wish you would have told her sooner. This complicates so many things. The hole just keeps getting deeper and deeper. You need to start being completely honest with Lindsay. Maybe if you had, we wouldn't be here. Figure it out, Robert, before she does."

"I don't need this right now, Jack. I really don't."

"None of us do, but here we are. Sam is going to be asking questions."

"I know. I don't need to be reminded."

"He's also, potentially going to be your Son-In-Law someday. He's probably the best one for you to be allies with to help you get through this with Lindsay. Make friends with him."

68

An hour later, Sam walked in to find Robert sleeping in the chair near Lindsay's bed. "Long morning? I hear Jack's arrived, finally."

"He got in late last night and spent some time being interrogated by the FBI."

"Imagine that. How long did they have you?"

"Not as long. Jack had more involvement with Ch…Lindsay."

"And you were going to say Charlie. Who was she?"

"Let's not do this now. Not here." Robert stared at Sam, then remembered Jack's words. "I'm sorry. We'll talk about Charlie but not here, not right now. I'm going to go to the hotel and shower. I'll be back in a few hours. Do you need anything?"

"Other than answers, no." Sam followed Robert out of Lindsay's room. But returned a few minutes later.

Sam settled into the chair near Lindsay's bed. He talked openly to Lindsay, even though he wasn't sure she could hear him.

"Linds, we are all here waiting for you to wake up. The boys are good. They're still at the ranch. I miss you, Linds. I need you to come back to me." Sam stared at her face. She seemed so peaceful, but he knew that was far from the truth.

He wasn't sure how long he had been lost in thought when Lindsay's lips moved. She was tying to say something. He moved closer, "Talk to me,

Linds. I'm here." He waited.

"Gray." She said it but Sam wasn't sure he heard it right. Her eyes were still closed and she appeared to be talking in her sleep.

"Linds, wake up. I'm here." Sam watched her face, but that was it. He pushed the button for the nurse. He kept watching and waiting.

"You called. What's going on?" The nurse didn't stop moving toward Lindsay as she came through the door.

"She was just talking! I thought she was waking up."

"What did she say? Did she open her eyes?"

"She just said, 'gray' but didn't open her eyes. What does that mean?"

"It's hard to say. She may be dreaming or still loopy from the sedation. I'll get Dr. Davis. He'll want to know." She continued checking Lindsay's vitals, then left the room.

Sam held Lindsay's hand and kept talking to her. He talked about some of the memories they had made. He talked about the boys. He talked about everything, except work and Robert Langston.

Dr. Davis, along with his nurse, entered Lindsay's room a few minutes later. "Good morning, Sam. How's our girl today?"

"I'm not sure, but I hope she's improving."

"Great. I'll take a look. Can you please excuse us for a few minutes while we check her out? Go grab a coffee or breakfast. We'll let you know when we are done."

Sam reluctantly left. He didn't go far. He wished he had left the blinds open in Lindsay's room. Now he couldn't see what they were doing.

The waiting was impossible.

Dr. Davis reduced Lindsay's sedatives and watched her vitals closely. He checked her pupils to see that they were looking better than yesterday when she was brought in. Things were definitely looking up for her and she was improving. He loved giving the family and friends good news.

Just as he turned to leave, Lindsay spoke again. "Gray." Dr. Davis leaned down closer to her. "Lindsay, do you know where you are?" He waited. Nothing. He tried again. He waited. Nothing.

He gave the nurse instructions and told her he would check back in later. He called Sam into Lindsay's room. "She's improving. We still won't know much until the sedative wears off more. In the meantime, we are still monitoring her closely."

Sam was ecstatic with the news. He texted Derek and told him. He asked Derek not to tell the others just yet.

Derek came into Lindsay's room with Robert and Jack right behind him.

"Anything yet? Has the doctor been in?" Robert looked expectant.

"She's doing okay. He was just here. Not much change." Sam spoke slowly and glanced at Derek with a warning look.

"Sam, let's give Robert and Jack some time to visit with Lindsay. Let's go eat." Derek understood the warning and couldn't wait to hear more about what was going on with Sam.

"Nah, I'll stay, thanks. Jack, why are you here? We all know Lindsay isn't your favorite person."

"Sam, Lindsay has been part of my life since she was fifteen. We may not always agree on things, but we have a history and I deeply care about her."

"Enough to shoot her." They glared at each other.

"Okay, Sam, let's go. You aren't doing this here. Not now." Derek put his arm on Sam's back and guided him out the door.

"Where's Deacon. I want more answers."

Derek waited until they were well beyond the agents standing outside Lindsay's room. "Tell me what happened with Lindsay earlier."

"She didn't open her eyes, but tried to talk. She said, 'gray'. Not sure what she meant. The doctor said she's improving but they are still watching her closely. Have you found any more about what happened or where Lindsay's been?"

"Deacon wants to see you to fill you in. He doesn't know Lindsay is Robert's daughter and I'm gonna' ask you not to enlighten him."

"Why not? If he knows, and investigates Robert, then maybe Lindsay will get the truth she's been looking for so desperately. We all will."

"That's not your decision, Sam. It's Lindsay's. There are things that Robert needs to tell her before she hears it from others. It's not your call."

"Whose side are you on? Robert's had more than enough time to tell her and yet, he hasn't. Part of how we got here, in case you missed any of this."

By now they had reached the conference room Deacon was using as a temporary office. "C'mon on in." was the response to their knock.

"Hey Deacon. Thanks for seeing me." Sam shook Deacon's hand and slumped into the chair.

"Rough morning? How's Lindsay?"

"Same. What happened out there yesterday?"

"As you know, we are still investigating and

it may take some time. But what I do have is that Lindsay was enjoying a boat ride when the game warden showed up with Ava. Apparently, there was someone else on the game warden's boat. Charlize, who shot the game warden. Charlize was shot by her own gun. She died. We don't have much on her, yet. If the game warden pulls through and when Lindsay wakes up, we'll have more. What we have right now is mostly Ava's testimony which is sketchy. She's quite frazzled."

"Who is exactly is Ava?" Sam didn't look convinced.

"Ava James. An old friend of Lindsay's."

"Why is the FBI involved in this? Because of the game warden? I thought it was an FBI agent that was shot, not a Game Warden."

"I'm not sure where you are getting information but I will caution you, Sam, be careful who you get information from. This time, you are correct. The Game Warden is an FBI agent. And why we are involved."

"That makes sense. Who is Charlize?"

"The information on Charlize is incomplete and still under investigation."

"What is the game warden, FBI agent's name?"

"That is classified. I'm sorry, Sam."

"Can you at least tell me if 'gray' means anything? Lindsay did say that earlier. She didn't wake up or open her eyes. Just said 'gray'. Any idea?"

Deacon appeared to be in deep thought. After a minute of complete silence, he simply said, "No."

"Thank you for talking to me, Deacon. I appreciate it. If you think of what that could mean, please let me know." Sam stood up slowly and walked out with his head down.

Deacon watched Sam leave. He remained standing and calm for two minutes after Sam left before he slammed his fist down on the table. He would need to be there when Lindsay woke up to protect both of them. He thought of cutting off anyone going into her room, but that was a fight he wasn't sure he was up for. It would also make them dig deeper. He didn't want that, either. It appeared that none of them knew more than he did. He didn't take Lindsay for someone to blurt information out, but if she were talking in her sleep... he couldn't have that.

69

Once Sam left Lindsay's room, Jack gave Robert a hard look, scrutinizing him. "That internal battle is a bitch, huh?"

Robert only glanced up at Jack for a second before looking at Lindsay lying still in the bed. "How did it get so out of control? We had a hard and fast plan that worked for everyone else. The most planning went into her. The one person it should have worked for, is now lying here in a hospital bed. Her tenacity and determination are admirable. I just wish she had used them on something…someone else. Where did we go wrong?"

"Underestimating her. I'm not sure where she got her morals and integrity from. By all means, she shouldn't have them so strongly." Jack stopped when Robert raised an eyebrow at him. "I'm just saying it's not like she was surrounded by people who taught her well. You were gone and we all know what a wretched woman she calls 'Mom' is, along with her useless brother. Face it, Robert, she would have been better off with you."

"You know I tried everything to make that happen. I was out of time and out of options. If I had taken her, it would have raised too many flags. She wasn't safe. They would have found her. I was able to stay out of view, she wouldn't have been. She needed to be a kid, with a normal life."

"There never has been anything 'normal' about Lindsay. Have you figured out how we are going to protect her now?"

"We?" Robert didn't miss the term Jack used.

"Yes, we. Robert, we've been in this a long time. I've always had your back. And Lindsay's. The truth is, I'm the closest person on earth to Lindsay. I know more about her than anyone. And that's not sayin' a lot right now with….this." He spread his hand toward Lindsay lying in the bed, motionless, with no apparent life and the unknown of her memory. He questioned how much her life was going to change with finding out the truth of her father and now, potentially losing her memory. He hated this. "Robert, the only way to protect Lindsay is to be completely honest about everything with her. You don't have a choice now."

"What if I was to disappear?" Robert had his finger across his bottom lip, one arm across his mid-section, supporting his other arm.

"What the hell are you thinking? She would hunt you down if it took the rest of her life. She wants answers. She wants truth. Even if you were to die this time, she would want to see your body and do full x-rays, blood samples and whatever else she could think of. You can't do that to her."

"If it's the only way to protect her, I will. And I see you've thought of the possibilities as well?"

"As much as you have, no doubt. Listen, Lindsay isn't five anymore. She's a smart woman. She can handle herself. She's proven that the past few months. Who knows, she may want to take them down herself."

"That's what I'm most afraid of. We haven't been able to. What makes you think she could?

Never mind. It's not an option."

"Look how close she got to Caro Aguilar. She got closer to him than anyone before her. Up close and personal."

"I can't put her in front of them." Robert massaged his temples.

"They know Lindsay Phillips to be your daughter. Not Kendall Thomas. Do you think they are still watching her after all this time? That may be their mistake. What if Lindsay Phillips were to die in that boating accident yesterday?"

70

Lindsay had woken up during the night but hadn't moved. She laid completely still, waiting for her foggy brain to clear. There was little light, just enough for her to see she was in a hospital room. Nothing was making sense. She slipped back to sleep.

She was in and out all day. Things were still more fuzzy than not. She could hear people talking but wasn't sure if she were awake or dreaming. She didn't have the strength to completely wake up and couldn't figure out why. She tried several times to piece things together but nothing made sense. She also couldn't stay awake long enough to wrap her head around anything, including the conversations happening around her.

Ava had arrived at noon and had stayed out of sight of everyone going in and out of Lindsay's room. Finally, in the late afternoon, she was able to slip into Lindsay's room without any of the others. She knew she wouldn't have much time before one of them would be back.

Ava hurried to Lindsay's side and began talking to her. She was talking fast and rambling again. But if there was a chance Lindsay could hear her, she was hoping it was now. "Lindsay, you have to come back to us. I don't know what to tell them and they have so many questions. I don't know who is who and how much they know about you. I'm playing the scattered old lady well, but they are relentless in their questioning. Sam is going to the house in a little while. He has more questions than anyone. I need you to come back and help me and I don't want to leave you right now. Oh, Lindsay, come back." Ava quieted her voice when she realized she was talking louder than she had meant to. "I'm pretty confused on what happened as well and not much of it is making any sense. I had just gotten to the house when the game warden showed up. He was friendly and looking for you. A few minutes later, that awful lady, named Charlie, showed up and forced us to drive to the game warden's office then onto his boat. You know the rest from there. Am I supposed to tell them all what happened? I can't keep playing dumb forever. I've told them I'm too shaken to remember."

Not seeing any indication that Lindsay heard her, Ava gave her hand a squeeze and left before anyone could stop her and ask more of those questions she didn't have answers for.

Lindsay tried to open her eyes while Ava was in the room and talk, but she couldn't manage. She heard what Ava said and remembered the boat. Then she drifted out again.

71

Sam and Derek had requested Ava and Dave meet them at the lake house. The FBI had cleared out and allowed them in. Ava and Dave had noticed the FBI had gone into the house next door but weren't sure why. The boat that Lindsay was on, wasn't brought back to Lindsay's dock, but instead taken by the FBI.

Sam greeted Ava and Dave with a head nod to Ava and a handshake to Dave. Derek followed suit. Ava invited them in and told them to make themselves at home. She went to the kitchen and brought ice water for everyone.

"That's a beautiful view of the lake. How long have you lived here, Ava?" Derek tried to sound nonchalant but wasn't sure he pulled it off.

"I lived here for several years, then met a man from Europe and got married. I've been gone for several years now. I just couldn't part with this home, though and visit often."

"So, you don't live here now? Were you here with Lindsay this whole time?" Sam didn't bother with the nonchalance and jumped right in.

"No, she's been here by herself for a few months. I talked to her not long after she arrived and promised to come visit. Well, that didn't work out as planned. We should be enjoying our time together not her laying in a hospital. I should have come home right when she did." Ava was wringing her hands again and it was clear she was heartbroken.

Derek recognized the signs and didn't want to push her. That explained some things. "Do you mind if we look around? I hate to ask as I know they've already invaded your privacy."

"Please make yourselves at home. There isn't much of anything personal here of mine or Lindsay's, except clothes."

Sam and Derek looked around downstairs. They both thought it was strange that there was no food in the kitchen or the pantry and the refrigerator looked like it hadn't been used. They headed upstairs. Everything was pretty meticulous as anyone who knew Lindsay would expect. Sam looked for the places that he knew Lindsay liked to hide things. He knew most of her secret stash places, but he had never been here.

At a glance, there was nothing of any importance. Sam looked around expecting to see a telltale sign as someone who knew her. He opened the closet in the master bedroom and was surprised there were no clothes. They finished looking around the rest of the upstairs. Then when satisfied they hadn't missed anything, rejoined Ava and Dave in the living room.

"Where was Lindsay sleeping?" Sam waited for Ava to answer.

"I assume in the master bedroom. When I got here, I was only here for a few minutes before the game warden showed up. I should have figured out something was wrong right away. Lindsay's suitcase was at the top of the stairs on the landing, but she was no where to be found. The car was still in the garage but the food had been emptied out, too."

Derek piped up, "It doesn't look like Lindsay, or anyone for that matter was living here. Are you sure she was staying here? Did you call her to tell her you were coming?"

"Yes, I called her the day before, but she didn't answer. I left her a voicemail. I may have called the wrong phone now that I think about it. With her having so many, sometimes it's hard to keep track."

"What do you mean by that?" Derek and Sam both look confused.

"What? Oh, I mean I forget her number or my friends' numbers or my husband's half the time, with so many to remember."

"Do you know what all the FBI took out of here?" Sam was not convinced she was telling the truth.

"Only her suitcase. I don't think there was much else really. Oh, they found something in the garbage and took that."

"Okay, is there anything else you can tell us, either of you?" Derek stood with his arms behind him, assuming an innocent, open stance.

They both looked at Derek, then at each other, then at Sam, then out the window, then back to Derek. Finally, Dave spoke. "Nothing that we can think of. They really aren't telling us much."

"Care to tell us what you guys know?" Dave asked with more confidence than he was feeling. He studied Sam.

"I think you both know more than we do at this point." Sam let out a long breath. His frustration was apparent and he wasn't trying to hide it.

"That lady, Charlie, that died, did you know her?" Ava had a worried look before they even answered her.

"No, neither one of us had ever heard of her. Did Lindsay know her?" Sam asked Ava because she was on the boat and witnessed what happened.

"No, but she knew Lindsay. I couldn't hear everything they said because the lady sent me down below, but I did hear her ask Lindsay if she enjoyed the dead roses. And I heard her ask Lindsay what her intentions were toward the organization. What organization was she referring to?"

"I don't know." Derek stood up and thanked Ava and Dave for speaking with them."

As Sam stood up, he looked out on the lake, then turned back to Ava. "Do you know the neighbors?"

"It's been a while since I lived here so I'm not even sure who is still here. I only talk to the caretaker once in a while, usually if he needs something. He lives two houses down. The last time I spoke with him was right after Lindsay got here. He said he wouldn't be by again unless one of us called him."

Derek and Sam thanked them again and headed toward their rental truck. Derek was driving and as soon as they hit the main road away from the lake, the only thing he could think to say was, "Nice place. Lindsay is on the deed."

Sam looked at him surprised. "You already checked? What else?"

"She's on the deed as Kendall James, niece of Ava James."

"Then how do you know it's Lindsay?" Sam was getting more frustrated with every new detail they found.

"We all have our 'go-to' place and this was Lindsay's."

"Damn Robert Langston!"

72

Deacon took six hallways, three elevators up and down to different floors and the stairs in between on his way to Lance's private hospital room. He knew where Robert and Jack were and he wasn't taking any chances on anyone following him. Sam and Derek were at Lake Dare with Ava and Dave.

When Deacon walked in, Lance was sitting up in the bed and staring out the window looking like he was contemplating the magnificence of the cement wall within his vision.

"Just happy to be alive?" Deacon leaned against the wall just inside the door, putting one foot on the wall and crossing his arms across his chest.

"I'm not so sure about that. Where's Charlie? No one will tell me anything."

"Has anyone been in to see you that would know?" Deacon raised an eyebrow.

"Only the FBI guys guarding my door. Am I under arrest or surveillance?" Lance turned to look at Deacon for the first time.

"Do you have any reason to be arrested?" Deacon still stood against the wall, not giving any indication of how this was going to go.

"Depends." Lance was tired. He wanted all this over with and to get back to life as he knew it.

"On?" Now Deacon was curious.

"On how much you know."

"Or maybe how much you want to tell me."

"I'm not a betting man but if I were, I would say you are on the verge of knowing everything I do."

"Lance, I'm listening. I know there's more to this story than meets the eye. Tell me the truth." "Where's Charlie?"

"I'll ask the questions, then, depending on your answers, you can ask your questions when I'm done. What were you doing at Lake Dare as a game warden?"

"Look, I'm going to make this easy for you. I was at Lake Dare as a game warden because Charlie was blackmailing me. She had gotten through the FBI system and changed some information to make it look like I did things that I didn't. Which, as you know, put me under investigation. I took a leave of absence so that I wasn't working on any more cases that she could make look suspicious." She also threatened my sister's life. I know she was having my sister watched, because I followed the guy who is following my sister. That's a fact. My sister is a COO for a major company. I believe she may have planted someone inside the company as well. She threated to ruin her then kill her and make it look like suicide."

"Okay, hold on. How do you know Charlie?"

"We worked together on a few cases five years ago. I was undercover. Then we crossed paths a few times."

"Did you have a strictly professional relationship?"

"Yeah, she wanted more but I always refused.

Although she was good at what she did, she was high maintenance, demanding and unreasonable most of the time."

"Why you?"

"She said we were good together and I figured it was her way of getting close to me in hopes of changing my mind. I don't know how well you know Charlie, but she's used to getting her way, in any way that she can. The woman is evil behind that polished exterior. She also knew how to get to my sister."

"What did she blackmail you to do?"

"Drive Kendall Thomas crazy, make her think she was losing her mind. She never told me why and I couldn't find any connection between the two of them. I sure didn't think it was to make Kendall vulnerable then kill her. I think she was looking for something to blackmail Kendall with also. I had gotten into Kendall's house a few times, looking for something, anything. She was too smart to leave anything hanging around, which I told Charlie. I think she got desperate and when she found Kendall at Lake Dare, alone, she figured she had her chance. She started blackmailing me a couple of weeks before Kendall got to Lake Dare. She had me break into her house, but there was nothing there worth blackmailing her over."

"How do you know Lindsay Phillips as Kendall Thomas?"

"Charlie told me her real name. I had heard of Kendall Thomas and knew of her reputation but hadn't met her until this."

"What did you do to Kendall? What did Charlie do?"

"I tried to get close to her, partly to see what

I could find for Charlie, to satisfy her delusions and to protect Kendall. Charlie did have me drug her a few times. One night in particular, I stayed at Kendall's waiting to see what Charlie was going to do. She never showed up. Kendall didn't know I was there. Then she would just have me move things around so Kendall would go crazy, knowing someone was watching her. Stupid stuff really."

Deacon was taking all this in and watching Lance closely. "What was Charlie's motivation?"

"I told you, I couldn't figure that out. I couldn't find a connection between them. I know Charlie's known Kendall for some time. You and I both know people are typically motivated by jealousy and/or greed. Charlie was eaten up with jealousy but wouldn't, or didn't, elaborate on it. I don't know if it was personal or professional. I could never tie the two together."

"What happened on the boat?"

"I had gone to Kendall's to check on her. I had seen a flower arrangement receipt in Charlie's car. The delivery address was Kendall's lake house. I wanted to see the card on the flowers, hoping for a clue to something. When I got there, I was greeted by Ava James, Kendall's aunt. Not two minutes after I got there, Charlie showed up. She had to have been close by already because she hadn't followed me. She had us get the game warden's boat and take it out on the lake. Once we got near Kendall and Grayson, she had me tie them up, saying she just wanted to meet Kendall face to face. I left Kendall's hands pretty loose. I know the guy on the boat was Grayson Tyler, Kendall's neighbor. Just as I turned from tying them up, Charlie shot me. As you know, a gunshot to the abdomen will take one down. I was in and out but at one point, Charlie got close enough to me for me to knock her off balance. I heard the gunshot but wasn't sure who shot who. Next thing I know, I'm on a helicopter, then waking up here."

"The Kimber was Charlie's gun?"

"Yeah, that's what she carried."

"How much do you know about Grayson Tyler?"

"Not much. I didn't think he was a threat of any kind. Assumed he was just Kendall's neighbor. He and Kendall had a little gunfight over a coyote. He checked out clean so I didn't give him much thought."

"I think that will be enough for now unless there's anything else you want to add."

"Where's Charlie?"

"That's classified." Deacon wanted to tell him, but couldn't until after the investigation closed and in case Lance thought of anything else.

"Get Charlie to admit she was blackmailing me. And please check on my sister."

"I can promise you we'll check on your sister." Deacon didn't move.

"Who is Grayson Tyler? Is he FBI or are you here because of me?" Lance was tiring and flinched as he adjusted himself in the bed.

"Grayson Tyler is just a short-term neighbor." Deacon started for the door when Lance stopped him.

"One more thing. I do know there was a female Charlie had frequent contact with. Her name came up a few times on her caller ID. Maria De-Marco. I was in the process of checking her out, but nothing yet."

"Thanks. Get some sleep."

73

Deacon made several calls after his visit with Lance. Deacon found Robert, Jack, Sam and Derek in Lindsay's room later that evening. As he entered her room, he was greeted by nods from everyone. "No change?"

They each looked at him and all nodded in the negative. "Do any of you know Maria DeMarco?"

They all thought for a moment and again, shook their heads. Jack was the one to ask, "Should we?"

Deacon took his time in responding. "Don't know yet. Her name came up, but nothing back from forensics. Thought it might be faster to find her if any of you knew her."

As Deacon turned to leave, Robert stopped him. "How is Lance?"

"He's recovering. Still weak and not well enough to be fully questioned." Then he nodded and left.

Robert knew a liar when he saw one. Deacon was lying. Where else would he have heard of Maria DeMarco. Robert waited about five minutes. "Jack and I are going to grab some food. What would you guys like?"

Both Sam and Derek declined. Robert pulled Jack along with him out of the room. When they were far enough away from the agents outside of

Lindsay's room, Robert gave Jack a hard look. "Do you know Maria DeMarco?"

Jack shook his head.

"Find out who Maria DeMarco is. And find Lance's room. See if he's awake. Text me when you have the info. His room is probably guarded as well."

Once Robert and Jack were out, Sam let out a breath. "Find out who Maria DeMarco is and find out if Lance is awake. Text me when you find out anything. And I need the truck keys."

Derek nodded. "Where are you going?"

"To the Lake House. There's more to this. Wait. Do you have a number for Dave and Ava? They aren't at the lake house. They are still here at the hotel, right? They can come here. I don't want to leave Lindsay alone right now."

"Yeah, I'll text them on my way out."

"Thanks, Derek. I don't know what I would do without you."

"Hey, she's going to be okay. She'll have answers when she wakes up. And she will."

Sam nodded and took his seat beside Lindsay's bed. After Derek was out of her room, Sam started talking to Lindsay again. "Come back to us Pretty Lady. We can get through this together." He continued to talk to her until he dozed off.

He wasn't sure how much time had passed, but he was awakened by Ava, who put her hand on his back. "Sam. We're here."

Sam thanked them for coming in and informed them there was no change with Lindsay.

"She just needs time. She's going to be fine, Sam."

"That's what everyone keeps saying. Do either of you know Maria DeMarco?"

They both shook their head. "Should we?" Dave's voice was a little strained and Sam noticed.

"I don't know. Her name came up but not sure how or why. You've never heard Lindsay talk about anyone with that name?"

"Nope. But remember, I've been gone for quite some time." Ava looked directly at Sam and was relieved to be able to finally give him an honest answer.

Sam noticed Dave wasn't looking at him and was, very much, looking uncomfortable. "Dave, are you sure you don't know her?"

"I don't think so. I'm trying to think if I even know anyone named Maria. Or DeMarco."

"Okay. I think I need to get some fresh air. Are you guys able to stick around for a little while and sit with Lindsay until I get back? Shouldn't be more than a few hours."

"Sure, we can stay. We wanted to visit with Lindsay anyway but don't want to crowd you all." Ava was relieved she could visit. She didn't mind the few hour drive but hated that she couldn't stay with Lindsay as much as she wanted while she was here.

"Sam, who are Robert, Jack and Derek? Are they FBI? Does Lindsay work for the FBI?"

"It's complicated. The less you know, for right now, the better off you are. I wouldn't ask any questions. It keeps you 'safe' so to speak."

"Interesting. Okay, I'll take your word for it." Dave couldn't wait for Lindsay to wake up and clear this up and he needed to know what do to, especially now.

"Best that way, Dave."

Sam thanked them again and headed out the door.

Ava and Dave waited for five full minutes to make sure no one came in. "There is definitely a lot of things we don't know going on. This is crazy." Dave raised an eyebrow and took a deep breath.

"Maybe the FBI is only involved because of the game warden. We shouldn't jump to conclusions." Ava put her hand on Dave's arm. "Lindsay will have answers."

"Yeah, I will." Lindsay hadn't moved but she definitely spoke. Ava and Dave rushed to the head of the bed to be able to hear her.

"Lindsay?"

"Don't tell anyone I'm awake. Please?" Lindsay was speaking softly and they had to strain to hear her. "Listen closely. You have to promise me that you won't tell any of them I'm awake and talking."

"We promise. Are you okay?"

"Sore laying in this bed." Lindsay was speaking slow and faint. But she kept talking as she looked at Drama Llama, "Keep denying you know Maria. Do you have anyone you trust in Baltimore to clean out your shop and move it to a storage unit immediately? Move it all to a storage unit for now under a different name. Do not tell them you know Maria. Understand?"

"Yes, I know people who can do that. But can you tell me why? Are you FBI?"

"Just do as I say. DL, I need you to go outside and watch for anyone coming back." Dave kissed Lindsay's cheek and left.

Now Lindsay turned her head slowly to look at Ava. "Keep telling the story you are. Play dumb.

I also need you to ask Sam about his dying and coming back. Got it?"

"Yes. What else can I do?"

"Nothing. Where is Grayson?"

"I don't' know. Agent Wyatt ordered me not to tell anyone anything about him or to even say his name. You've been saying 'gray' in your sleep. Sam's asking what it means."

"Don't tell him."

"Does the doctor know you're awake?"

"Sort of."

"Lindsay, I hate to ask, but do you have your memory? I overheard them talking about it."

Before Lindsay could answer, the door opened and Drama Llama came back in. "Derek's here."

Ava moved away from being so close to Lindsay's face, but kept her hand on Lindsay's head and stroked her hair, like any loving aunt would do.

"Hey. Good to see you guys. How is she?" Derek whizzed in and smiled. He seemed to be the only positive one of them all.

"Same. Has the doctor been in to see her?" Ava asked for lack of anything else to say.

"I'm sure, but not while I was here. Do you know where Sam is? I left him a while ago."

"He said he would be a few hours. He didn't say where he was going." Ava looked uncomfortable. Dave kept his eyes down.

"Are you guys okay? No one has probably asked you since they're all drowning in their own thoughts."

"Yeah, we're good. Just lots of questions that no one wants to answer."

"Ask away. If I can help you, I will."

"Who's Charlie?" Ava asked quickly in hopes

he would spit it out.

"I don't know. That's apparently classified."

Drama Llama took a turn. "Who are Robert and Jack?"

"Friends of Lindsay's." Derek shifted from one leg to the other, realizing he shouldn't have been so friendly.

"How did Sam come back from the dead?" Ava knew Lindsay told her to ask Sam himself but she couldn't help but take advantage of this situation.

"That you would have to ask him or Lindsay, when she wakes up. And she will. Just have to be patient with head injuries." Now Derek wanted to change the subject. "Tell me again how you're related to Lindsay, Ava. I'm not sure I heard this story."

Lindsay figured this would be a good time to intervene. "Gun. Gun. Gun." This time she moved around in her bed, but didn't open her eyes.

Drama Llama moved to Lindsay's bedside near Ava while Derek moved around to the other side close to Lindsay's face. "Is she awake?"

"No, she's been talking in her sleep."

"You sound pretty sure of that. What else has she said?" Derek gave Drama Llama a questioning look.

"This is the first time I've heard her but someone else, I don't remember who, mentioned it."

"What else has she said? I'm asking in hopes that it means she has her memory intact." Derek suspected they didn't know she had a photographic memory and he wasn't going to be the one to tell them.

Derek felt someone behind him and turned to

see Sam standing in the doorway. He hadn't wanted to interrupt the conversation. He suspected that most of them were tiptoeing around him and he was tired of it.

They all turned to look at Sam then. "The doctor said it's a good sign if she's talking in her sleep. I just wish I knew what some of the things meant."

"She clearly just said gun three times so maybe that's a great sign that she is remembering what happened on the boat, which means she has her memory intact." Derek was always trying to be positive.

"Maybe. Ava, Dave, are you guys hungry? I can stay while you go eat." Sam looked so lost it broke Ava's heart.

"No, thank you, Sam. We'll eat later. I know this may not be the best time, but since we have time, can you please tell me about your disappearance when you died? I mean what happened?" Ava was uncomfortable but told Lindsay she would ask. Now seemed the best chance of any.

"It's complicated, Ava. I wish I could take the circumstances back, but I can't. I really don't want to discuss it right now. I'm exhausted." Sam put his head down and didn't elaborate anymore.

Ava hoped that was enough for Lindsay. She wasn't sure what the purpose of all that was, but was sure Lindsay had her reasons.

Lindsay did get what she was looking for in Sam's answer. He didn't lie and he was sorry. She still hadn't decided if that meant that she could forgive him. The lies ran deep. Lindsay reminded herself again that the person you would take a bullet for is sometimes, the one on the other side of the trigger. Knowing who to trust was exhausting.

74

Lindsay's eyes fluttered and it only took a minute for her to keep them open.

"Well, well, well, I heard you were waking up. How do you feel?" Dr. Davis asked while feeling around her head with both of his hands.

"Alive. Barely. How long have I been here? The nurses won't tell me anything."

"One thing at a time. Let's run a couple of tests to see how things are looking."

Lindsay passed his tests with flying colors. "Can I get out of this bed? I can't remember ever lying down this long."

"Yes, if you are feeling up to it. Baby steps. Let the nurses help you stand up."

"Can you lock the door and tell the agents not to let anyone in first? I don't want anyone knowing anything right now." Lindsay was able to get up and be steady on her feet. She was able to take ten steps without getting lightheaded or nauseous. When the nurses tried to direct her back to the bed, she made her way to the reclining chair in the corner by the window. "All good signs, Lindsay. You should be able to leave by tomorrow."

"Please don't tell anyone. If they ask you questions, tell them a little more time. Only Ava and Dave need to know. As a matter of fact, just let them all think I'm still sleeping."

"Sure, I can do that. Doctor/patient confidentiality. Now, you have been here for almost four days. Do you remember what happened that brought you here?"

"I remember being on a boat but not sure who was there. I remember gunshots. I remember falling backwards. Do you know who was there?"

"No."

"Why are the FBI agents guarding my door?"

"There is an FBI agent that wants to talk to you before I let anyone else in. He says you know him, Special Agent Deacon Wyatt?"

"I know of him. Has he been around the last four days?"

"Yes. You definitely have an interesting group of friends and family."

"Who all has been in here?"

"Robert Langston, Jack Cooper, Ava James and David, Sam Stone and Derek something."

"A regular party. Sorry I missed it. And Special Agent Wyatt?"

"Yes, as a matter of fact, Agent Wyatt is on his way here. He left strict orders that once you woke up, he was to be the first to see you."

"I'm going to guess he didn't tell you why. It doesn't matter. I'll find out soon enough."

"Are you up for company?"

"I hardly would classify the FBI as company, but then again, they are more welcome than others. Please keep everyone except Ava and Dave out of here. I'll let SA Wyatt know."

"I was actually referring to everyone else, other than the FBI, but you've answered me." Dr. Davis had a kind smile and a great bedside manner.

"So, is my head fine? I'm not going to have

any long-term damage of any kind?"

"You shouldn't. How is your memory?"

"They told you, huh?"

"They did, but I also can see some variances in your scans. They are minor and most doctors wouldn't see them if they don't know what they are looking for. Your tests are normal. You shouldn't have any issues or problems. I do see that you've bumped your head a few times and they look recent. This is really why I kept you sedated. It was more for observation than anything else."

"Yeah, it's been a bumpy few months." Lindsay couldn't help but laugh at herself.

Dr. Davis chuckled. "I heard you have a great sense of humor. Glad to see it's still intact."

"In this life, one must have a sense of humor. If you can't laugh at yourself or laugh it off, you'll drown." It was at that moment Lindsay realized she may be taking things too hard and it wasn't good for her nor was it getting her anywhere. Maybe she would ease up on everyone. Her only other option was to kill them and start over, but that wasn't who she was. It was who they were. At that moment, she also realized that she would need to figure out who was really behind the scenes.

"Are you okay?" Dr. Davis's face not only showed compassion, but real concern.

"Yes, I am. Thank you for your excellent care Dr. Davis. I do appreciate it. I think I need to leave tonight if that is okay with you?"

"I will agree if you agree to a few more tests first. You seem to be as 'normal' as expected. Just take it easy and don't overdo it and you should be good. I would suggest you get a checkup in about six months or so. You may also want to consider a helmet if the road is going to continue to be bumpy." He smiled and turned to leave.

"Please don't tell anyone I'm leaving. Can you message Ava to be here later today. She's on my contact information I'm sure."

"Easy enough."

"Thank you, Dr. Davis. If you can meet me in radiology for those tests with the discharge paperwork, I would like to leave from there, without anyone knowing."

"I'll have a talk with Special Agent Wyatt and as long as he approves, we'll make it happen. You lead an interesting life, Miss Phillips."

75

Special Agent Deacon Wyatt knocked on Lindsay's door. He thought he heard her say to enter, but he wasn't sure so he knocked again. He didn't want to find her in an awkward position.

Lindsay opened the door without showing herself. "Special invitation needed?"

"Glad to see you up and about. No, just didn't want to walk in if you weren't…." Deacon's face didn't give anything away, but Lindsay grinned. She knew what he was going to say.

"Have a seat." Lindsay pointed to the chairs on the side of the bed. She didn't wait for him to get settled before she asked, "Where's Grayson?"

"Lindsay, I have to ask some ….."

"Yes, you do, but I want that one answered before we go any further."

"Fine. It's the least I can do. He's alive."

"Okay and where might he be?"

"That's classified."

"Deacon, I'm not playing this game with you. Was he there for me or Lance?"

"That's classified as well but I can say this, it wasn't you."

"Is he FBI?"

"Lindsay, I'm asking the questions." He gave her a steady gaze. "I can't imagine what you've been through and I respect that, but this is my investigation."

"One I knew nothing about but somehow got put smack in the freaking middle of!"

"You're right and I'm sorry for that. But you know I have to ask."

"Yes, you do, as do I. I hope I haven't lost my memory from the bumps to my head. All caused by your guys, I might add." Lindsay gave Deacon a straight look, with a blank expression and nothing showing in her eyes.

Deacon could see why Lindsay, or Kendall as he knew of her, had the reputation she did. She was all business, didn't pull any punches and knew what she wanted. "Okay, I will make you a deal. I will ask one question, then you ask one question. We'll take turns. Does that work for you?"

"Yes, as long as your answer isn't that it's classified. If you answer that way, I get another question. Does that work for you?"

Deacon laughed in spite of himself. "I'm quite sure that your head and memory are completely and entirely intact. Fair, but this could take a while."

"So be it. I'm not going anywhere yet." Lindsay stuck her hand toward Deacon, who just looked at it confused.

"You're kidding me, right? You want to shake on it?"

"No, I just want to touch you." Lindsay changed from a straight face to a seductive look in a split second. Then she couldn't help but laugh again. "Fool. Go."

"Can you tell me what you remember?"

"Most of my whole life. Where would you like me to start?" Lindsay couldn't help but give him the sweet and innocent look. "Now my turn. Who ….."

"No, you just asked me one." Now it was Deacon's turn to give her back the sweet and innocent look. "I would like you to start with how you met Lance Becker and Grayson Tyler."

"Damn, you're good, Special Agent. I met Lance Becker the night my neighbor at the lake, Mrs. Wigley, got into my house. She is old and delusional and thought she was in her own house. Lance Becker was out looking for her when he heard her yelling in my house. I met Grayson Tyler the night I heard a woman scream and run through my backyard. I had gone out looking for her. When I couldn't find her, I started across my yard when I realized someone was standing by my back door. There as very little light, but enough that I realized he had a gun pointed at me. We both fired. I shot him and he grazed my arm." Lindsay stopped and waited.

"You aren't going to leave that meeting right there. You have to continue to answer in full."

"He wasn't shooting at me. He was shooting at the coyote behind me. I didn't realize it was there and thought he was shooting at me." Again, she waited.

"Okay. Fair enough. Ask away."

"What was Grayson Tyler doing at the lake house as my neighbor?"

"He was involved with Lance Becker. Did you get close to either Lance or Grayson? When I say 'close' I mean, did you become friends or intimate with either of them? I'm sorry, Lindsay, I have to ask."

"Lance had continuously asked me out. He

would randomly stop by and bring coffee. Grayson and I became 'friends' so to speak. Did either Grayson or Lance know who I was, my true identity?"

Deacon didn't miss that she didn't answer the 'intimate' part of his question. "Good question. Yes, Lance did. Grayson didn't know who you were until the day on the boat. Did either of them cause you any harm or distress?"

"I'm not sure. My house was broken into several times. At first, I thought it was Mrs. Wigley's grandson or some camp kids who were bored. Lance led me to believe that they were breaking into other houses. Then I was accused of robbing the local jewelry store. I was poisoned on at least two occasions. I'm going to guess you found the dead roses in the trash can? I'll save you a question on those. Every few years, I got them delivered on the death anniversary of my father. I've never figured out who was sending them, until Charlie mentioned them on the boat." As far as Lindsay knew, Deacon didn't know Robert Langston is her birth father.

Lindsay gave Deacon a few seconds to take all that in before she asked her next question. "Who is Charlie?"

Deacon hesitated. He wasn't sure how much to tell her or how much she knew. "Charlie's real name was Charlize Torrington." Deacon studied Lindsay's face. He didn't see any recognition flicker there.

"Was?" Lindsay's face didn't change but the color drained from her face. "What happened?"

"She died at the scene. She fell off the boat."

Lindsay seemed to be trying to remember.

"How?"

"Lindsay, we can stop for right now if you are too tired."

"Tell me! I don't remember the last few minutes on the boat. I only remember Lance knocking her off balance and that's when I plowed my body into her. I don't remember anything after that. Oh God! Tell me! Did I knock her off the boat?"

"Lindsay, please calm down. Take a deep breath."

"Just tell me." Lindsay stared at Deacon and hissed through her teeth.

"From what I've been able to assess, you and she had a scuffle. You both had marks on you that indicated a struggle. She did fall of the boat, but the cause of death was fatal chest wound. We don't know who shot her but it was her gun."

"She was shot with her own gun? No, I need to know more about her and why she did what she did. How much do you know that you aren't telling me? Deacon, please do not lie to me. I doubt I'll get the truth out of anyone else. Why was she doing those things to me? Are you sure she's dead? Did you see her body at the morgue?"

"Yes, she's dead. I saw her body. I think we need to stop here. There are some pieces to this puzzle I haven't put together yet."

"No, I need answers that only you can give me. Please, Deacon?" Lindsay didn't try to hide her frustration.

"What are you not telling me, Lindsay?"

"I don't know. I have so many unanswered questions. Can you tell me why Grayson was investigating Lance? Or at least if it had anything to do with me. If Lance knew who I was, why didn't he say so or give me some indication? He was there for no good?"

"I didn't say Grayson was investigating Lance. It didn't have anything to do with you. But you became part of the equation where Charlie was concerned. I'm not sure why yet." He studied her face and believed she truly didn't know either.

Lindsay slammed her fist against the wall. She began to pace. After a full minute, she slumped into the opposite chair from Deacon and let out a sigh. "Okay, stop me if I'm wrong. Lance is not FBI and was being investigated by Grayson Tyler, who is FBI and both just happen to be at the same lake as me."

"Stop. I never confirmed nor denied if Lance or Grayson were FBI. I also never used the word investigate. I said involved."

"I'm not an idiot, Deacon. At least one of them is an FBI agent for you to be here. Unless, Charlie was. There is obviously something to this, with two FBI guards at my door. Lance is here somewhere in an undisclosed room, also guarded. And no one except Ava, me and you know Grayson was there. But now only you know where Grayson is?" Lindsay did wonder if she heard the word 'investigate' while she was sedated.

Deacon held her hard stare. "I didn't tell you that. Okay, go on."

"For some reason, Charlie has known me for a very long time and hated me, tortured me, and was probably going to kill me, and I have no idea why? Give me something, Deacon."

"Lindsay, I need to continue my investigation. You know everything I do, except what's classified."

"That, my friend, is a whole lot of nothing. I'm tired now. I need to lie down. Oh, and please don't tell anyone that I'm awake. I don't want anyone knowing just yet."

"I already gave Dr. Davis the go ahead with releasing you. I will need you to keep in contact with me, but somehow, I know you will."

"Because you have answers that I don't and I want them."

"Okay, Lindsay, thank you for your information. By the way, I never asked you why you disappeared?"

"How do you know I disappeared?"

"Robert Langston called me a while ago and wanted help locating you. Jack, Sam, Derek, and Joe were also not aware of your location. You disappeared. I declined, just for the record. I know you weren't kidnapped or forced."

"How do you know that?"

"If you were, it would have been the first thing you told me. Why were you hiding, or should I ask from who were you hiding?"

"I was vacationing."

"Uh huh. And why are you escaping through radiology tonight and don't want anyone to know you're awake?"

"I have my reasons for leaving without anyone knowing, but I told you, so there's that. I'm not hiding from you. So, again, I'm vacationing."

"And I'm the pope. See ya' soon, Lindsay. Feel better."

Lindsay pondered the conversation with Deacon as she climbed into her hospital bed. She decided Grayson was FBI because he was investigating Lance. Lance knew who she was and suspected he was working with Charlie. While she was sedated, she had heard conversations, but she wasn't sure if they were real or dreams and still couldn't make sense out of it all. Lots of it was too far-fetched, but so was her life.

She had just dozed off when she was awakened by Ava rushing in to her room. "I just saw Sam and the others leave the hotel and suspect they are their way here. They can't be far behind me. How are we going to get you out of here with all them here?"

"Go let the nurses know I'm ready for the test. I will leave from there and meet you in the back of the hospital by radiology. Is Drama Llama with you? Are you ready to head to the lake house?"

"Yes, and yes. I'll go now before they see me. Be careful." Ava rushed out.

Lindsay chuckled at the way Ava was acting so grandmotherly. She wasn't that much older than her but she seemed to have aged a lot since Lindsay last saw her. She did hope that silliness would end once she was back at the lake house. She had never had anyone baby her and didn't need anyone doing that now.

———

76

Sam, Robert, Derek and Joe had been sitting in Lindsay's room for almost two hours when they couldn't take the silence any longer. Robert got up and said he would go find a nurse to see how much longer Lindsay would be in testing.

Coming back in to Lindsay's room, Robert informed them she may not be back for some time. Just as they all decided to clear out and go for a walk, Deacon popped in, looking quite gloomy.

"Hey guys. I'm glad you are all here. Except Jack. Anyone know if he's coming in?"

"No, he had something to do so he probably won't be back today. What's going on?" Robert could tell something was wrong.

"Did any of you know Lance Becker?" Deacon waited for a response.

They all shook their heads. "I didn't think so. Well, sadly he has passed away. He had to be rushed back into surgery and well, he didn't make it."

They each said they were sorry and put their heads down. Each lost in their own thoughts of what that could mean to Deacon's investigation and none of them getting any answers. "Robert, can I see you in the hallway, please?"

"Sure." Robert followed Deacon out. The others wondered what that was about.

"Apparently, Charlie had worked with Lance

before. You aren't aware of this? You don't know of any cases they were on together or did you just not want to tell me and hope with Charlie gone, I wouldn't find out?"

"No, I don't recall. Unless he used a different name. I don't know anyone by the name of Lance Becker. Was that his real name or could he have used another name?"

"Naturally. Thanks." Deacon shook Robert's hand and walked off.

Robert stood in the same position, staring blankly at the white wall of the hallway. It was quiet here for a hospital. With Charlie and Lance dead and Lindsay unconscious, they didn't have any way of knowing what happened. If Lindsay doesn't regain consciousness and her memory, they may never know. He needed to talk to Jack more before Lindsay woke up. With Lance dead, his secret regarding Charlie may be safer than ever now.

77

Lindsay had her test done and met with Dr. Davis. He agreed not to update Lindsay's file with her release for two hours. It would look like she was still having tests done. At least this would give her a head start on leaving. She might be sneaking out, but she wasn't disappearing this time. They would know where she went.

Dave and Ava were waiting for her outside of the hospital, at the place she requested. Dave was driving and once Ava saw Lindsay, she got out and got in the backseat. They had brought Ava's car from the lake house.

"Ahhh, it's good to be sitting up and not laying down. Drama Llama, please watch for suspicious activity behind us. I may doze off and on."

"You got it." Drama Llama reached over and patted her arm. "I'm starting to feel like a get-a-way car driver. Would that be accurate?"

Lindsay looked at him with a smirk. "You call yourself anything you like. I may start calling you my ass saver at this point."

"I'm glad I can be here for you, Lindsay. Although…"

Lindsay interrupted him. "Please don't. Not now. I will admit there are a lot of strange things going on and sadly, I don't have answers for them.

We do have to talk about Maria."

"Yeah, what's up with cleaning out the shop and moving it into storage so quickly and quietly?"

"Is she still around? I'm going to say no."

"No. She disappeared right after I did that thing for you in Philadelphia. Basically, she said she was going to be doing a lot of traveling on the west coast for work, so see ya' later. I have a feeling I'm not going to like this."

"Did she have access to your computer system, specifically, the programs that you used for my IDs, rental cars and clothes list and where they were sent?"

"No. I guess it's possible she could have gotten into the system. She had only been to the shop a few times. Now that I think about it, she was there more right before your trip a few months ago. "

"How sure are you about who she is and what she really does for work?"

"I'm going with 'not sure enough' because she must have been involved in something if you're asking me all these questions. I mean, I thought I did. But, it's weird now that I think about it. She knew I went to the bar almost everyday to eat and she never wanted to come with me. She always had some reason and I never thought much about it. She was always such an easy-going person and carefree. I guess I figured it was just her way of giving me my freedom to do what I wanted."

"Did she ever tell you anything about her background, or did you ever meet her family? Anything?"

"Nope. Said her parents had died in a car accident when she was in college. She has a brother, but he's a doctor in Texas and never comes to visit her. She said she had never been married and extended family is spread out all over the country and not close."

"Next time someone tells me their parents died in a car crash while they were in college, I'm not buying it. Seems to be the lie of those who aren't who they say they are." She kind of chuckled to herself at the realization. "I wouldn't plan on hearing from her again. Sorry. She isn't who she said she was. She was involved with someone who, for reasons unbeknownst to me, was trying to get to me. Not sure if they intended to kill me or what the ultimate goal was, but here we are."

"Sooooooo, can you enlighten us on anything. Can you at least tell us who you work for?"

"I can't. I work for the good guys is about all I can say, but that's sometimes questionable, too. I do go undercover. With the alias's you give me, those are outside of the organization and personal. No one, and I mean no one, needs to know what you do. As a matter of fact, just stick to everything that you do that is legal. Never admit to anyone the illegal stuff. By the way, did you get the car in Maryland that I asked you to get?"

"Lindsay, that goes without saying." Drama Llama looked at her and wondered if they released her too soon. "Yeah, and you aren't going to like this. There was a tracker on it. I've never seen one like it. You wouldn't have found it. I'm not sure the detector would pick it up, but my guys are testing it. We've never seen anything like it. To the lake house, I presume?"

"Yes. At least there, I can control who comes and goes and still have some privacy. Let me know what you get on the tracker. Did either of you see the FBI go to the house next door at any time? Not Mrs. Wigley's but the other side?"

Ava, who had been quiet as a church mouse, spoke up. "Yes, they had the yellow caution tape up over there, too. I asked them why, but no one would give me an answer. Do you know why? I'm sorry, do you want me to call you Lindsay or Kendall. I guess while we are the lake house, Kendall?"

"Kendall would be best while at the house." Lindsay hesitated on answering if she knew why the Feds were at Grayson's. Damn it, she hated lying. "I'm not sure, but when we get back, I'm going over there. You said they had caution tape up? Damn, now everyone in town will be nosing around."

"The place looked like an ant hill that had just been disturbed. No one could miss the FBI agents crawling around our house, the neighbors and the boat. But you did specifically ask about the house next door. You don't have any idea, or you don't want to tell us." Ava was scrunching her nose in the backseat, even though Lindsay couldn't see it, Drama Llama saw her through the rear-view mirror.

Lindsay put her hand over her face. "Now I have two detectives with me." She shook her head. "Ok, you guys win. I'm an undercover agent for a secret organization. We do work for the FBI, CIA, Cartels and Mafia. We play both sides of the fence. Happy? Now pray you aren't ever sorry you know that." Lindsay had said it very casually and hoped they took her as being sarcastic.

Drama Llama looked at her, then back at the road, then back at her, then back at the road. His mouth opened and closed as much as his head turned back and forth. Ava was quiet.

"I knew it!" Drama Llama was almost drooling.

"Shut up and drive. I need a nap." Lindsay wasn't sure if they believed her but didn't care right now. She guessed the sarcasm didn't work as planned. She dozed off.

78

Drama Llama nudged Lindsay. "Hey, we're here. Lindsay?"

"I can't believe I slept that long. Are we good? No followers?"

"Nope. Nothing. Want me to go in and check the house before you go in?"

"Yeah, do that. Ava stay here. I'm going next door while I have time. No one is to mention anything about the neighbors to anyone other than me."

"Oh, here you might want these." Drama Llama handed her a gun and a cell phone.

She looked at them and smiled. "Good choice in firearms, my friend. How did you know I would need these?" She checked and was happy to see it was loaded. Not that she thought she would need it.

"Are you sure you don't want me to go over with you? Or do you at least want a flashlight?"

"See ya' in a few minutes." Lindsay opened the car door, went in the garage for a minute, then disappeared across the side yard, toward the trees separating her house from Grayson's.

She didn't bother to try the door, but started to pick the lock, when the door opened. She jumped back. She didn't expect that. Now, she drew her gun and walked in. She didn't turn any lights on, but instead waited only a moment for her eyes to adjust to the darkness. She silently made her way through the downstairs, then started up the stairs.

At the top, Lindsay stopped and listened. Not hearing anything but complete silence, she moved in to the master bedroom. Everything was quiet. She checked the rest of the upstairs. It was empty. She was alone.

Lindsay went to the fireplace and opened the tile drawer. She put her hand in to feel if it was empty. She felt the photos. Lifting them out of the drawer, she made her way to the bathroom. She locked the door and turned the light on.

She expected to see the same photos as before, but now there were more. There were several with Lance and Charlie together. This confirmed that Grayson was investigating Lance, who was working with Charlie. In the photos, Lance didn't look like he was enjoying being with Charlie. He looked angry in all of them. Charlie however, was smiling in a few of the photos. Her green eyes went from smoldering, to excited. This confirmed only a few things. But left her with more questions. If Grayson was working with Deacon, why didn't Grayson tell Deacon about the photos in the fireplace?

Lindsay had no choice but to meet with the guys.

79

As Lindsay entered her lake house, Drama Llama handed her a cup of coffee. "Thank you! You are so good to me."

"Yes, I am." Drama Llama gave her an expectant look.

"Ahhh, you want something. Seriously, why?"

"Because I'm your friend and I care about you. Lindsay, it's easy to see that you are full of chaos and uncertainty. I may not know much, but you aren't the fun loving, easy go lucky, Lindsay I've always known. What's going on? And don't tell me the less I know, the better off I am."

"The fact that you are my friend is all I need. If I tell you 'things', it isn't going to change anything, except maybe for the worse. There are things about my life that the less that know, the better off. I'm asking you, as my friend, to just roll with it. You can't do anything to help other than everything you have already done. I know it's confusing. I know it's complicated. One of the reasons I love you is because you don't complicate anything. But asking me questions that I can't answer or that have no positive outcome, is complicating things for me. I'm asking you not to do that. I know it's a big ask. Look, I promise you, that you are the best friend I have and everything you have done for me, is huge. Don't think it goes unnoticed. It doesn't.

But, please accept that I can only involve you so much."

"You know that you contradict yourself, right?"

Lindsay let out a breath. If only it were simpler. "I do. I know it's asking a lot."

"Okay, if that's how you want it." He shrugged and Lindsay could see the change in him and she didn't like it.

Lindsay slammed her hand down on the counter. Drama Llama jumped. "Damn it, Dave, it's not that simple. This isn't about trust, because you are the only person in my life, along with Ava, that I can actually trust right now. I'm not happy about it. I'm pissed if you want to know the truth. My life was rolling along just fine. Then I got obsessed with having to know the truth about some things in my life, and that's when everything got complicated. I don't want to drag anyone else down and knowing the truth isn't always black and white. It can be convoluted. And apparently, deadly. Please trust me on this and let it go."

"I just want to help, Lindsay."

"Don't you see, you are helping me. You are solid, trustworthy and I don't have to guess where we stand. That's what I need right now and that's what you are. Please don't let this change. Not right now."

Drama Llama didn't say anything but walked over to Lindsay and hugged her. They stayed that way for a few minutes. When Drama Llama let her go, he smiled and wiped away the wetness on her face. "Okay, Lindsay. We'll do this your way and I'll trust you."

Lindsay whispered, "Thank you." She bent

her head and walked upstairs with her cup of coffee.

Drama Llama stood there wondering if he should let it go as she asked him or if he should pursue this more. Ava interrupted him when she whizzed into the kitchen. She walked behind him to the coffee maker. She whispered to his back, "Well, that was warm and fuzzy and neither of us have any more answers than before. I guess we can just be here for her and whatever she needs."

"Yup, no choice unless we go against what she just asked of me. In the meantime, we know nothing when questioned by others."

"Well, we ain't lyin'." Ava shook her head and walked back into the living room. Drama Llama followed her for lack of anything else to do.

Lindsay washed her face in the sink then stood looking at herself in the mirror. She looked like crap. She made her mind up right then. She would gather the guys, ask the questions she had, then regardless of the answers, she would move on. She had to accept this life change and move on or it would destroy her. She needed to get back to living. Things were buried too deep. The truth would eventually come out. She had to believe that.

She didn't have to wait long. They got there faster than she calculated.

80

Lindsay walked down the stairs into the living room. All eyes were on her. They all stood as she walked down. Sam was the first to move. Lindsay held up her hand and he stood still.

"Please, everyone, have a seat. I know you have questions but so do I. You are now in my house. I will ask the questions, if you can't answer honestly, then please just show yourself to the door. I don't want any more lies. You all have been playing a game where there are no winners."

Robert, Jack, Joe, Derek, and Sam sat. Drama Llama and Ava had left as Lindsay had asked them. She warned them the guys would all show up.

Before Lindsay could get started, Joe did cough and raised his hand. "I think there is something we should tell y...."

Lindsay raised an eyebrow and interrupted him. "Really, Joe? I think there are a million things that you all should tell me, but please, go ahead."

"Lance Becker died in surgery."

"I'm sorry to hear that. Can you tell me who he really was, Joe?"

"I have a reliable source that told me he was FBI. He was being investigated by the FBI, but before he could be questioned, he had taken a leave of absence. Apparently, he was being blackmailed and was here to clear himself. You know what he was up to while being here, I assume."

"Who was blackmailing him?" Sam asked with puzzlement.

Joe looked directly at Lindsay even though Sam asked the question. "I don't know."

"Which leads to my first question. Robert or Jack, which of you would like to tell me the truth about Charlie and who she really was?"

Lindsay had barely gotten the question out when there was a blast of shattering glass, and the lights went out. Everyone hit the floor and drew their weapons when the chaos broke out. The room filled with people with masks covering their faces and dressed completely in black. The noise from the gunshots was deafening.

Since Lindsay had been the only one standing, she was able to move the fastest and hit the floor up against the wall just below the stairs. Her eyes adjusted quicky and she was surprised at the number of people now in her house. She only fired once at the masked man approaching her. They were fast, in and out. One of them grabbed the man she had shot and drug him out.

Once she realized they were heading out, she stood and ran to the kitchen, hoping to cut them off outside. They would need to get away by the road. She cautiously started out the back door expecting to see them, but it was clear and quiet. Then she heard the roar from the motor of a boat. She ran outside and around the house. She was met by the guys when the FBI appeared in tactical gear, guns drawn. The first voice Lindsay heard was Deacon.

"Kendall! Kendall!"

"Right here!"

"Is everyone okay?"

"I think so." She started naming the guys off even though she couldn't see them too well in the dark of the yard. "Sam?"

"Here with Derek."

"Robert?"

There was no answer. She tried again. Still no answer. "Jack, Joe?"

Joe and Jack answered in unison. Then Joe, "Dammit, they have Robert."

"Who is they?" Lindsay and Deacon asked in unison.

"I don't know. Whoever just ambushed us."

81

One month later…

"Lindsay, I can't keep doing this with you. You are driving me crazy!" Sam slumped into the chair behind him, defeated.

Lindsay could clearly see Sam was having a hard time. The dark circles under his eyes hadn't dissipated since she came out of the hospital. He was grumpy and she had never known him to be. Oh, at first, he was caring, sweet, and couldn't get enough of her. He wasn't smothering her, but giving her time and she had to admit, he was being patient. But now that had worn off.

Over the past few weeks, she stayed distant and noncommittal. Quietly, she said, "I don't know what you expect of me, Sam. My life is completely in chaos, I don't know who I am and I'm still chasing my tail around like some lost puppy. I don't have any more answers now than I did when I met Robert. In fact, I have even more questions, like who the hell was Charlie and why was she blackmailing Lance and what did he have to do with anything." Lindsay didn't mention Grayson and in fact, she didn't think anyone, other than Ava, knew he was involved or on the boat that day. No one had said his name. Like he never existed.

"Maybe it's time to start letting go of whatever it is you are holding onto." Sam took a deep breath. "I'm sorry, Lindsay. I know you want answers. Look at what you do know."

"Really, Sam, why don't you tell me what it is I do know."

Now Sam stood up, hoping they were making progress. "Okay, let's go through this one more time. Then I'm done. You know Robert's been at an FBI safehouse. You know the guys that took him aren't talking so no idea who they are or what they wanted. You know Jack and Joe are lying low, working on Robert's kidnappers. They aren't ignoring you, Linds. And you need to hear things from Robert for yourself. You know the organization is part of the FBI Black Ops, which means off the books. You know Lance was being blackmailed by Charlie, although we still don't know who Charlie was or what she wanted from you. Tall One might be in the wind now, but I talked to him myself and believe him when he said he went to you for help but wasn't sure if he could trust you. He only snuck in because he didn't know what he was walking into. You know when you do get to see Robert again, he will fill in the blanks. I know you've made several trips out west, chasing leads, although I don't know where you are getting them. And you know the next time you see Robert; he has promised to tell you why he did what he did. You know I 'died' to protect you, and we agree, it was a poor decision on all our parts. We've apologized repeatedly and frankly, I'm tired of apologizing for doing what I thought was best at the time. I've told you I will spend the rest of my life making it up to you. I don't know what else you want from me. I know what I want, but I'm tired of begging."

"And I'm tired of trying to understand all the lies. You know when you tell the truth, it becomes part of your past. When you tell a lie, it becomes part of your future. But it seems in this case, everyone else can lie and move on. I'm the one paying the consequences of others' lies with my life. You all stabbed me then act like you are the ones bleeding."

Lindsay wouldn't tell Sam those trips out west weren't leads regarding Robert. They were trips to find Grayson to get answers that no one else wanted to supply. She thought he may know more than what she was able to find out. She had hoped she would find him in Seattle, near his parents or his sisters. She needed to let go of finding him. Deacon wouldn't tell her anything and all her leads were dead ends. She also wanted to clear the air with him. She had a thought creep up that bothered her. While at the lake, hadn't she told herself that omittance of facts was the same as a lie? Did her finding Grayson have anything to do with Sam? Now she was trying to excuse her own behavior because it was benefitting her. How would Sam see it?

After a few moments of silence, Lindsay added, "Let me see if you can relate to how I feel. Imagine someone stabs you in the back, then asks you why you are bleeding. That's how I feel. Everyone is acting like I'm the problem. Since when did finding out the truth become so impossible? Is it really asking too much? I suspect Robert could sledge through a swamp of shit and still come out smelling like roses. I just want a basic human need. Truth. It seems the more I look for it, or ask for it, the deeper the lies get. It's like I'm drowning in the lies and those that caused it are acting like it's no big deal and I should trust them. I'm not getting any air but drug down deeper, never to surface again. Like I once told Joe, you can't put a band aid on a bullet hole."

"Look, I am not going to pretend to understand how you feel. The only thing I can say is, you'll get answers in time. I know you want them now and I know you were depending on Deacon to give you more answers when you met with him two weeks ago. The truth will come out in time, on its own."

"How can you be sure the truth will come out when the lies are buried so deeply. They still aren't out after how many years? Are you sure you don't know who Charlie was?"

"Linds, I can't do this. I have told you everything I know. I need your answer. I need to know if we are together or not. You may never get the answers you are looking for and I'm not putting my life on hold any longer. I love you and want to marry you, but I can't wait forever. Lindsay, the truth always comes out. Trust me, Lindsay, please."

"Stop asking me to trust you while I'm still coughing up water from the last time you let me drown!" Lindsay was surprised by how high pitched her voice just came out. It was louder than she had ever used with Sam. They had never had an argument that she could recall, let alone a fight. Sam just didn't get it. She wondered if he ever would. She took a deep breath, "Here's the problem, Sam, I don't know how deeply involved you truly are. Do I even know you?"

Sam covered his face with his hands for a moment, then just looked at Lindsay. The sadness in his eyes was stark. He didn't say another word. He looked at her, then closed his eyes.

Lindsay turned away from Sam, running her fingers through her hair. She needed a moment to gather her thoughts. Being this mad, if she opened her mouth now, she had no doubt she would say something she would regret later. He had been extremely patient with her. But she was angry at being put on the spot like this. She didn't think before she answered her phone when it rang. Whipping it out of her pocket, she answered, "What?"

"It's Deacon. Don't say my name. Are you alone?"

"No."

"Just listen. I need your help. I hate to ask but I'm out of options. This is off record."

Lindsay hissed into the phone, "You have nerve asking me for anything. All I want is a few answers and it appears to be too much."

"I know you can't trust anyone right now, but you can trust me."

Lindsay thought to herself, here we go again, no coming up for air. But instead of saying what she thought, she retorted with, "Prove it. I'll wait." Lindsay didn't expect a fast comeback to that challenge, but she got it.

"Charlie was your sister."

The End

Did you enjoy Web of Lies?

Please consider leaving a review wherever you purchased this book.

For more information on The Truth or Die Series and future books, please follow
Alex Clayborn
at www.authoralexclayborn.com
and also on Facebook
at www.facebook.com/alex.clayborn.author

About the Author

A L E X   C L A Y B O R N

Alex Clayborn has two grown daughters and has lived from northern Maine to southern Florida and many states in between. Alex's hobbies include traveling, downhill skiing, anything on top of the water and reading a good mystery novel. Alex has an accounting degree and worked in the forensic accounting field for many years, loving the chase of uncovering assets people try to hide.

www.ingramcontent.com/pod-product-compliance
Lightning Source LLC
Chambersburg PA
CBHW031606100726
47898CB00006B/1668